Pretty

Fin

A

Smokey Moment

Novel

This book is fiction based on the imagination of the writer. Names, characters, places and incidents are creations of the writer for entertainment purposes and any resemblance to actual people, living or deceased, is purely coincidental.

Published by BookBabe Publishing

Cover designed by angelahaddon.com

Follow me on:

Twitter: smokeymomentbo1

Instagram: smokeymomentbooks

Facebook: smokeymomentbooks

<u>Visit my website:</u>

http://www.smokeymomentbooks.com

Acknowledgments

Dedicated to all the readers who love a good book that keeps you guessing, laughing, cursing, crying and all caught up in your emotions. A good book is powerful. You get to escape and use your own imagination to fill in the blanks. You get to travel all around the globe. Sometimes even to another planet. Possibly discover a new species. A good love story will have you daydreaming and fantasizing about what is and what could be. Or it could have you shaking your head in disbelief while you watch the *train wreck* of a life unfold. And then you hope that fate intervenes and saves your potentially awesome love story. Whatever type of books you like, the one common theme amongst all book lovers is we want to enjoy them. So, I hope you enjoy!

Table of Contents

1

The Story of Fin

The crackling sound of thunder made Isla uneasy. She peeked out from under the sheets. Her father had told her she needed to be a big girl. "You're a big girl. You're a big girl," she chanted, her eyes tightly closed. She wanted to be. If her father could only see her, he would be so proud. But he was sound asleep in the room down the hall. It seemed he was miles away.

She was still in her own bed. She was being brave. Thunderstorms would take some getting used to. But the sheets over her head helped. Being wrapped under the warmth kept her calm, as the weather made its presence known. Her father was training her to sleep in her own room. But the crashing sounds were powerful. It shook their home.

Lightning shot through the sky, dancing like electric arms. It was all very dramatic. Isla closed her eyes. Thunderstorms felt intense. Her sensitive ears amplifying the intensity. Everything was an experience. She usually looked forward to the discoveries. But not this one. It was too much for her delicate spirit.

"Daddy," Isla called out. Soon her small feet hit the floor. She scurried down the hall towards her father's bedroom overlooking the water. Their large contemporary glass and stone home was impressive by most standards. Isla climbed into her father's bed. "Daddy wake up," she said, as she shook his shoulder.

"Huh," he mumbled, then turned his back to her. He was unaware that his precious baby girl had climbed out of her bed and into his. "Daddy, daddy," she shook him again. He rose, still half sleep and taking a moment to gather himself. A bolt of lightning lit up the sky taking with it the remnants of his peaceful slumber.

"What baby girl," he said, as he turned his head, his eyes half open. "What's wrong? You can't sleep?" he asked. "No! I'm scared. I want to hear the story. Read me the story," she said. Her father smiled. It was the same thing with Isla. Sleepless nights, followed by a request for her favorite book.

The story always soothed her. She was always able to go to sleep soon after.

He stacked the pillows so she could lay back. Isla got comfortable. Her father looked dotingly at her. He adored her. She was all he had of a love he lost. A beautiful reminder of the woman he gave his heart to. And Isla was a splitting image of her. Even down to her personality. She was so full of life. So clear in what she cared about and what was important. What she loved and didn't love. And what she loved above all else was her father.

The person whose love never waned. Her loving yet fierce protector. His patience was admirable. If he only got two hours of sleep each night, it would be worth it for his baby girl. She was adjusting well, given the circumstances. And he would see to it that she was comfortable and happy.

Her father kissed her on the cheek. He laid back, cleared his throat, then opened the book to page one. He chuckled as she wiggled her feet in anticipation. He turned the page. A familiar sight. Before the words, there was the woman. Isla smiled at the beautifully etched drawing. It was perfectly accurate. A mermaid. Her scales small and well-defined. Her long hair covering the top half of her well-toned body. She looked happy. Something in her eyes looked authentic.

He started at the beginning. He had finished the last part a few nights before He had a feeling Isla was already aware that this story was special. He wondered how bright she really was. She was gifted. And he didn't doubt that she knew more than what she led on. Lance opened the book. "Ok Issie. We're going to go back to the beginning. We read the whole book already. You sure you don't want to read one of the books your uncle Allan gave you," he asked. Isla shot him a look. Her adorable pout on display. "No daddy. I want to read Pretty Fin," she said.

He kissed the top of her head and then started at paragraph one. Isla became giddy. She always acted as if it were her first time hearing the words. Each time he read it, she listened with the same intensity. The story sometimes making him emotional. It was therapeutic for him. Theirs was an epic love story. Something dreams were made of. He had never known love could feel so complete. And Isla's little face, a constant reminder that he was not dreaming. Mermaids did exist. And he would give his daughter a piece of an extraordinary woman. One page at a time.

The sounds of the storm seemed insignificant. Its power fading into the background. Her father glanced at her. He gave her a moment. She stared at the drawing. The eyes seemed to stare back. The artist who drew it, had rendered it in remarkable detail. Her hair. Her eyes. Her small delicate hands. The fading of color along her tail. Her exquisite and undeniable beauty.

Isla looked up at her dad again. He smiled at her then turned the page. He could see she was ready. She'd had her fill. Isla still bore the scars of a child without its mother. She had the memory of an elephant. She had not forgotten the mother she had been separated from since she was an infant. The story helped ease her deeply rooted pain. A void that was felt every day. He hoped her mother would return. Until then, he would tell her about a woman of the sea. A story about two people from different worlds, who found love against all odds. This was the story of Fin.

"Get back here. Fin! Come back," Queen Aterra yelled. "Uh," Finora grunted, as she wiped the tears from her eyes. Her strong, small legs fast enough to keep a significant distance from her mother. "Should I stop her sir," the kings trusted young guard Lark asked. "No. Let her go. She'll be back," King Zander replied.

Lark had been by his side since he was nine years old. He was now a fifteen-year-old young warrior who protected the king fiercely. King Zander was beloved by all of his subjects. He commanded Mojarro fiercely yet fairly. And he made himself available to them. Going into the villages and talking with the citizens, face to face. He loved the people. His army. The city. His castle. He ruled over the city with pride. The land was one of the richest in Madaka. And he had plans to make Madaka great.

But of all King Zander's prized possessions, his most valuable was his outgoing, outspoken and free-spirited daughter he affectionately called Fin. He doted on her. Gave her a wonderful life. But there was one thing he could not give her. The freedom she so desperately sought.

Finora was getting frustrated with the rules that imprisoned her. She darted out the door, several times before, out of anger. Usually the king would send Lark to catch her. But there was something different about this time. King Zander saw it coming. She was inquisitive. She was asking a lot of questions. She wondered why she was not allowed to do things others could. And the same explanations were no longer working.

Things weren't adding up. Fin was smart. She could see through the mask. She could read between the lines. She wanted to go in the water like all nermeins did, yet she wasn't allowed. She wanted to hold her mother's hand and travel the easterly or westerly rivers into town. Go shopping or visit the locals, as all the other citizens did. The king told her it was for her protection. That she could not mingle with the common people. And for a while that explanation worked. Until Fin asked to swim in her own backyards. In the *Trojian Sea*, right behind the castle. And when the king gave his final answer, she rebelled in defiance. She was told terrible tales about the water. That she was different and could not go in it. But the princess seemed determined to do just that. And nothing was going to stop her.

"Fin! Fin no!" the Queen continued to yell. Finora continued to the cliff's edge. She could see the vast sea. Its beautiful clear blueish green hue had spoken to her soul since she was too small to walk. Finora had a fascination with water. A desire to feel it. Move in it. See the aquatic-life contained inside. It didn't seem fair that she was not allowed near it. Her father warned that she would die if she submerged herself. Finora wanted to see. That wasn't likely. Everyone got in the water. It was a way of life for them. She didn't understand what made her different and why she would not be able to partake in the same activities, other little mermaids her age did.

"Fin! Stop!" the Queen yelled. Her young and defiant daughter was not stopping. She hadn't even slowed. King Zander ran behind his wife. His personal guards Sparrow and Arfusei alongside him. Running close behind was Lark. A young, future soldier who was like a son. Lark was the son of his father's personal guard, who had died in the waters of the Palimora Sea. And after the death of the boy's mother, the king allowed him to stay in the living quarters behind the castle. He promised himself he would look after the orphaned boy who was becoming a young man. And Lark was turning out to be a fierce and loyal addition to his inner circle.

"Aterra!" the king yelled. She ignored his call, running after her daughter and nearing the edge of a steep cliff. He hoped his beloved queen didn't make a mistake and fall in. She didn't swim and the currents could pull her under. "Aterra no! I will get her. Stop!" the King yelled. Aterra couldn't stop. Not until she got to the edge and saved her daughter from going in. It could end badly. If she didn't change, the waters could take control. The Trojian Sea was vast. Deep. She would need a tail. And more importantly, gills.

The truth was, neither of them knew for certain what would happen. They both feared that their young Princess would have the same struggles as her mother. No affinity to water. Unable to sustain inside its unique composition.

Aterra always believed, as did the king, that Finora was like her. Unable to tolerate water. Unable to exist in it. Perhaps a genetic flaw. And Aterra was the only one in Madaka who suffered from it. And she believed her daughter had been dealt the same fate. Missing were the special skin between the legs and the flaps on the sides of her chest. The gills. They opened when air was released and water taken in. But if she were like Aterra, she could die trying.

Finora was only six years old. But she was wise beyond her young years. She questioned everything; Her parent's decision to home school her. Her lack of playmates. The reasons behind her mother not allowing her to swim. Her mother's own reasons for not swimming. They were an aquatic species. Half human and half fish. Able to change their legs to tails, in order to aid them in the water. Fin had seen it. She was fascinated by it. She knew how. She had practiced in her tub when her mother wasn't looking. It was a joyous occasion. And she yearned to test it in real water. The Trojian Sea.

Her two toned dark blue and aqua colored scaled were beautiful. Different from her father's tail, which she knew was a gold, red and orange. Finora believed the color difference was because he was a man. She flopped her tail fiercely. She splashed in the water. She made waves and giggled at her abilities then changed back as Aterra walked in. It was one of a few memories that would help her understand who she was. Her inquisitive nature had her standing, ready to jump. Finora planned to close her eyes and turn her legs just as she did in the tub. "Ok Fin. You can do it," she said, as she calmed herself. She balled her little fists and closed her eyes.

"Fin please," the Queen pleaded. "No mommy! Stay back. Or I will jump," she warned. Queen Aterra looked back. Her husband and his guards were approaching. "She won't listen," she said. King Zander stepped up. The Queen took a step back. Her husband would handle it. Fin would listen to him. He had a commanding way. A strong presence. And Fin only went so far with him. He seemed stressed lately. A side of his personality that Fin seemed to be bringing out with her stubborn and unpredictable behavior.

"Don't you take another step young lady. The water is deep. It is a far drop. You will hurt yourself. Step away from the edge," he said. Fin didn't understand his fears. She stared at the beautiful water. It was more than ten feet below the edge of the cliff. It was a long drop. She had never jumped from that height. The water was green and blue with a gold shimmer. Much too beautiful to cause pain. She looked back at her father. He looked serious. He needed to look strong and stern, in an effort to get her to listen to him. The king doubted she would. His heart raced.

The cliff was majestic. It normally had a calming affect for King Zander. He had stood at that very spot during times of reflection. And now he stood there, terrified. Fin was scared. He could see her shaking. But she wanted to prove that she was right. That the water was safe. That she would know how to change. She wanted to show them she could. This was more than proving something to herself. If they saw she could handle the water, maybe they would allow her to swim in it. Fin was skilled. Graceful. She was one with the water. Their fears were unfounded.

Fin closed her eyes tight and leaped. "No!" he shouted, as he tried grabbing her. "Fin!" the Queen shouted. Their fears made worse in an instant. Fin hit the warm water and turned her legs into a beautiful tail. She looked at her body. She was thrilled. She had done it. She had changed in an environment she could now swim in. She looked around trying to gage where she was and where she wanted to go. She looked at her tail again. "Wow!"

She giggled at her resemblance to the water animals that swam in abundance around her. Some of them seemed drawn to her. They approached her curiously. She tried to reach out. She became startled when a yellow tailed fish got close, then quickly darted away. Fin noted the way he moved. She watched how he swam. She was amazed at his use of his fin and tail. His ability to turn and avoid her touch. She giggled again then tried to coax the fish to her. She hummed and held her hand out. The fish floated. She looked at its gills then looked at the side of her body. Her skin had parted. It was similar to the Yellowtail. Thin separations in its structure. Fin touched her gills. She hadn't noticed them in the tub. She was unaware of why her skin separated into folds. It was another unique experience. She watched as the fish got closer. It came to her unhurriedly, before becoming spooked and swimming away.

Fin's tail was magnificent. A beautiful, blue scaled extension, that had her in awe. She wiggled it then chuckled. This wasn't at all like the times she changed in the tub. Here she could be free. Finora stopped admiring her tail and swam quickly to get away from the area. It wouldn't be long before her father would enter in after her. She swam, trying to see as much as she could. It was a breathtaking sight. Sea anemones lit the way. She swam up to the brightly lit reef and touched the live reef. Sea cucumbers tucked inside their folds. Small pink sea urchins moved slowly across the rock. Everything glowed. The reef was natural light. Fin was amazed. It was more beautiful than she had imagined.

"I'll get her," Lark blurted. "No. I'll get her. She would never come to you," he said, as he ran and leaped into the water below. His guards watching from above. He hit the water. His legs turning into a massive, beautiful black tail.

Small amounts of silver, barely visible, on its underside. A tail powerful enough to propel him at high speeds through the warm, clear blue-green water. He looked around. He spotted Fin immediately. His eyes widened from the shock of seeing her.

He wasn't prepared for what he saw. She had a tail. A beautiful green and blue tail. At times, depending on the angle, camouflaging her in the water that surrounded her. Zander stared in awe. He had no idea Fin was capable. It was a wonderful yet scary reality. He and the queen were not ready to face this part of their reality. Fin was different. But they had no idea the extent of her difference. Whether she could change was a mystery they had no answers for. But she was a nermein. There was no reason she should not have been able to form a tail. But Aterra could not. And so, it was feared that neither could Fin.

Aterra's inability at change was a mystery that had not been solved. And it turned into a secret the castle and its occupants worked hard to cover up. King Zanders parents never talked about it. And one day they were sworn to secrecy. But Zander was not ready for Fin to discover anything. She wa difficult enough to control. This would make her want to enter the water more. Their waters were vast. She could swim to Panga or enter the Palimora Sea and swim to Eulachon. It was a lot to worry about. She would need to heed the warnings. Obey the travel rules. Respect the property lines. Keep from the dangerous animals that dwelled within. And above all else, keep away from the deadly dunes.

Fin saw her father and swam away. Zander swam quickly, trying to catch her, but Fin was too fast. He was shocked at her speed in the water. She had an innate ability to use her whole body in a quiver and flex motion, along with her tail, to propel herself. It was a brilliant sight. Her natural abilities made him proud. He couldn't tell what she was doing. It was seamless. Her body not appearing to move, as she glided through the water. Like that of a skilled swimmer.

It took nermeins years to learn to move with little effort. A skill one would want to master if they planned to travel through the *Arapaimas*. Small rivers used for travel. They ran east, west north and south. Zander watched her. Fin came to a stop. He approached slowly from behind, trying not to make his presence felt. One small ripple would give him away. Her back was to him. Her attention was on the undersea life that surrounded her. Bioluminescent algae, plankton and other aquatic animals crawled and swam near the rocks and floor below. It was a jeweled city. A world all its own.

Fin marveled at their colors. The swaying movements of the anemone. Small schools of shrimp fish and sea cucumbers. She looked to her right and saw a huge fish. She tried to get it to come to her. She hummed. The fish stopped. She hummed again, and it turned and approached her slowly. Its body was three different colors, mostly blue and green. She looked down at her tail. Her color was similar. She looked similar to them. But then, she wasn't. Fin reached out and touched the fish. It allowed her to rub along the top of its body. Soon the fish dashed away. Fin giggled. She was thrilled. She was used to seeing the fish on her plate. But it was quite different seeing them alive. In their habitat. Her habitat. A world filled with more light. It was an underwater light show. Fin saw the algae and moss that glowed at night on land. But these were creatures of the water. Slightly different in size and appearance. Something she had not witnessed.

"Wow!" she exclaimed, as she tried to touch a plankton as it slowly moved through the water. As Fin neared the animal, it darted away. Fin giggled, unaware her father was approaching from behind. He moved slowly though the water. Suddenly her focus was on the small ripples in the water. How they changed. A slight variation that alarmed her. Fin turned around and scurried from him. "Fin!" he called out.

His telepathic yell just as loud as it would be on land. She stopped and stared at him then took off again. Zander was growing frustrated.

"This is not play time. Come here now! If you come to me, I will not ground you," he said. Fin looked around. She wasn't ready to get out of the water yet. She wanted to go further out. Deeper towards the floor. She had gills, lungs and a sophisticated internal system designed to sustain her life in the water. The same as her father. The same as all nermeins. This was their life. Some chose to live in the water. Some on land. They were equipped for both. And it was obvious that Fin would be preferring the water. It was a personal preference. And it was allowed so long as no one lived in the seas. There were large lakes and rivers if one wanted to live their lives in the water. The seas were off limits. Patrolled by men called uarus'.

"Fin... Do you hear me? I know you can hear me. This is transference. We use it to communicate when in water. Your speaking voice doesn't work down here," he said. Fin looked at her father. His desperate attempts to remove her from a natural part of their lives was puzzling. "Why can't I stay poppa," she asked, maintaining her distance. King Zander wasn't prepared to answer her. He was her protector. The disciplinary. The King of Mojarro. Talks about life and the uniqueness of her bloodline was new territory. This was his wife's job. And he and his wife tried to keep her from knowing anything until she was old enough to understand. They believed they were doing right by their daughter. They never expected her to be capable of changing or living and breathing underwater. She needed to be educated on life in the waters. It was different. It seemed exciting. But it could be dangerous.

"Oh Fin… There is so much to know. You are much too young to understand the complexities of our world. One day I promise to show you all there is to know. The power of water. The mystique of it. How to use it to strengthen yourself. How to use it to heal. To travel. To relieve stress. One day you will be Queen of Mojarro. Queen of these waters. Right now, you should be having fun. Not worried about these things. Come to me Fin," he said, extending his hand. "No," she replied.

It was no use trying to grab her. Zander would wear himself out. She moved like a guppy in a large body of water. Able to maneuver and make quick turns effortlessly. "No… Then what is your plan? Why are you in the water? Haven't you seen enough? Yes, you can change your legs to a tail. No, the water will not kill you. I was not lying to you when I told you that. I believed you were not capable. It is a long story. One day your mother and I will explain it to you. Now let's go home," he said. Fin stayed back. She wasn't convinced her father was being honest. "No Daddy. I'm different," she said, as she turned and swam further.

The dunes were not too far away. He hoped she would stay captivated by the reefs. Not venture into the dark depths of Trojian. Zander approached slowly. Fin could feel him. The pounding of his heart. The speed and rise of his chest. He was uneasy. She was fine. No damage had been done. His ordeal should have been over. She was not dead. She had survived the fall, and the entry into the water. Fin wondered what he was hiding.

"You are no different from any other nermein. And if you were, it wouldn't matter. Your mother and I would love you just the same," he said. Fin didn't believe him. Yes, they loved her. But he wasn't honest in saying she wasn't different. She was. And at six years old, she could tell.

A game of cat and mouse continued as Fin scurried away each time her father got near. Zander sighed, then took off after her. The water was clear. Nothing had stirred up the sediment and sand of the bottom. He could see his daughter clearly. She moved fast toward the darker waters. An area avoided by the citizens. He tried to keep up. He shouted in vain. His telepathic voice as loud and strong as his speaking voice. But it was no use. Fin wasn't listening. And the speed at which she travelled was impossible to try to keep up with. Zander wondered how it was possible. She was faster than anything he'd ever seen. And she was moving toward the dune. An area that sat just off *The Dark Lair;* One of the most feared places in all of Madaka. A mystical place. It held secrets. It was forbidden. And no nermein had gone there and lived to talk about it.

It was difficult to approach. The heat alone could kill their kind. Zander panicked. He knew something about the lair. It was known as death valley and he knew of only one man who successfully went through and returned. His father King Zaire.

The area surrounding the lair, called the dune, was comprised of chemicals and heat from the earth's core. Dangerous gases escaped from the ground bubbling up to the surface and making the whole area hazardous. On the other side of the dunes was a mountain. It spanned from the water to the sky. Its surface made of pointy, razor sharp barbs that could slice skin like a knife. No one touch or scaled the rock.

King Zander believed the gods of Madaka built it that way, to keep them from reaching the top. It was the only mountain of its kind. And at the base was a hole. Called the Dark Lair.

If one survived swimming over the hot layers of the dune, there was still the lair to contend with. A tunnel of concentrated gas trapped from the lava. Uninhabitable by their kind and lethal if inhaled. The depth of the hole was impossible to go through without breathing, and one breath was enough.

Zander stopped just shy of the dune. It was as beautiful as it was dangerous. The ground glowed and yellowish orange hue. It seemed to move. And every now and then a huge yellow bubble would pop, like a light show. Zander wanted to get out of the area. They were too close. One touch of the lava and he would not make it back. He looked around. Fin was nowhere to be found. He panicked. He hoped she didn't travel over the dune. Soon he spotted her. She had made it half way.

"Stop right there. Turn around now!" he shouted. She was in awe of her surroundings. The bubbles popping up from the brightly lit ground was interesting. She hoovered over the bubbles. King Zander watched, horrified. She should be weary. Sick and having trouble breathing. But she wasn't. She seemed unaffected. "Fin! Come to me. Please. Come to me," he commanded telepathically, hoping to reach her on a deeper level. Fin wondered why he stopped at the dunes edge. She was just a few feet away. Yet he stayed back.

"Why daddy?" she replied, using the same telepathic power. "Just do it. Come to me now," he replied. Fin looked around. King Zander became more nervous. He believed she was holding her breath. It was impossible to survive the gases that escaped. Fin wasn't ready to go to him. But she could sense that her father was at the end of his rope.

She swam back to him as he waited with his arms outstretched. She swam fast into his arms and he held her tight. "Don't you ever do that again. This area is forbidden," he said. "But why?" she asked. "Because it is dangerous. You could have died. Do you understand?" he scolded. Fin paused. She was confused. She looked back at the bubbles. She didn't understand. She was fine. "Do you understand Fin?" he repeated. "Yes daddy."

"Fin!" the Queen shouted, as she waited for the King to scale up the rock back to where they were. His men reached for him and pulled him up as he got close to the top. "Mommy," Fin said, as she ran to her mother. Aterra picked her daughter up and hugged her. "You can't do that. It's not safe," she said, as she wept. She was filled with emotion. Zander smiled at her. The Queen nodded at her husband. He had saved the day again. He usually did. Aterra turned and walked back to the castle, holding her daughter close. She carried her the entire way. The flash of danger still in her heart, mind and spirit. Fin kept her head on her mother shoulders. She enjoyed the touch. It was rare. Her mother hadn't hugged or held her in years.

King Zander stood looking over his kingdom. The city of Mojarro was a spectacular place. A city beneath the earth's ocean with its own atmosphere. A vast land surrounded by mountains, trees and water. It was covered in bioluminescent moss and algae that made the land a unique and beautiful light show. Night life was important. It was the time to enjoy the lights of the ground, trees and mountains even more. One could stand on the cliffs edge and see lighted sea creatures swimming in the water. The coral reefs lit the waters of Madaka, unless deep in the ocean. There, sea creatures lit the way. Madaka was a unique place and its people, a unique species. A peaceful civilization. There were no more wars. No weapons. No hunger. No ill will. Wars from generations prior had created the nonviolent world they were living in now. And it seemed all nermeins lived happily and were at peace with their lives. Everyone, except little Fin.

King Zander stood at the cliff's edge. His guards Arfusei, Ziege, Sparrow and Lark at his side. He was surprised at Finora's abilities. "You ok Sire," Arfusei, one of his most trusted body guards asked. "Yes," he said, as his mind raced. "What is it?" Arfusei asked. King Zander looked at him. "She swam like she'd been swimming all her life. Better than anyone. Faster than anyone. She swam over the dune. She was right at the entrance to the lair."

Arfusei furrowed his brow. "How is that possible? Others have tried. No one has been able to swim over the dune, let alone go into the lair. Those that have tried, have perished. That can't be? How?" he questioned. "I don't know."

2

Unanswered Questions

The grass was coming in nicely near the castle. The king had imported soil and grass seeds and the result had amazed the princess. She walked barefoot through it. It had come in thick. Luscious. And soon more would grow on all sides. King Zander was trading more gold and alexandrite for soil and plants. Mojarro stood to benefit from King Nephrus of Panga and Queen Rasbora of Piratchu's blessings. His city had the jewels. And their cities had the soil. It was a perfect system.

Fin was celebrating another milestone. She was turning eighteen. Her friend Rae was on her way. The two planned to eat the special meal prepared. It was Fin's favorite. Jellyfish and karra beans shipped in from Eulachon. Her father had a surprise for her but he decided to hold off on telling her. He wasn't sure how she would take it. They hadn't spoken of it. But the king had taken notice to his daughter's affinity towards the opposite sex. She was showing interest. Good news for him. He had several options open to him. It was well known that she was the most beautiful princess in all the land. And with beauty came suitors. He was content for now, just allowing her to be happy on her special day. And all she wanted was time with her friend and freedom from prying eyes. He obliged her. No guards were permitted to close. They were to watch her from a distance.

"Fin! Rae is here," shouted her lady's maid Lillia. Fin turned back to the castle. "Coming," she shouted, looking up to the window. Lillia smiled and walked away. Fin was excited. She had been so busy going to events with her mother, that she barely had a moment to herself. All local events that didn't require much in the way of travel. Which meant no need to swim in the travel streams. Fin wanted to go further. She wanted to jump in one of the traveling rivers and go somewhere far. Anywhere. Just to feel alive. To feel a part of her world.

"Rae," she exclaimed. Rae was a small in stature. She was slightly shorter than Fin with a petite frame. She was beautiful with delicate pale skin and long golden hair. "Fin. I missed you. My mother sent you something," she said, handing her a box. "Wow! What is it?" she asked. "I won't tell. Open it," Rae replied. Fin excitedly sat down and opened the handmade wood box covered in leaves. It was a kind gesture since plants with large leaves were rare in Mojarro. The Queen looked on. She would need to thank Rae's mother later. It was obvious the wrapping came from Panga since they were the only ones with such rare plants.

"Oh my. What is this?" she marveled, as she removed the small round jewel from the box. "I don't know. I found it inside a sea creature. I have never seen one before. There were more creatures. But I couldn't one with another jewel," she said of the pearl. Queen Aterra was surprised. She was familiar with the rare mineral. She had seen one on Queen Rasbora once.

"That is so beautiful Rae. Thank you. I will have it fastened to gold. Fin can wear it as a ring," Aterra stated. "Oh mom. Please," she asked. Aterra smiled. Fin jumped up and kissed her mother on the cheek and left to go to her room.

"Shut the door," Fin said, as she plopped down on her bed. "I am so bored. I wish I could go out," she complained. "Why don't you? Why is your father so strict about where you go? I don't understand. What could happen. Nothing ever happens," she stated. "I know." Fin looked around. She sat up. "Not today. This is my day. Come on," she said, jumping from her bed. "Fin! What are you up to," Rae said, as she followed Fin to the door. "Shh," she gestured, as she placed her ear to the door.

Fin opened her door slowly and looked down the long hall. She looked the other way then shut her door carefully. "Ok. No one is around. My father is probably in his quarters. My mom is surely sleep. And Lillia is probably with one of the guards. Let's just go," she said. "What? Why would she be with a guard?" Rae naively asked. "Because she is. Let's go while we can."

Fin went to her closet and pulled a hat made of stiff fibers from a moss tree. She had received it as a gift from the dressmaker. A woman who lived in town who dressed the royal family. She wrapped a scarf around half of her face, keeping her eyes exposed. "Here. Cover your face. The guards will think we are visitors."

Rae took the thin, soft scarf and wrapped it around her nose and mouth. "Like this?" she asked. "Yes. Perfect!"

The two walked slowly down the hall and down to the entryway. Fin opened the door and looked around. Suddenly a guard came from around the side of the castle. "Look down. Just speak and don't look in his eyes," she cautioned. "Hello. Is the exit this way?" Fin asked, as her and Rae walked past the guard. He nodded then furrowed his brow as he walked towards the side of the castle. Fin chuckled. It worked. She expected Sparrow to recognize her. Fin looked back. "Is he looking?" Rae asked. "No. Don't look nervous. Just look forward. One more guard and were clear.

"Thank you. Have a good day," Fin said, as her and Rae exited through the gate. "Have a nice day madame," he replied. Fin looked back. Lark was coming. She would have been unable to fool him. He knew her from head to toe. He had paid close attention. He had been her father's faithful protector since she was a baby. He was young when Zander first took him in. Orphaned with nowhere to go, he became like family. And he was in love with Fin.

"Oh no! Lark," she said, as she sped up. "Walk faster," she said to Rae. "Alright," Rae replied. Fin feared looking back again. It would surely look like the behavior of someone who was nervous. "Don't look back. Just keep walking until we get to the water," she said. The women approached the westerly arapaima. A travel stream that would dump them into the Trojian Sea. Rae jumped in. Her legs turning into a beautiful orange, yellow and gold colored tail and fin. Finora looked back. Lark was quickly approaching. She jumped in the water. She changed her legs to a beautiful tail and raced from sight, with Rae tagging behind her. "Slow down Fin. I can't keep up," she complained. Rae tried her best. She followed her into deeper waters, the women looking back to make sure they weren't being followed. "Did he get in the water?" Fin asked. "No. I didn't see anything," she replied, looking at Fin's tail. Fin looked down. She instantly became self-conscious. The difference in their tails made her feel awkward.

"What?" she asked, her voice sounding agitated. "Well…Your tail. It's blue. I have never seen a blue tail. I have never seen you in water," she said, appearing stunned by the revelation. Fin was immediately hurt. Rae was behaving as if there was something wrong. Fin hadn't given it any thought. She was banned from entering the water and Aterra never changed in front of her. So, her knowledge of the color of tails and fins, was limited. All she knew was her father's tail was black.

"My father's tail is black. Mine is blue and a little green. So what! Yours is orange and yellow. What difference does it make," she said, offended that Rae had brought it up.

Fin was embarrassed that she had no reference point. This was a new revelation. She had seen a few women traveling along the canals when she was younger. She recalled their tails being orange and yellow. And when she turned at five years old for the first time, she assumed that some of them had yellow tails and some were blue.

"It's no big deal Fin. I just never seen a blue tail. Yes…The male tails are black. Our tails are orange and yellow. It's beautiful. Don't get upset," Rae said. Fin looked around in the water. She wanted to change the subject. She was unaware she was different and this was a terrible way to make the discovery. On her birthday, at a time when she should be enjoying what little freedom she had. Soon her father would send his army. Soon she would be found and forced back home. "Never mind. Let's look around," Fin said.

The waters were clear and beautiful. They swam towards the mountain rocks to see the beautiful reef. Fin remembered it being the most beautiful place she had ever seen. She could see it up ahead. Then something caught her eye. Fin slowed. A group of men were hanging around the reef. They wore metal vest. They were soldiers. But their vest were not the ones worn by Mojarroian soldiers. She looked at

Rae. The women stayed back. Soon one of the men looked their way.

"Who are they? This is Mojarro waters," Fin said, as they quickly approached. Fin panicked and swam swiftly away, leaving Rae trailing far behind. She was faster in water than any nermein. A fact that she soon forgot as she hurried to distance herself. *Rae,* she thought, as she turned around.

"Rae!" she called out, as she swam back. Rae looked back for her as she engaged in conversation with one of the soldiers. "Princess," the handsome man said, as Fin approached. He looked at her tail. He stared at her. Fin felt strange again. He seemed familiar even though she was sure she had never met him. "And you are?" Fin asked. "Prince Andreus," he replied.

Rae looked at Fin and smiled. But Fin was not amused. He was far from home. She had heard of him. Her father had mentioned him as a possible suitor. A possible mate. "My pleasure," he said. Fin looked at his guards. She felt on display. It seemed everyone was staring at her tail.

"Why are you here? You are far from home. How did you get past the Uaru's?" she asked. "Prince Andreus smirked. He had his ways. "These waters are vast. They cannot occupy it from all areas," he noted. Fin didn't like his quiet invasion. His brashness at bending rules set in place to preserve each cities wealth and property. It was bold and dangerous. Trade was important. The cities had agreed to keep from unauthorized entry unless they were a citizen. Born and bred.

"You shouldn't be here," she said. "Neither should you. Where are your guards?" he asked. Fin became furious. It was none of his business where her guards were and why she was in the water. She thought of her father. It was obvious he had told King Orfe a few things about her. Which would explain Prince Andreus's knowledge of her being forbidden to enter water.

"I have more rights to be here than you. Please leave," she said, as she turned and swam away. "Uh…Nice to meet you your Highness," Rae said, as she swam to catch up with Fin. Rae was infatuated with the handsome future king. Andreus stared at Fin, catching a last look. She was breathtakingly beautiful. It was a pleasant surprise. He never expected to see her. He was there to see what was growing on their mountains. Eulachon was void of such beauty. They were plentiful in oil and metal. Nothing beautiful. And he wanted to import it. But he wasn't sure it would grow. Nothing would. And the mysteries behind it was startling. He figured it was the heat. A lack of understanding of the lava that he and his citizens had become used to had him perplexed.

"She was beautiful," a guard said, as he swam up beside the prince. "That's my wife. I will marry her one day."

"What an arrogant finny," Fin complained, as she swam towards the dune. "He was handsome," Rae replied. Fin shot her a look. "Who cares about handsome, when you're a trout," she teased. Rae chuckled at her friend's candor. Fin was high spirited and always open and frank when expressing her thoughts. It was a trait that lacked in so many others. And Rae found it refreshing. She had picked up a few of her ways, since they were lifelong friends. "He wasn't that bad," Rae interjected.

"Yes. He was. When I marry, my husband will be a good man. A great communicator. He will love me unconditionally. And I will touch him," she said. Rae stopped swimming. "What? Why would you want to do that?" she said, appalled at Fin's revelation. "Because Rae, it is natural. Normal. Something is wrong with our world. Why don't we touch. Why does it stop after you turn a certain age? My mom hugged me when I was six. It was the best feeling in the world. I can only imagine what it would feel like if a man hugged me. Held my hand. Don't you ever desire that?" she asked.

Rae looked perplexed. "No Fin. That is disgusting. I can't imagine it. Not my mother and surely not some man," she replied. "Not just any man. The man you love. Ok. For instance…Take the trout. What if he touched you? Don't you think you would get some pleasure from the attention?" she asked. Rae slowly shook her head *no*. "No Way. And if he did, I would run from him. I would never see him again. I would throw up. I can't stand to touch myself. My skin doesn't like it. Neither does yours. What are you thinking? You are so weird Fin," Rae said.

Fin stared off. She was again, feeling embarrassed at her differences. Now it was more than physical. She was different in the way she felt. What she desired. And again, she changed the subject. "Let's go this way," she said, turning from Rae. Her friend didn't understand her. A sad moment, since Rae was all she had. Her mother Aterra was not open for such discussions. And neither was her father. Fin decided to keep such thoughts to herself. One day the world would make sense to her.

The two continued swimming, going further out, into the abyss. Rae became nervous. "Where are we going? We're getting far," Rae said. "I know. I want to go to this place I saw when I was a little girl," Fin replied, as she continued going further out. Towards the *Ayu Mountain*. Rae continued following her. She trusted that Fin knew where they were headed. It was an area she hadn't been to. Rae only travelled the shallow travel canals and rivers called *Arapaimas*. This was deeper than she'd ever ventured. "Isn't that dangerous mountain with the sharp rocky surface this way? We should turn back. That mountain will cut you up pretty bad. I will get in trouble. My mom will know I was here," Rae said in fear.

Fin ignored Rae. She wanted to show her the beautiful yellow bubbles that escaped from the sea floor. She approached the dunes. Rae stopped and moved back. "I heard about this place. We shouldn't be here. Let's go! There's a reason no others are around. This is a dangerous place," Rae warned. Fin approached slowly. She remembered swimming over it. "Fin! No!" she shouted.

"It's ok. I've done this before. I'll be back. Wait there," she said, as she moved across the bubbling floor. Rae tried to approach but felt herself getting ill. Her gills becoming clogged. She backed away, but stayed within view of Finora. The move seemed to clear the feeling immediately. "Oh no," she worried. Rae thought about going for help. She didn't see how Fin would make it. Soon she saw men approaching. "Help!" she shouted, as they emerged from the darkness. It was Prince Andreus.

"What's wrong?" he asked. "It's Fin. She went over the dangerous part. Please help her," she pleaded. Prince Andreus became alarmed. He wasn't sure what Rae meant by dangerous. It was what he and his soldiers swam over to get to Mojarro. "Where is she? And what do you mean by dangerous?" he asked. "The bubbles! I got sick just getting close to it. And she swam all the way to the rock," she said. Andreus looked at his soldiers. "I'll see if she's ok."

Andreus swam with his soldiers behind him, over the dune. Rae looked in astonishment at their ability to breathe what the floor produced. Andreus looked around. He didn't see Fin. "Go that way. You... go to the other side," he ordered. It was a huge undertaking. The area was large. She could be anywhere. The heat was the worse of it. Their land had lava and gases all around. Centuries of living near it helped them build an immunity to it. But the heat felt like it was cooking them slowly. Andreus swam hurriedly around. He wanted to remove himself from the area fast.

Fin had made it to the lair, and was swimming up its long narrow cave. She vaguely remembered it. And she was determined to see where it led. She sped up. Soon the water changed temperatures. As she continued, the water temperature continued to drop. Fin tolerated the change even if it was a bit uncomfortable. Her ascension seemed never ending. Soon temperatures were frigid. But Fin continued on. She continued to speed up. She worried about Rae. She had left her behind. *She will be alright. I'll just go see what up this tunnel,* she thought, as she continued on.

Fin could sense the elements changing. She was approaching something. It was too dark to make out. And even though nermeins had great night vision, she was unable to see it clearly. Soon, Fin was swimming through a layer of thick soot. She closed her gills and held her breath. She hoped it would turn back into water. This was unbreathable. Fin panicked. She didn't have much time. She sped up again. Now using more energy and needing to breathe. But to breathe in the soot would surely kill her. She knew enough to know that the thick slime would clog her gills up. It was already irritating the skin on the rest of her body. Her gills were the most sensitive part on her body. It was not safe for the thick gaseous water to enter them.

After a few seconds and what she was certain was her impending death, Fin emerged from the soot and took a deep breath. Her gills opening to allow for the gas exchange and the flow of water through. Fin stopped. She looked around then stopped when she saw something in the distance. She swam to it. Her body stirring up the sediment of the ocean floor. She marveled at the large, diverse number of creatures that crawled across it. Her memory was clear. She was sure these were new creatures. They were never part of the trade. Never in the local market. And were not present in the water during her brief but memorable time in the Trojian Sea. She remembered every fish. Every crustacean. Every anemone. And this was unlike anything she'd seen. Clearly a new place with new animals.

Fin reached down and picked up one of the illuminating creatures and put it in her mouth. She tried chewing it but quickly spit it out. The flavor too bitter and harsh. She opened her mouth to allow the water to rinse it. Soon she saw another small creature. It's sparkly lights illuminating brightly. Reminding her of the crustaceans near the reef.

She grabbed it. The animal crawled across her hand then suddenly stung her. She looked closely at it. Unaffected by its poisonous barb. She pulled the stinger out, then placed the creature in her mouth. She chewed it slowly prepared to spit it into the water. She was hungry. The swim there, had her famished. She continued to chew. The flavor was better. She saw another. She grabbed it and pulled the barb and popped it in her mouth, chewing aggressively, as she enjoyed the flavors. Soon she grabbed a few more.

After consuming several more, Fin swam towards the object that was growing in size, the closer she got. Soon the magnitude of the object overwhelmed her. She stared at the large metal ship. It was foreign to her. She swam slowly towards it. She was mystified. This was something built. In her world they had metal items but nothing this massive. Fin reached out and touched the rusted, badly damaged ship. The large letters *Adr* faded, but still clearly seen on its side. Fin wondered what the strange lettering was. The writing was unlike that of anything she'd seen. There was no other writing. All other letters had been eaten away by time, bacteria and the elements.

The ship was broken and rusted. Fin swam into a huge opening in the ship's hull. She looked around then quickly exited. Her surroundings were interesting. She wanted to go further. She figured her father was probably looking for her, but she had come too far not to see more. She knew she would never get another chance. *Ok. Just a peek. Let's see what else there is. There has to be something if I go up*, she thought.

Fin swam up. Soon several minutes had gone by. She was surprised that she had not made contact with any surface. She decided to test her speed, suddenly shooting up like a rocket. Her speed so fast, that it hindered her taking deep breaths. She decided to shallow breath and keep her speed until she explored the new environment. Fin tired. It was daunting.

Just as she was about to give up the water changed temperature. She looked up. She could see a dim glow. She pressed on and soon the water warmed. The dim glow turned into a bright light. Fin smiled. She slowed down and took a deep breath and then continued her ascent to the surface. Fin broke through. She chuckled. It was exciting. She looked around. There was nothing. The bright sun was warm like lava. She wondered if the new place had lava in their skies.

A quick glance to her left startled her. A ship in the distance. It was the same as the large metal object she'd seen on the bottom. Fin swam to get a closer look. The large oil carrier had men walking on its deck. Fin could see them. She gasped. Their clothes. Their hats. Some had their eyes covered by small plastic items. *What is this? Where is this? Who are they?* she thought.

"Sir! There's a woman in the water," the young ship mate said, as he ran into the ships bridge. "Excuse me! What did you say? Carter... Have you been drinking?" the captain asked. "No Sir. Come quick," he said, running out onto the deck and towards the bow.

"There!" he pointed. Fin could see the men pointing at her. Her anxiety about the strange new world took hold. The ship blew its horn. Fin covered her ears and ducked under the water. "What the... Did you see that! She ducked under the water. She actually swam down," the young man said.

"No! Something grabbed her. Maybe a shark. Call the coastguards. Call for help," the captain said. "Should we drop in the water?" the man asked. "Whatever got her, took her under. There's nothing we can do but report it. We'll stay for a minute. But I'm sure she's gone son," he said to his young helper. The ship called in the sighting but were asked to update them on whether it was a search and rescue or a recover.

After an hour, the ship's captain confirmed that she was no longer visible. The coast guard stated they were in route. They asked for the coordinates in case the ship had to leave the area. The ship's captain was asked if he could stay in the area but he stated it was not safe to do so. They had a ship full of oil and it was important to get to their destination.

"Let's get underway. There's nothing here. We couldn't save her," the captain said. His men walked away. The youngest ship mate stared intensely at him. He knew what he saw. A woman had ducked into the water. She wasn't pulled down, as one would expect to see if someone was dragged under. The captain nodded and walked away. It would not be discussed. He too was still puzzled by what he observed. He didn't want to spook the young man. But the woman ducked. And he had no way to explain it. Her movements were unnatural.

"Fin!" Rae exclaimed when she emerged from the dunes. Rae stood alongside Andreus and his men. "We looked for you. Were you ok? Where did you go?" the prince asked. Fin looked fiercely at him. "I'm fine. You should go. I'm surprised my father isn't here. I suspect his personal guard saw me get in the water. If he finds you here, he will not be happy. Please go," she said of Lark. Andreus looked intensely at her. He did not fear her father. He did not fear anything.

But he wanted to make a good impression. He liked Fin's tenacity. He liked her energy. Her fearlessness.

"This area is not safe. I will go if you leave here now," he replied. Fin looked at his men. Then at Rae. She paused, then turned from him and swam away. Rae turned and followed. Andreus watched her. He wondered about her. Why she swam so fast. Why her tail was a different color. How she was able to handle the gases of the dune. Only Eulachonians were able. And not all of them.

"Where did she go. We looked everywhere?" the guard asked Andreus. "I don't know. We covered the whole area pretty good. She's crafty. I like her. She has no fear. I want this place searched thoroughly once more. She went somewhere. She seemed shaken. Somethings got her spooked."

$\mathcal{I}$t was a quiet afternoon. Fin sat on her bed. She counted down the time until her door would open. It was the same routine. Never a surprise to look forward to. No leisure games or fun. No freedom, to go and enjoy life. Everything was about following the rules her father had in place. The only joys in life was the discoveries she made. She had become quite skilled at making things. Homemade beauty products that she tested and improved on. She had refined her processes and was making things for her body. Lotions and balms scented from flowers were her favorite. And when she discovered an ant that when squished, left a red stain, she got to work finding the right ingredients to create a paste.

Soon she was using the ants to make colorings for her nails and toes. She used petals from flowers to make lipstick and blush. Fin was crafty. And Rae was using the items to trade for other things. Fin's only request was pearls. And Rae searched the arapaimas for more. She found three and Fin promised to make her several containers of the colored paste to apply to the face. It was fun. Fin enjoyed it. She didn't need the money. She did it for the love of creating the product.

The King and Queen were loving but strict parents. Fin knew that they too lived sheltered lives. They were the royal family. Expected to be available to the citizens. Expected to stay safe. To be ready for anything which meant staying home. Making good of one's time. Fin had tired of it all. She wished to be normal. And she wished to be in love. She had noticed men. She noticed Lark. He was handsome. Built. Charming. And intense. But he was like a brother. She felt torn. They were close. They'd known each other since she was a child. But the king would never allow it. And so, he would need to stay a close family friend. And even though Fin had come to the conclusion, she still noticed him. And she knew he noticed her. He tried to hide it. But it was clear.

"Time for studies," Aterra said, as she opened her daughter's bedroom door. Fin sighed. "Can I do it at dusk mom? Please! Rae and I are painting our nails tonight. I am going to teach her how to prepare the mix and make the colors," Fin said. Aterra gave her a sharp look. "We spoke about that Fin. No! You are not to do such silly things. You can visit her. But you are to mind yourself. You are a princess."

Aterra wanted Fin to stay home. To start her studies. It was important. She was studying the laws of the city for the day she would be queen. There was a lot of ground to cover. She was expected to know the land. The price of all their commodities. Each rare and precious jewel. The minerals that they came from. She was expected to know trade values. And all the local citizens who made life possible by helping harvest the items for consumption or for sale. Aterra had taught Fin a lot. She worried about pushing her daughter too much. Fin could be unpredictable when cornered or pressed to do something she didn't want to do. She lashed out and ran away in defiance. And so, Aterra would allow the break. So long as the guards tagged along.

"You can go. But you must take Lark and a few of the others with you," Aterra said. "Fine," Fin huffed. It was better than not going. She was ready to go. She hoped to visit her friend Rae before it got late. The nights were spectacular but she was the princess. It was still not respectable for her to be out at night, amongst the commoners. Fin planned on taking Rae her hemini plant. It glowed brighter than the moss and ferigone plants that grew on mountains and the bark of trees.

Hemini was rare. A gift from King Nephrus to her father. It grew naturally in Panga. And it was highly sought after for its ability to shine bright. Fin had two. And she was expecting more. The king of Panga sent them when he discovered that King Zanders daughter loved them. A gesture to improve trade between the two cities.

Fin was ready to go. Her and Rae talked about attending a gathering at one of Rae's classmates house. Fin kept that part of the plan private. Her parents would never allow it and so she decided against going. King Zander had rules and he had become tougher on enforcing them. And as much as she wanted to run free, she couldn't. The source of her lifelong frustration with her parents. There was no time for such nonsense. Only what her father had planned for her.

But Finora was maturing. She had grown into a responsible young lady. Even still, Zander had reason to be concerned. Fin was a princess and her protection was vital. She would be "Queen of Mojarro" someday. She was becoming a woman and was growing into a position she was reluctant to fill. It would come with a husband she had never met. Fin was unaware that Zander had bequeathed her to King Orfe's son. A decision he had not yet relayed to the cities of

Madaka. He was still hoping to meet Prince Andreus. To endure he was suitable.

Fin walked the halls of the castle looking for her father. She wanted to ask a favor. To be allowed to leave, this one time, without the guards. "Mom, where's dad?" she asked. "He is in his quarters. Please don't disturb him. He is having a meeting with the King of Panga. It is important." Fin walked out of her mother's quarters and down the hall. She bent the corner and headed for her father meeting chambers. A room stocked with wine, gold jewels and any other valuables her father sometimes used to bargain on the spot. Finora approached the door. She was stopped by a guard.

"Your father is in a meeting. He asked not to be disturbed," he said. "This is important. He'll want to speak to me. Now if you'll excuse me," Fin said, as she walked past the guard. This wasn't the first time Finora disobeyed her father. The guards were used to it.

"Fin. Uhmm. Excuse me King Nephrus. This is my daughter Finora," King Zander said, as he stepped away to see what she wanted. King Nephrus bowed. Finora smiled nervously. She could see her father was not happy with her entry into his chambers.

"I specifically asked not to be disturbed," he noted. Finora glanced back at King Nephrus. He hadn't taken his eyes off of her. He had never seen King Zander's daughter. Finora smiled and then turned her attention back to her father.

"Dad. Please. I have to ask a favor," she said, looking desperate. "What is it Fin?" he asked. "Well…," she hesitated. "I want to go out alone. Please dad. This one time. It's just to Rae's house. I will only be there for a little while," she stated. Zander looked at King Nephrus. "Excuse me. I need a private moment with my daughter," he announced. King Nephrus was shown to an adjoining room and the door was closed.

"You have disrupted me to ask what you already know the answer to? No! You must follow the rules. Why is this so difficult? I put them in place for your protection and happiness." Fin looked down. She felt ashamed for being so demanding. She had been, since she was a little girl. She didn't like to see her father upset. Usually he huffed and gave warnings. But she never took him seriously because he never followed through on any of his threats.

"I'm sorry dad," she replied. The King sighed. Fin looked around. King Zander felt her pain. His daughter was always too large and bright of a spirit for the confinements of their life. "It's not important dad. Sorry to interrupt. I promise

I will start listening," she said. The king chuckled. "No... You won't. It's not in you. You are just like me when I was your age. And no, you cannot go there without an escort. Now, can I get back to my meeting. King Nephrus has travelled a long way to meet with me. He travelled by land and by water. So, I must finish up so he has time to get back."

Fin shook her head and left the room. She walked slowly though the castle, disappointed that she was still being treated like a child. She walked past a locked room. A reminder of her limitations in life. "This house and its secrets. Can't do anything. Can't go anywhere. Can't even go inside that room," she mumbled.

The castle was a house of secrets. There was a locked room Fin never entered. A room she had tried to gain access to, so many times in the past. The door was made of thick hard wood and iron. The handle, sturdy and impenetrable. She wondered what was kept inside. What item was so important, so valuable, that it needed to be locked away. Even her mother never entered. The room had never been opened. Finora used to go up to the door and listen. She thought she heard noises. She tried peeking in the peephole. Other than being able to see bright colors, there was nothing noteworthy. Zander had the only key. And its location was also a mystery.

Fin was sure it was hidden somewhere in their vast castle. And one day she would find it. If it took a lifetime.

King Nephrus was escorted back into the room. "Please...Sit," Zander said. King Nephrus had a devilish grin. Zander already figured what the smile was about. "I never seen the princess before. She is the most beautiful in all the land. Her hair. Her skin. Her features. Perfect. Instead of due trade with soil and gold, I would like to make a proposition. Your daughters' hand in marriage to my son Osiris, for enough soil to cover most of this land. I will have my army carry it here on their backs. Plenty of soil," he offered.

King Zander paused. It was quite an offer. He wanted the soil. It was rich in nutrients and their city was mostly black sand. Soil meant other species of flowers and plants for consumption. There were trees and plants that thrived in the black sand. But they were inedible. Most were poisonous. It would benefit the city, to grow their own versus trading for it with Panga and Piratchu. Other than fish, mussels, shellfish and jellyfish, there wasn't much more to consume. The world of Madaka had limited items safe for consumption and so rich soil was just as valuable as the taaffeites, alexandrites, diamonds and gold.

It was a thought. King Zander pondered it. It would mean the joining of the cities and access to all the soil they needed. But he had already had this conversation with King Orfe. And had already promised his daughter to Prince Andreus.

"She is already spoken for. I am waiting until she gets a little older. I'm sorry. She is to be married to Prince Andreus one day," he said. King Nephrus was shocked. He shook his head slowly back and forth. He was disappointed. And he was verbal about it.

"Prince Andreus! That boy is an abomination. Pure evil. I noticed it when he was just ten years old. You mark my word…You will regret that decision. It will end bad for her." Zander looked puzzled. He had heard nothing of the sort. But if there was any truth to it, then he would need to find some way of backing out of the deal. Prince Andreus had laid eyes on Fin. He spoke of nothing else. He was smitten with her and was looking forward to her being his queen. A promise of joining the lands would make life easier for both sides. But not at the expense of his daughter's happiness. King Zander stood up. The men bowed instead of shaking hands. Nermeins refrained from touch. It was considered dirty. Foul. Forbidden. And they never kissed. Babies were made in water. In pools of sperm secreted by the males. It was an informal and planned event. That was their way of life.

King Zander's army led King Nephrus and his men to the westerly arapaimas. One of the main arteries for traveling west. The men dove in and changed. Their legs immediately taking form. Their tails now propelling them quickly through the water. King Nephrus was strong. Fast. His army would need to work hard to keep up with him. He swam thinking of King Zanders words. He wanted another meeting. He was sure Osiris would love Fin. He had failed at setting his son up. Two failed attempts had him worried. But not anymore. Fin was perfect.

What Fin called home, was a large castle that sat high on Mount Sabalo, in a world called *Madaka*. Madaka was split into four lands The four lands were eventually turned into four cities; *Mojarro, Eulachon, Piratchu* and *Panga*. The land was unequally divided and occupied by a race of mermaids called *Nermeins*. A half-fish, half-man species, able to survive in water. The nermeins were capable of changing their legs into tails for speed in water. Once in water, their gills, small folds of skin on the sides of their chest, opened up. They were a unique species. They had two sets of lungs. Large ones for water and small lungs for land. Because they were better in water and many preferred to be in water. Some lived in pockets of water beneath the surface. Others chose to live on land. And even land dwellers frequently entered water. Water was a way of life. It sustained them. Avoiding water was not an option.

Water was their method of travel. Their speed in water was ten times that of walking on land. Madaka was equipped with thousands of small rivers called Arapaima's that flowed through each city. Some rivers were wide and deep. Others thin and shallow. Many rivers flowed throughout the lands, connecting some of the four cities like a railroad and making travel to a neighboring town quick and easy. Not every city connected by small rivers. Pitachu and Eulachon were far away from Mojarro. Travel happened by way of a vast body of water called the Palimora Sea. Travel from Mojarro to Panga, was much faster. They were closer in proximity, separated by the Trojian Sea.

The seas were guarded by water soldiers called *Uaru*. Each city had their own guards who protected their own cities natural resources. Travel was limited in and out of the cities. And each of the four cities had its own lakes and rivers that were not accessible by the seas. It was intricate. A natural way of life for them.

*****

One of the four cities was the city of Mojarro. Fin was lucky. Her father was king of the most sought-after land in Madaka. It was known as the land of riches. Abundant in diamonds, jadeite, red and green emeralds, gold and several other metals. Precious stone such as alexandrite and the rare black opal, were also found in its mountains and in rock inside its streams. The presence of the jewels embedded along the surface of the mountains and their cone-like rock structures scattered throughout the city, made Mojarro a beauty like no other.

King Zander mined them carefully. Jewels removed by force, took a long time to be re-created. It was better to wait until the elements caused them to loosen and fall. There was always a crew working the ground near the mountains to collect the casted gems for trade. A full-time job since the city had hundreds of mountains covered with thousands of gems.

No other city sparkled with such radiant charm. And the addition of soil imported from Panga over the years, helped the land. They were able to grow their own plants and trees, lessening the need to acquire it in trade. Something that had Piratchu and Eulachon nervous. If Mojarro got to the point where they were saturated with soil, it could affect the value of trade. But Mojarro was too vast. And half the land was covered in useless black sand. They would always want soil, mud and plants.

Part of Mojarro's charm was the many waterfalls they had. Some were a beautiful blue hue. Moss and dark blue waters gave the massive rocks their beauty. Some were green and gold. A result of gold metal and the rich green color of the water and the algae. The winds and moisture in the surrounding air, resulted in all the mountains being covered in vibrant blue and green colored moss and algae. Adding to the beauty were the addition of stones such as; emeralds, alexandrite and jadeite embedded right into the surface. Making Mojarro the most beautiful in all of Madaka. Rubies were found on some of the more northern mountains. And King Zander had soldiers protecting the jewels twenty-four hours a day.

On the opposite side of the Trojian Sea, sat the city of Panga. The smallest of the four cities. Panga had the most nutrient soil in Madaka. Their land was mostly flat with small amounts of gold in their clear green streams. The land was colorful, with four shades of green grass and plenty of vegetation. But Panga lacked jewels and precious metals. Something highly sought after, as they enjoyed adorning themselves with it. There were two mountains in the entire city and both were abundant in one stone that was unique to them. The sapphire. Its beautiful rich blue color was popular to all the other cities except Mojarro, would was heavy in jewels and had no desire for the stone. It yielded high trade value with Eulachon and Piratchu, but their most valuable resource was their soil and exotic and edible plants. Panga was ruled by King Nephrus. He was a strong leader who kept the peace between the lands by constantly traveling to speak with each leader. Panga's claim to fame was their ability to grow plants not found anywhere else. All thanks to their soil.

Adjacent to Panga, across a large body of water, was the city of Piratchu. A small city, in comparison to Mojarro and Eulachon. It was the only city ruled by a woman. A Queen named Rasbora, who was a strong and fearless woman. Her army was large and the men were committed to her. She had the most aggressive army in Madaka. Her men would die to save her honor. Queen Rasbora had two daughters. Princess Eilena and Princess Darbee. Her city, Piratchu, was also rich in plants, soil and wood and was the only city with an abundance of pearls in their waters. They had the largest and tallest trees. And men were employed to keep the trees healthy and ready for extraction. The wood was cut down and traded for jewels like emeralds, alexandrite, gold and other metals.

Then there was Eulachon, the largest city in Madaka. A large section of land with huge mountains. Eulachon was not adorned with jewels. It was a city once beautiful and vibrant. But decades of heat, gases and aggressive farming, had all but ravaged the land. Their natural and most abundant resource was oil and edible aquatic life. Their rivers and lakes were teaming with rare and delicious sea animals. And their oil was used for everything from cooking to personal use. Eulachon's beloved leader, King Orfe, was a gentle and mild-mannered man.

He led by example, often going to the people and engaging with them. And the citizens of Eulachon looked up to him. He doted on his one and only child. A son. Prince Andreus. And young man who didn't share in his father's ideals and beliefs. Prince Andreus had plans. He liked the power. And he had plans to execute his own political agenda. They were the largest land with the smallest amount of highly sought-after resources. And yet they were the most powerful.

Eulachon was partially surrounded by land that spewed molten lava. It was unique to that area. Eulachonians had become adept to the gases emitted from the seeping gaps in the ground. And Fin's father, King Zander, always believed that if their people came to Mojarro, they would be the only ones capable of crossing over the dune and entering the lair. A highly protective opening that no one ventured to. Its existence was kept from all the people of the four nations. King Zander was one of a few people aware of its existence.

It was called the *gates of hell* by Madaka's forefathers. The gods and goddesses of the ocean; The creators of the oceanic world. And no one wanted the species on the other side to invade their world. A group of people known for extreme violence. Deceivers who would rape the land and claim it as their own. King Zander had been taught about the *Dry Land Dwellers.* A race of people that he would need to always stay hidden from. It was a precaution that the old wise men of Mojarro were the first to talk about. Many believed it was a tale made up to entertain the young and control the old. But Zander knew better. His father had proof. And the *Dark Lair* was kept a secret.

Of all the cities, Eulachon was the most feared. They had the largest army and the largest population. Although the world of Madaka existed in peace, each city still kept an active military and each leader travels with guards and soldiers close by. There wasn't always peace. What tranquility they experienced, was the result of years of fighting. Peace had come at a cost. And only after thousands of lives were lost.

King Zander was well aware that other leaders sought his land. He had built a formidable army himself. He too, sought to gain access to things he did not have. His solution was easy. Marry off his daughter and gain a second city through the joining of two leaders. Queen Rasbora also had two daughters that she could marry off. She too had a chance to join forces and combine wealth and resources. But no princess was as beautiful as Finora. The king was sure he would have the opportunity to choose successfully. There was Panga, which would be ruled by Price Osiris one day. Then there was Eulachon, and Prince Andreus. He had reasons for interest in both lands. But there was a problem. Fin was not docile. She was not demure or easy to control. It would take time and convincing. And unknown to the king was the fact that his daughter *was* different. She was much more complex. It was more than the color of her tail. She had a different spirit. Different desires. Much more than he could have ever imagined. And she would seek love. Real love. The tangible kind. And she would find it in the unlikeliest of places.

3

An Unfulfilled Life

"Ok, so listen. The new owner is on his way here. His name is…" the man said, as he walked through the office of *Bandz Technology Firm.* David looked at a fax he had just received. Everything was going so fast. It had been just a few days since the owner passed away. And a team of lawyers scurried to find an heir. Howard Reed had left behind a vast fortune. A will drafted in his own handwriting and tucked into a safe, dispelled all rumors. Erased any fear. The company would continue on. Mr. Reed had a son. A man ironically in the same line of work. The move would be seamless. He had been brought up to speed on the current state of affairs for *Bandz Technology.* A firm that was made reputable by their tablet style cell phones.

The lawyers located a long-lost son, who himself owned a small but successful technology company in Boston. The handwritten will left his son and only child, everything. IT was Howards way of repaying for time lost. He hadn't laid eyes on his son in years. This was a way to pay him back for not being in his life. His brief encounter with the man's mother had left him a father. A role he never wanted.

"What's his name? Do we know anything?" the secretary said. "Barely! He will be here shortly. I want you to make an announcement and have everyone come to Conference Room C."

Dave grabbed his things and headed to the conference room to brief the employees. He wasn't sure what he would say. Some people had quit upon the death of their beloved boss. Others waited. It was a strong company with vast holdings and a bright future. They were on the cutting edge of technology. No one wanted to see the company fail. Not with several promising inventions set to change the course of communication, ready to be unveiled.

"Ok everyone. Sorry for the last-minute meeting. I'll make this quick. As you all have probably heard by now, Howard had a son," he said. The room went quiet. Whisperes suddenly halted. "No! I haven't heard that. What son?" one of the computer scientists said. Dave looked intently at him. "He had a son George. That's all I know right now. If you let me finish. Can everyone hold off comments until I have finished," he said, giving George a stern look.

"As I was saying. Howard had a son. He is also into communications and technology. He had his own business based out of Boston. He had decided to join us here at Bandz. In fact, he is on his way here now. I wanted to brief you before he got here. Please make him feel welcomed. It can't be easy losing your father and stepping into his place at a company you are unfamiliar with. I expect George, Thomas and Lionel to bring him up to speed. Kathy and Marisa will meet with him separately to go over sales projections and what's coming up," Dave said. Soon whispers filled the room.

"Hold on. Let me finish," he interjected. "No. Wait Dave. No one said anything about a son. Some young cat's going to just come here. Run the place? Does he have a degree? Does he know anything about this business? We have lost half our workforce already. Half! We can't survive without engineers and scientist. Some of our account executives have left. The meat and potatoes of our company. Who is this kid?" the man said, as people around him shook their head in agreeance.

"My name is Lance Neilson Reed. But please, call me Lance," a voice said from the doorway. Everyone quickly turned around. The room went silent. Lance was no kid. He looked like a man with a plan. He was confident. Charming. Handsome. Sophisticated. It was obvious he was already a success. His well-tailored suit and expensive shirt and tie, couldn't be missed. He wore it well.

Lance was the personification of male perfection. His thick lashes and eyebrows coupled with almond shaped, powerful looking eyes, were mesmerizing. It seemed the gods had showed him favor. His mustache and goatee finished his look. And his clothes fit him impeccably, showing off the fact that there was a trim and muscular physique beneath the two thousand dollar wool blend suit. Every woman in attendance of the impromptu meeting took notice.

The women swooned. His presence was captivating. Lance cleared his throat. He didn't mean to cause panic or take anyone by surprise. But the silence was deafening. "Oh. Mr. Reed. Welcome. Glad you could make it. Everyone, this is Lance Reed. The new owner of Bandz Technology. Please make him feel at home," Dave said.

"Thank you, Dave. I just want to say hello to everyone. And thank each and every one of you for staying on with the company. I'm sure my father's sudden death was a shock to you all. But we will mourn together and honor him by building on his legacy. I have a lot to learn. And I am hoping to sit with each of you to get your thoughts on the company's strengths and weaknesses. Just so you know, my background is in technology. I have a Master's Degree in Computer Science and Engineering. Bandz will continue to thrive and grow. Please be patient. And anyone who needs to talk, my door is always open," Lance assured.

"Thank you, Mr. Reed. Welcome," one woman said. She was the manager of Human Resources and she was already looking forward to working with him. "Hi," Angel, the sales assistant greeted. Soon everyone said hello. The secretary looked at one of the female account executives and grinned. He was impressive. He was more than eye candy. He seemed down to earth. They looked forward to working with him.

Dave introduced every person in the conference room. Some women gave each other looks. One kicked her co-worker. He was intimidating. Sexy and sophisticated. And obviously intelligent. He came with a lengthy and successful career in technology and had several degrees to his credit.

But Lance was humbled. He was aware of his attraction to the opposite sex. But being visual perfection had not saved him from heartache and pain. If the employees of Bandz were expecting some male whore, hell bent on showing his prowess, they would be mistaken. Lance was picky. He had tried his hand at dating. But it wasn't for him. He had been in several long-standing relationships. The last one, testing his strength and perseverance as a man and human being. He had suffered a great loss. And as a result, was single and not ready to jump back into the dating pool. He had overcome a lot. And now he was in a new city running a new company. A major move from him. And there was no one there to lean on. He knew no one in California. He didn't even know his father.

Lance spent nearly an hour talking to his employees and being brought up to speed on some of the more urgent matters. He and Dave excused themselves and had a private meeting to cover more serious issues. Dave was impressed with Lance's credentials. He was a man of considerable education and wealth himself. And now he was inheriting a huge fortune. He was also inheriting his father's cars, homes, properties, land and other valuables. His father's watch collection alone was valued at more than five million dollars.

Lance was overwhelmed. He hadn't had a chance to even mourn for the man whose face he saw only through Forbes.

"Thanks Dave. Thanks for everything. I have to get going. I am meeting movers at the house in Malibu. It's the only property that I may keep. I haven't decided," he said. Dave smiled. He knew his boss well. Howard was an opulent man. He had more homes than any one man would ever need. "Yeah. Your father loved cars and homes. He just liked to own things," Dave said. "Yeah. I see," Lance replied. Dave looked at Lance. He was friendly but he seemed like the type of man that liked his privacy. Dave wasn't sure he should question him. But he was curious.

"So, you have family? Wife? Kids?" he asked. "No. Not yet. It's just me for now," he replied. Dave chuckled. He was a newlywed with twins. "Well, don't be too much in a hurry. Your life isn't yours after the family starts growing."

Lance laughed. He agreed. But he was still a romantic at heart. And no matter what, he still looked forward to marriage and children. But it seemed fleeting. He had been on a few dates. But his heart wasn't in it. He hated the casualness of it. The uncertainty. And he was confused as to why he didn't seem destined for marital bliss. Within the last year alone, he'd been on six dates and two almost dates that he ended after seeing their online profiles. Most of the dates were set up by his half-brother, Allan. He meant well.

Allan had worried about his younger brother. He was still mourning the death of his unborn child. A tragedy he and his fiancé could not overcome. After the miscarriage, Paula went into a depression and their relationship could not handle the strain. The marriage was called off and Lance suffered in silence. Paula was in her eighth month of pregnancy. A rare condition was to blame. But Lance blamed himself. He believed she was under stress from his hectic travelling schedule, and the fact that he always wanted her to accompany him. Allan stepped in to pick up the pieces when Paula left. He began setting him up on dates with women he knew. Various women from different backgrounds. All beautiful and intelligent women. But one after the other, Lance found a reason not to go on a second date. He was particular. And he wasn't sure what he was looking for. All he knew was he would know it when he felt it.

"Thank you for all your help. See you in the morning," Lance said to his secretary. He was adjusting well. It had been a great first few months. Maria smiled and shut her computer down for the day. She was attracted to her new boss. But Maria was no fool. She needed her job. An office romance with the owner could end badly and she would probably be out of work. So, she snickered at the thought. He was eye candy that she would have the pleasure of working with every day. Nothing more. Lance walked with Dave out together. The men talked about the meeting they had lined up as they made their way through the parking structure. "See you in the morning," Dave said as Lance walked up to his SUV parked in a private spot with his name on it. "Yep. I'll see you tomorrow," Lance replied.

It was a scenic drive to his home in Malibu. Lance open the double doors of his gate and pulled into the driveway. The Oceanfront property was breathtaking. A custom-built home, that sat close to the ocean. Its structure, a part of the rock it sat on. A long, man-made wood dock stretched from the home, out into the ocean. Howard Reed was a man who loved his toys. And his most cherished was his water toys.

"Mr. Reed," the man said, as he approached Lance's car. Lance rolled the window down and shook the man's hand. "Hi. Am I all set?" he asked. "Almost. Just a few more things," the man replied. Lance sighed. He saw movers taking furniture inside. He had left the door unlocked and had an interior designer furnish the home. "I will be right back. I saw you out here and just wanted to update you. There are just a few more items that need to be placed and we will be all set," he said.

Lance sat back. He scratched his head and then looked around. His favorite part of the property. Where it was built set it apart from the other homes. Beachfront property was prime real estate. And the views were spectacular. Lance looked forward to sunsets. He yearned for the outdoors. He was a water guy. He loved beaches. Long walks. He used to surf but had given it up. This was perfect for him.

"All done Mr. Reed," the man said. Lance was so consumed with his thoughts, that he didn't see the man walk up. "Yes," he said, as he rolled the window down. "Come take a tour. We are all done. I want to make sure everything is to your liking," he said.

Lance walked the house, room to room, making sure there were no other changes he wanted. "This is great. I love it. I have no changes. It's perfect," he said. "I'll make the final charge to your card. Would you like me to mail you the receipt?": he asked. "Sure. Thanks a lot," Lance replied. He walked the man and his crew to the door and then walked into his newly decorated great-room and plopped down. His timing was perfect.

He watched the sun as it set. It was a spectacular sight. The last time he saw a perfect sunset was on a beach in Hawaii. He was hypnotized by its beauty. And he would now get to see it every evening. Lance got comfortable. He had dinner in the fridge. He got up and heated the plate and sat back down. He tried to relax and get acclimated to his new life. Thoughts of his father consumed him. A man who had no time for him. A man he had tried to contact before being stopped by his mother. Her words cutting deep like a knife. Naomi told her young son that his father was ready to be a dad. That he abandoned his responsibilities. But Lance pressed on anyway. And when he heard his voice one day when he called his office, fear consumed him and he hung up. Lance decided to write a letter. In it he detailed how he admired him. How he hoped to meet him one day. That he loved him regardless of his decision to not be in his life. Lance never heard from Howard. And when his lawyers showed up on his doorstep, it was all overwhelming.

He hated himself for admiring a man he barely knew. But it was Howards success that would mold him into the man he ultimately became. He learned everything he could about the elusive Howard Reed. The man who abandoned his pregnant girlfriend before she gave birth to their son. His only child. He wanted to feel like they had something in common.

And so, he followed the same path. Took the same classes. All in an effort, to be like him. All in an effort to make Howard pay attention to him. He didn't think it worked. Howard never attended one ceremony. Never watched as his son accepted award after award. It wasn't until the lawyers handed him a letter they found along with the will, that he got a glimpse of what Howard thought about him. The letter read;

Dear Son,

If you are reading this, then I have passed on. I cannot begin to explain to you my life. My childhood. The complications that led to me deciding to never father children. It was not your fault. You did not ask to be here. And I spared you the trouble of knowing the horrible person I was on the inside. My success came from a deep seeded passion to never fail at anything. And a fear of being poor. I grew up eating out of garbage cans and I promised myself I would never go hungry again. I over compensated, I guess. But of all my accomplishments and vast wealth, my greatest accomplishment was you.

I watched you from afar. I was there when you got your diploma. I was there at Boston U when you got your Bachelors and again when you received your Master's from Harvard. I was so proud of you. I wanted so desperately to tell you how sorry I was. How much I regretted not being there. But it was too late. And you were a grown man. I couldn't face you. That's when I discovered I was a coward. I know money doesn't erase pain. I know that first hand. But I still feel I owe you something. And money is all I have to give. The only good thing I had to give.

I have left everything to you. It was the least I could do. Do with it what you want. If you turn away from it or burn it, no one could blame you. I know you don't need it. You have done well. I even came to the hospital to see you. Your mother never saw me. But you did. You seemed to look me straight in the eyes. I stared at you through the glass. Wishing you would forgive me one day. And then I turned and left. It was the first time I ever cried in my life. I love you son. Take Care!

Lance didn't understand how a man could have a son and not reach out to him. And Lance wanted to know his father. He had tried contacting him over the years. He wished for just one meeting. One chance. And when it never happened, he was resentful. Howard couldn't help himself. He was never the fatherly type. Naomi Stiles already had one son when she found out she was pregnant with Lance. And when she contacted her lover to inform him that they were expecting a child, he instantly froze up. And Naomi felt the burn. Howard feared what that meant. He felt overwhelmed. He left soon after, leaving a large amount of cash. Naomi, heartbroken and devastated, relocated and raised her sons alone. She used the money to educate both her sons and never looked back.

"Good morning Mr. Reed," the secretary greeted "Good morning. Can you announce a meeting? I want to meet with the engineers and scientist. I will have a separate meeting with sales later this week," he said. "Yes sir," she replied. Maria watched her handsome boss walk away. She couldn't help but be attracted, even though she promised herself she would keep her lustful thoughts to a minimum. She was a professional and good at appearing that way. But her attraction was more than physical. He was brilliant.

Lance had made good on his promises and she stood behind him as did many others at the firm. Good changes were happening. And their first quarter with the new owner was better than predicted. He had an impeccable reputation according to Dave who had done some research of his own. And every contact in Boston said the same thing. That Lance was a charismatic and shrewd businessman with a near perfect GPA from one of the most prestigious schools in Boston.

"Good morning," the employee said as he took a seat. Lance stood at the head of the conference room table. He smiled at each employee as they entered. His phone buzzed. He looked at the text message. It was his brother Allan. He sent a message asking if he should fly there. Lance smiled. He missed his brother. They had a tight bond. This was just like Allan to take time out from his busy schedule to make sure his baby brother was adjusting well. Their mother Naomi was deteriorating and it was devastating for them. Allan had a different father and his father was in his life. He was also married with a son and daughter, so he had a much stronger support system than Lance. Lance was unmarried with no children. And with his mother's mental frailty, he had no one to lean on except Allan.

"Excuse me. I need to make a call. Please look over the meeting notes. We will discuss projects in detail. I need an idea of what needs my immediate attention and what can wait," he said, as he walked out into the hall and called Allan.

"Hey. Just got your message," he said. "Hey. Just calling. How are things?" Allan asked. "Good. I'm at work right now. Got an important meeting. We need to go over some of the projects my father was working on. Allan...When I tell you this man was brilliant. I mean...He has things in the works that are revolutionary. Game changers. It's impressive," Lance said. Allan held the phone. He wasn't convinced Lance was ready for such a massive change in his life. But his brother was strong. Stubborn. And when he has his mind made up, there was no changing it.

"I mean…It's a lot. But I can handle it. You know me," Lance said. Allan chuckled. "Yeah. That's what worries me. You take on a lot. And you don't say anything. Won't ask for help. Then get overwhelmed. You want me to come there? Help you with the company? Kerry and I have come to an agreement for now. She wants to separate. Work on herself. In the meantime, I have to take the kids. She can't cope. They have been with me a few weeks now. The timing couldn't be worse. But we could come there if you needed us to," Allan offered. "No. I'm good for now. But you should come in a few months. When things settle. The house is fabulous. I have plenty room for you and the kids," he said.

Allan agreed. It sounded like a plan. He would bring his children to visit. Malibu was a beautiful place with great views and premium waterfront properties. Allan was not as accomplished as his younger brother. And his father was a man of minimal means. But what he lacked in financial resources he made up for in love and support. Lance held a high regard for Allan's father. He was a surrogate father to him. Always there when he needed a man's guidance. He and Allan were important men in his life.

And Allan was no slouch. Lance watched him slide through school with ease, always getting the best grades. He had finished law school and had his degree. But the activist in him had him taking on a lot of pro-bono work, and so he didn't earn what he could have. Lance opened his wallet and helped save Allan's house by paying the mortgage in full. He knew Allan was brilliant. He believed Allan would be wealthy, if he would stop trying to save the world. But Allan did try and save the world and Lance saw to it that he never suffered financially.

"Hey. Gotta go. My meeting is starting. You need anything?" Lance asked. "No. I'm good. Call me later."

$\mathcal{L}$ance walked inside his home exhausted. He sat his keys on the console and sorted through his father's mail. There was nothing that needed his attention. He tossed the pile in a small wicker basket and walked into the great-room. The sun had already set. Not completely ruining his evening, but almost.

The homes outdoor solar lights came on automatically. Lance walked to the wall and turned on the high-powered lights that lined the rocks and exterior porch. He flicked on the lights that angled towards the water. And the ones that lined the floor.

"I wish we could have talked. It would have been nice to meet you. We are a lot alike. Well…That's what your employees say. I wouldn't know. You never gave me the chance. You leave me all this. Yet I would return it for a chance to have known you," he said, in a low voice as he stared out at the water.

It was all so humbling. The waves of the water were calming. Lance reminisced on his life. He was a family man. This was a lot for a single man. He longed to meet a woman he could marry and start a life with. He had tired of his single life. His last relationship lasted just six months. It was the closest he'd come to a serious commitment since his fiancé Paula. He blamed himself. He was unwilling to compromise. Partly due to not being over Paula. But that was all behind him. He had a new life.

There was no regret. Lance was comfortable. He was surprised how much so. Owning his father's company felt right. As if built, with the sole purpose of him being the owner. Lance shook his head. He could do this. He shed a tear for his father. He stood in the window. The letter from Howard clutched in his hand. It was bittersweet. This was his new life. And he had a feeling there was more in store for him. Something big. Something meaningful.

4

Father Knows Best

"Excuse me Princess. The King would like to see you," the guard stated, as he approached from behind. Fin sat perched on a stump. A downed tree covered in moss. Her feet in the beautiful green water. She could see small yellow tail fish. Finora sighed. She was enjoying the water. The view. The sky. It was a beautiful day. "Sure," she said, as she turned around and smiled at Lark. Her father's trusted personal guard. He gave her a look and then turned and walked away. Fin watched him walk away then stared at the water. There was something about Lark that was appealing. Something charming. She was surprised that she never noticed him before. She hadn't realized she was a woman. No one made much mention of it. Her mother never told her she would feel different. Want different things. Notice a lot more. Mostly men. But it was noted. It was the reason King Zander felt she was ready. Finora was bequeathed to Prince Andreus of Eulachon and he was ready to inform her.

"Yes poppa," she said, as she slowly entered his chambers. "Fin. Come in. Sit," he said, as he sat drinking fresh *Haku.* A wine made from seagrass, local fruits and yeast. Finora was nervous. Her father seemed very formal. He looked like a man with a lot on his mind. She sat down close to the edge of the chair. Her uncomfortableness apparent. King Zander took a sip of haku. He looked at his daughter. She wasn't ready and he had been patient. Prince Andreus was pressuring him to produce her. He had grown into a powerful man. He would soon run a vast kingdom. He had a party planned. All in the hopes of impressing his future queen. He had proven himself worthy. He had been victorious in battle and in the tasks given to him. Battles won on land and in the sea. His strength and cunning ability displayed before his people. A necessity, in order to lead the people of Eulachon. He had fought the great animals of the sea. He was victorious. Proving he was ready to be crowned and take his seat at the throne when his father passed. Prince Andreus had plans. And Fin was a big part of a bigger picture.

"Father…," Prince Andreus said, as he kneeled at his beloved father's bedside. King Orfe reached out and held his hand. Andreus wept. He could see his father was weak. He felt his father was slowly slipping away. But Andreus had faith. He was in denial. King Orfe didn't have much longer. Time was near. The king stared at his only son. His mouth moving. Andreus got close. "Yes father," he said. King Orfe took a deep breath. "I said…Make me proud. Be better than I was," he said. "Yes father," Andreus replied. The king found the strength to speak. He cleared his throat. He spoke. This time louder. His son needed the message. It was a vast undertaking. And his son would be king soon.

"Son. You have a responsibility to the people. I want you to make me proud. Eulachon is yours. But it is a city that looks to its leader for guidance, protection and strength. I want you to move forward, taking us into the future. Your marriage to King Zander's daughter will combine the two most powerful lands. I hope I am still here to witness your union," he said. Andreus became angered. He wanted his father there. And if King Zander would make coming to Eulachon a priority, he would be. But King Zander was procrastinating. He was taking a long time responding to the invitation. Andreus wondered why. He had a sinking feeling about it.

"I don't think she wants to marry, father. It is taking too long. I sent a message to the King asking that we proceed with the union. He sent a message back requesting more time."

King Orfe looked off. He remembered a conversation between himself and King Zander. When the subject of marriage between their offspring came up, his demeanor changed.

"She will be your wife. She probably wants time to prepare. She knows her life will change. Once you two are brought together, she will not see her parents. That is a lot to accept. Give her time," he said. "No father! They don't have much longer. You are ill. I want you there."

Prince Andreus held his father's hand. The King closed his eyes. He grunted as he winced in pain. Andreus stared at him. His father was becoming weaker. It wasn't the first time he was sick. And this time was more serious. He hadn't been out of bed in days. It seemed time was running out. He wanted his father to live to see him do as was he was expected. Marry and take his seat at the throne. Follow in his father's footsteps. Theirs was the greatest nation. The strongest.

He turned and left his father's chambers. Andreus walked with purpose. It was time to force his hand. Eulachon was double the size of Mojarro. Their army, three times the size of King Zanders. He saw no reason to play fair. His father was a kind man. He kept the peace, allowing trade with the three cities. Prince Andreus saw no reason to trade. Why not take what he wanted. In return, a promise of peace. Madaka was not evenly divided. They had the majority of land. The majority of food. The other nations would not want to survive on plants alone.

But above all else, he wanted Fin. He would play by the rules if he could begin his life the way his father planned. He would continue to do fair trade and keep the peace between the lands. But if Finora would not be his, then the future of Mojarro was uncertain. So was the future of the other two cities. He would take her. Even if it meant killing the King. And he would make his demands. There hadn't been war in the land of Madaka in over four hundred years. But Prince Andreus was a wild card. He had visions that weren't typical of their kind. They were a normally peaceful species. It was their natural way. But Prince Andreus was different. He had been since he was a child.

He was aggressive, forceful, overbearing, domineering and bossy. And with no intervention from his doting father, his behavior culminated into that of a small dictator. And now he was poised to take over. And he had plans. Madaka would be ran in a more streamlined way. Eulachon was the largest and more powerful, therefore it would lead. Andreus was prepared to tell the other leaders. But first he would need to make his home the home he envisioned. One with Fin sitting at her throne beside him.

Fin waited patiently while her father spoke with his guard. He was being informed that King Nephrus wanted to take a meeting with him. "Send a message back that I will come to Panga tomorrow. Please do not disturb me again," he said. King Zander shut the door and returned to his chair and sat next to Fin. He looked her in the eyes. Her mother, Queen Aterra, was waiting in her room. She gave them privacy. This was a conversation between father and daughter. It was time. And her father had chosen.

"Fin. It is time that you live your life. It is time that you move towards a future that will best suit you. One that will ensure the growth and stability of Mojarro. And the other cities," he said. He paused. Fin's eyes widened. She felt knots in her stomach. "Please father!" she pleaded. She had a feeling what he would say. The king continued. He held Fin's hand. She slowly pulled it away.

"Prince Anreas wishes for your hand. He is waiting for an answer. The marriage will mean better trade opportunities between Mojarro and Eulachon. You will have the best of both cities. And we are the two largest cities. Panga and Piratchu will offer the best of their cities as gifts and as peace offerings. In our entire history, no one has ever wed someone from another city. This will be the first of its kind. It opens the doors to other possibilities. Your children can grow up and marry a prince or princess from Panga. From Piratchu. We can move towards a more unified existence. And great things can happen."

Fin shook her head slowly back and forth. "I have met him. He is not nice. He is arrogant. Self-centered. And condescending with his words. I would rather die a thousand deaths. Please father. Can't I pick my own mate. Can't I feel deeply for someone and then marry. I want to be happy," she said. King Zander stood up. He walked over to his gold inlay wine cabinet and poured himself another drink.

"There is much at stake Fin. There is a bigger picture here. He will honor you as his wife. He will give favor unto you. It will take time. Once he has become enamored with you. Once you give him children. He will be humble. Because he will not want to lose you. You will be valuable to him.

Marry him and you will have control over him. Over trade. He will give in to you. He will be under your influence," he assured. Fin stared. She was too shocked to speak. King Zander could see she was displeased.

"You will be delivered to him tomorrow. The guards will escort us through the town towards the Palimora Sea. We will be with you. Do not be afraid. It will work out. Please trust in this union. This marriage will be a grand celebration. The world will envy you."

The room went silent. Fin's eyes teared up. She didn't see herself married to him. She didn't want to have children with him. "Go to your room and get yourself together. Prepare yourself. We leave in the morning," Zander said. "I don't get a say?" she asked. "No," he said, in a low tone. Fin turned and walked out. She never had a choice. Her father had already decided.

Zander took one gulp of what was in his cup. He felt bad. He wanted her happy. It was not supposed to be torturous. But their union was important. And he believed Fin's opinion about the prince was unfounded. He believed it was based off of fears. And all would be well once she got over her jitters and opened up to the idea. She would be the most powerful woman in all the land. She was making history.

Lark stood outside the door talking to two guards. Fin looked at him and rolled her eyes. She was angry at the world. She felt bad afterwards. He had done nothing. Said nothing. She wondered if he knew. If he did, then she wouldn't regret rolling her eyes. He could have said something. Prepared her some sort of way. Fin was tired of secrets. It seemed everyone had an agenda.

"Excuse me," Lark said, as he pushed past the soldiers. "You ok?" he asked. Fin continued walking. "Fin! What's wrong?" he asked. Fin quickly turned around. "You tell me. You are with my father every day. He trusts you. He tells you everything. And you always speak to me. You're always near me. Looking at me. Yet you would know I am to marry, and not say anything," she said, looking intensely at him. Lark narrowed his eyes. "What," he said, his eyes filled with pain. Fin looked intensely at him. He looked troubled. As though hearing it for the first time himself.

"You didn't know?" she said, shocked that her father kept it from him. Lark shook his head no, slowly. Fin could see something change in him. He looked at her differently. A longing. A sadness. She felt like a woman for the first time. Lark was a man. A man's man. Particular and loyal. He had his pick of single females and yet he remained single. Fin always wondered why. He was skilled at keeping his eyes to himself. He stole looks and glances whenever he could. Most men his age was married with children. But he lived a single life. He still lived in the servant's house behind the castle, even though he had the means to live on his own. He could take breaks. But he never did. And something in his eyes told her it was because of her.

******

"Gather the soldiers. It is time," King Zander commanded. He walked down the hall towards his wife's chambers. "It is time. Can you help Fin get ready?" he said. Queen Aterra smiled. She too, wanted the union. She envisioned her grandchildren being the future of all of Madaka. The four cities could one day be united. "I will help her get ready. Give us a moment," she replied.

Aterra walked the long hall to Fin's room. She was happy for her daughter. A result from the fact that her motherly instincts were never honed. She had failed to notice Fin's hesitation. Her anxiety. Most marriages in Madaka were set up by the father. And one was expected to be happy. Especially if they were marrying a prince. Not that Aterra would understand. She didn't have first-hand knowledge of what it felt like. She'd had the privilege of marrying someone she'd known her whole life. She had fell in love with, and married, her prince charming. They were raised in the same household. The castle of Mojarro.

"Can I come in," Aterra said, as she knocked gently on her daughter's door. She waited for a reply. It was quiet. Aterra knocked again. She narrowed her eyes then slowly opened the door. "Fin!" she called out, as she walked inside. Aterra walked through her daughter's oversized room. The walls lined in gold colored silk. Fin's love of plants was displayed prominently throughout. Rare hemini plants imported from Piratchu were her favorite. They glowed at night. A natural bright light that gave off a bright yellow hue. The world of Madaka glowed naturally at night. There was no electricity. No light bulbs. During the day, light from a sun like source in their beautiful blue skies shined down on the land. And at night, moss and algae came to life as their bioluminescent properties illuminated the ground and surrounding mountains. It was a remarkable sight. Madaka was beautiful.

Aterra was perplexed. Fin was nowhere to be found. "Fin!" she called again. Soon Finora emerged from her bath. "My goodness. Didn't you hear me calling you?' she asked. "Yes mother," she replied. Her voice harsh. He words abrupt. She wasn't in a good mood. Fin felt strange about going to meet with the man she would be marrying. The man she met in the sea one day. She was unimpressed. He acted arrogant and entitled. She never told her father that Eulachonians were in the water. The prince himself. Near their mountains under the sea. That he acted as though he had a right to be there. She didn't like him. But now she would be marrying him. It was overwhelming.

"Come sit. Let's talk," Aterra said. Fin looked at her. This was unlike her mother. She was rarely available for talks. Even at times when she had so many questions. What she learned about life she had to observe or get from Rae. Aterra was secretive. Quiet. Private. And usually absent. Fin walked over to the bed and sat next to her mother. Aterra touched her hand. Fin was in shock.

"Are you worried. Don't be. You are ready. You will make him a great wife," she said. Fin bit her lip. Her mother had never touched her. Touch was avoided in their world. Their happiness came from conversation and their surroundings. Bonding came from families having dinner as one. Giving gifts. Doing favors. Touch was irritating. Their sensitive skin too delicate for it. Even a husband didn't touch his wife. You were touched as a baby. Once you were big enough to walk, touching all but disappeared. Aterra was innately familiar with it. She had a desire for touch that perplexed the king. Aterra was rare in many different ways. And her daughter was even rarer.

She longed for a touch. She remembered it as a child. And she never forgot how it comforted her. Soothed her frightened spirit at times. The absence of it propelled Fin into a life of mischievous behavior. Like the time at five years old when she jumped into the sea. And the times she hid from her mother. Behavior that stemmed from a deep-rooted hatred at her worlds disconnect. And the confusion she felt for desiring something no one else seemed to care about. She remained defiant in her youth. A trait she was outgrowing. But old habits die hard. She was being defiant once again. She didn't want to go and she thought of running away. Prince Andreus embodied old world values. He would not be open to change. He would not seek truth. Or a different kind of love. He would love without personal involvement. Babies made from pools of sperm floating in contained tubs. No sex involved, even though they had the means. Not that Fin knew.

She was unaware that what she felt was called sexual desires. It was unique for her. No one else desired to be close. Their private organs were void of sensation. Sexual intercourse not a part of intimacy for them. There was no joining together. No physical closeness or copulation. Their satisfaction came from smell. Sight. And the knowledge that they were cared for through one's actions.

Fin felt betrayed by her own body. She believed something was wrong with her. That the sensations she felt was a sign of sickness. She hid it. Acknowledging what she was experiencing would only bring ridicule and confusion. So, she kept it to herself. Always wondering if there were any others who felt that way. Namely her mother.

"What's wrong Fin? Why do you seem so unhappy? It is normal to be nervous," she stated. Fin pulled her hand away. Her mother had not been honest. She could feel it. She wondered why the secrets. What was she not saying.

"Mom? Do you ever feel strange? Like…Do you ever want to touch dad?" she asked. Aterra narrowed her eyes and looked away in confusion. This was not the conversation she wanted to have. She looked back at Fin. "Strange? What do you mean?" she asked. "I don't know. In your body. In your special parts. Where the babies come from?" she asked. Aterra was floored. This was a conversation they shouldn't be having. "I mean. Don't you ever want to touch dad. Hold his hand. Hold him close. Why don't you? Why doesn't anyone? What are we afraid of?" she asked.

Aterra had heard enough. It was an abomination. No one touched. No one held hands. Only small children and it was only as needed. It wasn't necessary to express love. Words, energy, emotional transference were the ways to a person's heart. And loyalty. Always being available. It was unheard of, to physically touch one another. Babies were the result of sperm pools. Timed perfectly during ovulation, as the female entered water in a controlled, confined space after the male exited. It was their way of life. It had been since their existence. They were a lot like fish. Sex was unknown. Their minds and bodies did not yearn sexual pleasures.

But Fin was different. Something had been going on in her body for quite some time. She panicked at first. And then hid what was happening after Rae shamed her. But Fin was to be married. She didn't want to lay in sperm pools. Something in her wanted touch. Wanted to be close. And she hoped to get answers. And even though she was free-spirited and was known to say anything, Aterra was unprepared. She considered Fin's behavior a clever ploy to get out of her duties and responsibilities. That fear was guiding her. And she was being dramatic.

"What? No! Good grief child. Where do you get such things?" she said, as she shook her head slowly. Fin could feel the tension. She could see her mother's poise change. Something had her edgy. Tense. Aterra was a woman of few words. But this should have been a conversation that would yield more. Fin became frustrated. There was something her mother was not saying.

"Why don't you ever get in the water mom?" she asked. Aterra gasped, placing her hand on her chest. She was not used to being questioned. And surely not by her child. "Fin! Stop this now! All of these ridiculous questions. Where does your mind go? Stop this now before people think you are insane," she said, looking away. The queen was shocked at her daughter's candor. "What people ma! We are talking in private. I am your daughter. If you can't talk to me who can you talk to? Dad? About things regarding a woman's body? No, you can't" she said, taking a deep breath and releasing it slowly.

"There are things I've noticed. And you never talk about them. And there have been times I needed you and you weren't there. And when I was confused and tried to touch you, you pulled away. You cut me off from you as a child. It was very painful. I tried to hold onto your leg one day. I was frightened by a loud noise. But you pushed me away," she said. Finora continued on as Aterra listened.

"I don't understand why I desire things I can't have. And my body...I have these weird sensations. I can't explain them. Down where the water comes out. And I have strange feelings in my chest. I tried to tell you before. You looked so uncomfortable. And you started talking about something else. And now I am to marry," she said. Aterra stood up. She couldn't take much more. She'd had enough. "Get ready Fin. We leave soon," she replied. Fin fumed.

"Did you hear anything I just said? Do you know me at all? Do you not know your own child? I don't want him. I have no interest. He never crosses my mind. I don't want to. I can't explain why. I just think bad of him. Please don't make me do it," she pleaded.

Aterra looked like a woman with a thousand secrets. Fin looked at her. She hoped her mother would ease the stress. Open up. Be on her side. No one was around. It was safe. They could speak on things their world didn't think about. Things that was foreign to them. Finora could tell what she was experiencing was unique. And she wondered why that was.

"You are to marry him Fin. What you describe I have no answers for. I only know that you are to marry Prince Andreus. He promised your father to make you comfortable. He promised to be a good mate. You will have whatever you want. It is really the best thing for you. He will be king of the largest land. When you are his queen, you two can decide how to bring the two lands together. After your father and I have passed on, this will all be yours. You will be free to do with it as you please. Now get ready. It is time for you to meet him," she said as she walked to the door.

Aterra was unable to look Fin in the eyes. She opened the door and glanced back. She gave a half-hearted smile. Fin became emotional. But she held her head high. The one person who should help her navigate through life was determined not to do so at the risk of exposure. She wouldn't tell what she knew. Or what she felt. Fin was devastated.

The royal family and their soldiers walked through the village, towards the waters. King Zander chose not to take chariots since they were so close. It was a chance for him to greet his citizens. Walk by and nod, as they lined the streets or looked out their windows. Zander and Aterra waved. Oblivious to Fin's bitterness. She walked ahead, refusing to look at anyone. The citizens weren't fazed. It was normal to be nervous for one's upcoming nuptials. "You're so beautiful princess," someone shouted from the crowd.

Fin gave a forced smile. She rarely came to town. The streets were crowded. It was an opportunity to see the elusive Princess Fin. Many had heard of her. Rumors of the beautiful yet spoiled child ran rampant. But years had passed. No one heard any updates. Surely, she was no longer a brat. And they were right. They stood in awe. She was like nothing they had ever seen. Her eyes seemed to glow they were so striking. And coupled with her dark hair, she stood out. She was the only black-haired maiden. She was an anomaly.

"You look lovely Queen," a woman yelled out. Aterra smiled. She was gracious. And she loved the attention. She looked at Fin. Although she couldn't see her face, she could feel her mood. Fin stayed her distance. Her parents behind her and Lark at her side. Aterra could see some of the citizens becoming frustrated. They tried to get Fin's attention. They wanted the princess to acknowledge them. But Fin looked ahead. Her head held high. It was the worst day of her life. But she didn't plan on letting it show. She was sorry she wasn't in a more festive mood. And looking in the eyes of people who appeared happy for her, would surely make her break down. They hadn't a clue how she felt. How torn she was. How hurt and afraid she was. But this was her duty. And she was going. She just wasn't sure how it would end. She would rather burn in molten lava.

The soldiers walked as one. Their steps in sync. The sea shore was close. Soon the large group was out of the local village and walking on plain land towards the white sands. The beautiful clear blue water would get them to Eulachon. The waters were perfect for travelling. Eulachon was miles away. There would be guards waiting to escort them the rest of the way. To a castle known as *Pearl Palace*. It was a strikingly beautiful estate with pearls and gold embedded in the rock. It was the oldest of all the castles, built hundreds of years prior. The pearls were rare for Eulachon. Only Piratchu had them in abundance. All who got a chance to get close enough, were left in awe. No one could figure out how the forefathers were able to acquire so many of the rare and precious minerals.

$\mathcal{T}$he Palimora Sea of was filled with guards navigating their way towards Eulachon. It was a dangerous yet necessary mission. The waters were filled with some of the most dangerous fish in their world. There was no easy way to get to Prince Andreus. Unlike Panga, which was separated by a smaller body of water, Eulachon was further. And Piratchu was even further, located on the other side of Eulachon.

The water swelled like a tsunami. The force from their movement near its surface was powerful. An intimidating sight as they swam together in unison. Never breaking line and staying in-sync. Hundreds, on a mission to get King Zander, the Queen and Princess Finora, to Eulachon. The Queen had to be carted by guards that carried her in a specially crafted wooden crate. It was lined for comfort and adorned with jewels. The crate was carved out like a chair and designed to be carried. Straps all around were fastened to the men's backs. Three in a row, to carry it seamless above the water. No one ever questioned why the queen did not swim. There were whispers. But all concerns were disregarded when King Zander gave an explanation. He stated that queens of a particular age didn't swim. That they were above such exhaustive burdens. And so, she was carried everywhere, when travel by water was necessary.

Finora swam next to Lark. Her father on the other side. The men with their massive and powerful tails moving them closer to their destination. Some of the soldiers looked at Fin. They had never seen her tail. A beautiful rich and vibrant blue tail and fin. She swam elegantly. They were proud of her. She had grown into a stunning beauty.

Everyone except Lark, hoped she was marrying a prince who would be great for her. Good to her. He was jealous of the pending union. He had secretly loved her his whole life. But princesses did not marry guards. And Zander would never have allowed the union. He could tell she was unhappy. And he hoped the meeting was at least pleasant. They did not war. It was unheard of. But the soldiers protected her fiercely. They would go to battle. And Lark would kill a stone.

Fin never looked at anyone. She kept her eyes ahead. Lark looked helplessly at her. Another stolen glimpse. Everyone's eyes were on the waters around and below them. He looked at her again. She could see him looking. She turned her head slightly his way, then back. He could see she was angry. He wanted her to look at him. To know he didn't agree with it. She would know if she looked. Just one peek. Lark was one of the few males in touch with his emotional side. It was rare and he kept it hidden. Something Fin seemed to bring it out of him unknowingly. He would touch her. He would allow her to touch him. She had before. When they were young. And he never forgot. It was the most pleasuring experience of his life.

But she pressed on, never giving him the eye contact he craved. She couldn't Her disappointment was profound. King Zander glanced at her then continued forward. He wondered if it weren't just nerves. Finora lived in a fantasy world. He had watched her as a youngster at play. He noticed early on, his daughter's penchant for make-believe. He never understood her mind. Her desires. She seemed to want so much more than necessary.

Lark turned his attention back to the waters. He looked beneath him to check that there were no lurking dangers. He noticed lights. He realized what it was. It was the pink and blue lights of a Baika. The Palimora Sea was teaming with aquatic life that could be dangerous. The soldiers were layered from the top down. The soldiers of the last row were the protectors of the convoy. Ready to destroy any large water mammals that they encountered. And a large glowing whale known as a Baika, swam beneath them.

It was massive, at 29 meters and moved slowly in the water. The animal illuminated beautifully, lighting the waters below. The soldiers alerted one another and pointed. Baika's would attack. Especially if it were a female and her young was near. The soldiers looked around. The lone animal had no reason to attack. And it looked to be on a mission and not interested in the foreign travelers. The soldiers kept an eye on it but otherwise, deemed it safe. There was no need to kill it. It would take twenty of them to kill a Baika. And they had limited soldiers. It would not be good to lose so many men on a journey that should be pleasant and joyous.

Lark looked back at Finora. His anxiety mounting. He always liked her even though she was like family. Like a little sister. But things had changed. And he noticed. She was not his sister. And she was not little. She was a woman. And she was gorgeous. But the king would never hear of it. So, he kept his eyes to himself admiring her beauty from a distance. She usually smelled of flowers and he wondered how she was able to make herself smell so sweet. Finora had a lot of talents. She knew how to make polish, perfume, oils and body balms. She was the only one. Nermein women didn't typically use such items. And after Aterra discovered her daughter's hidden gifts, she prohibited her from speaking or sharing her talents with anyone. She told her daughter citizens would consider her wild. A reputation she would not want. Wild meant mentally deranged and unstable. She needed to be like everyone else. Not stand out. After Finora ignored her mother's request, she was banned from making the items altogether.

The large group neared the shore. Finora got nervous. She looked at Lark. He looked back at her. She turned her head swiftly away. She didn't want him to see her sadness. She swam closer to shore as her tail turned back to legs. She stood and walked the rest of the way. The water up to her chest. The waves crashing into her. She looked down into the water. The guards were beginning to change their tails to legs. She could see men standing on the shore. They looked intimidating. Prince Andreus stood amongst them.

He smiled at Finora. She looked away and over at her mother. Queen Aterra smiled. Finora looked back to Andreus. He was thrilled. He looked pleased. She did not share the sentiment of the moment. "Princess," he said, as he stared into her eyes. "Prince Andreus," she replied. She looked intensely at him. He was excited. Smitten. And elated that she had finally arrived.

Her eyes did not deceive. They were pure of her thoughts. She looked at him with contempt. And she wondered why he didn't feel her sting. Her visual cues were hard to miss. It was their second encounter. He should have felt the first one. That day in the water. The day she rendered a harsh judgment of him. He was *The Trout*. The self-absorbed, egocentric, entitled man who wouldn't know the way to her heart if he had a personal tour guide.

"This way," he said, as he stepped to the side. A chariot awaited her. One adorned in gold, rubies and pearls. A gift from Queen Rasbora. Finora walked to it. She looked around at his massive army. They outnumbered her men by ten to one. It was intimidating. He should have known better. She would have appreciated a much more intimate introduction. Maybe himself and a few guards. She couldn't figure why he felt it necessary to protect himself. Was he at war. Were there assassins hunting him.

Finora stepped to the chariot. A guard in leg wraps and a black vest adorned with gold medallions, opened the door. It was an impressive soldiers' uniform. All his men wore it. The outfits would be expensive and time consuming to create. "I must meet your dressmaker," Fin said, to break the ice. "You will. She is at the castle," Andreus replied.

Finora entered the carriage. She glanced around the land. She didn't like the view. Eulachon lacked luster. The land was covered in tall straw like grass that went on for miles. There were a few scattered trees and other shrubs. One of the enchanting parts of the city were the mountains. They looked like perfectly shaped rocks sitting side by side in a neat row. Fin hoped there were scenic parts elsewhere. It would be depressing if the whole city looked that way. There was a shortage of colorful plants. "Do you not trade for plants from Panga?" she asked. "Yes. But nothing will grow. We are waiting She was unimpressed with her possible new home.

Guards bent down and grabbed the poles that extended from the chariot. Finora looked behind her. There was a separate chariot for her parents. They walked up and got in. "Your Highness," the guard said, as he opened the door to the King and Queens chariot. The men bowed as Queen Aterra entered and sat down. King Zander got in and sat next to her. "This place looks desolate," she said in a low voice. King Zander chuckled. His wife could be opinionated. Eulachon was nothing like Mojarro. Not even close.

Prince Andreus was himself, nervous. He got in and sat next to her. She looked briefly at him then out the window. It was an uncomfortable moment. "Are you as nervous as I am," he asked. Fin sighed. She wanted to meet and get it over with. "No. I'm fine," she said. He cleared his throat. She was more beautiful than when he saw her in the water. She was breathtaking. He had heard rumors that she was difficult. Weird. Strange even. But he saw nothing of the sort. She was hard to get through to. Feisty. Ice cold when nervous or unsure. But she was wonderful. Unique. He liked her.

"You smell, um… like flowers," he commented. It was the balm. The water had not rinsed all of its contents off of her skin. Finora smiled. His compliments helped ease the tension. It was a start. "Thank you."

The large convoy of soldiers and chariots approached the Pearl Palace. King Orfe walked from the window. He wished his wife, Queen Inga, had lived to see the day. There was a grand party awaiting them. A buffet, filled with the best sea life and plants available. Queen Rasbora sent the chariot as well as sea kelp from her clean and healthy waters. She had kelp only native to her waters. King Nephrus, although disappointed that Finora would not be marrying his son, sent a buffet of shellfish and sweet tasting plants from his land.

He also sent, as a gift to Prince Andreus, a solid gold crown made of rubies and emeralds. Jewels he received from King Zander himself. It was a grand gesture. King Zander did not share his emeralds and rubies. He gave King Nephrus just a few, as a thank you. King Nephrus had sent him soil in exchange for Finora's hand. And the jewels were a way to apologize for not being able to give his daughters hand in marriage to his son. King Zander wanted no bad blood. He had only one daughter. He could not make all the princes within Madaka happy.

******

"Welcome to Pearl Palace," King Orfe greeted. King Zander, Queen Aterra and Princess Finora walked through the palace doors. "This way," the house servant said, as she led the way to the grand ballroom. The door opened to a large gathering of Eulachonians. All smiling and waiting to get a glimpse of the princess, whose beauty was known throughout the lands. Finora smiled and nodded as she walked past the citizens. "Your Highness," King Orfe said, as his men escorted the King and Queen to their chairs, beside his throne. Finora had a special seat in front of her parents and the King of Eulachon. She sat and waited. Andreus stared from the sidelines. He stood amongst his personal body guards. The men whispered to him. He was the envy of the party. The men were intrigued by her. And she was his.

Fin sat, ready to be entertained. First by a man who was able to make fire dance in his hand. A nice trick Finora had never seen before. Then there was a woman who danced on the tops of her toes to nothing but the beat of a drum. It was the only instrument in their world. Many found the sounds it made jarring and unpleasant. Finora relaxed. She liked drums. She wanted to see what they offered her. Being able to entertain the queen was important. It was a sign of a city's creativity. Of their spirit. The only entertainment Mojarro had were drums and men who could make fish do tricks. She had tired of it. She found Eulachonians refreshing. And they welcomed her with open arms.

"Can I have a moment with you in private," the prince whispered in Finora's ear. She glanced back at her parents. King Zander nodded. It was obvious the prince had already asked for permission. "Sure," she said, as she stood up. Suddenly the music stopped. "Carry on," King Orfe commanded.

Prince Andreus showed Fin to a private room off the hall. He shut the door. She turned from him. She was nervous. He walked up from behind her and smelled her hair. Finora's eyes darted from side to side. She turned around to face him. "What are you doing? Don't! I am not even sure we should go through with this," she said. Andreus narrowed his eyes. "Why not," he said. Finora shrugged her shoulders. "I don't know. Because we are not connected. I have no desire," she said. Andreus walked to a table filled with haku, wine sent by Queen Rasbora. He poured a cup.

"That will come. I am fond of you. I desire you. You will feel the same one day," he said. "How do you know?" she asked. "Because that's the way it happens. You will have everything you need. Don't worry. You will be happy," he said. Finora looked terrified. Andreus stared at her in confusion. He wasn't sure what her problem was. Women and men were brought together. They stayed together. They raised their offspring and lived happily ever after. It was time. She was a woman. He was a man. It was what they did.

"No," she said. Andreus walked closer. "Yes. It is already done. The wedding is near. I have chosen you. Your father has agreed. We will marry. And you will make me happy," he said. "No! I can't. And I won't," she said, as she hurried to the door. Prince Andreus followed closely behind. "What will you do. Where will you go. You belong to me. No one else can have you. Don't you know that once you're selected, you have to be mated," he said. Finora was fuming. "What! And I have no say. Stop following me!" she griped, as she continued walking to the entrance. "Wait!" he shouted. The guards heard their prince and stood in front of the door, blocking Fin. Finora turned around.

"Tell them to let me past now! I need to go out. I need to be outdoors," Fin shouted. "Let her by," he ordered. Finora pushed past the men and opened the door. "Do you want us to follow her, Your Highness?" a guard asked. "Yes. But stay back."

Finora cried hysterically, as she walked through the land. She could see his guards trailing her. She felt he was among them. She hoped not. She had nothing else to say. His description of their union was disgusting. And his attempts at forcing her hand had fallen on deaf ears. She would not be forced to do anything. He almost won her over. His vulnerability on the ride there, gave her hope. Fin walked briskly through the vegetation. Suddenly a memory flashed. Something she saw as a child. Her father was in her mother's face. Standing close. Much closer than he should have been. She wondered what they were doing. Her mother had a look on her face she hadn't seen since. A look of enchantment. No words needed. Her mother looked captivated.

She looked out to in the distance. The ocean lie ahead. She thought of swimming back home. It was getting dark. These were unfamiliar waters. Filled with unfamiliar living creatures. It was dangerous. But she didn't care. Finora ran towards the water. She heard the guards yell out for her to stop. It was too dark to enter the water. "Stop," they continued to shout. Finora's hair bounced about. Some of it strewn across her face. She bit her lip in anticipation. Freedom lie ahead. The waters she loved since she was a child would be her deliverance. It was more than a way to travel. It was more that another world to live in. It was life.

The water splashed, as her feet hit its shoreline. She continued, looking back. The guards were getting near. Some entered after her. Finora jumped into the air, arms outstretched. She was almost at the promise land. All she needed was the water to hit her body and she could turn her legs into her powerful tail. The guards dove in. Finora hit the water. Her legs now a tail. It was useless for the guards to continue pursuing her. She was the fastest thing in the water. And with her innate abilities, she dove deep so the guards would not be able to see her as easily. Her tail was not bright yellow able to be viewed in dark water. It was blue with small hints of green. She blended with the environment. She swam fast, leaving them in her undercurrent. Finora snickered. She would not be getting married. Not to him.

King Orfe saw the commotion. His guards walked towards him with purpose. "What is it?" he said, as he sat forward. "The princess sir," the lead guard spoke. "What about her?" he asked. "The guard glanced at King Zander. "She's gone, your Highness. She ran to the waters," he said. "What!" King Zander shouted. He jumped from his seat and walked out of the hall. Aterra got up from her chair and followed behind her husband. "Where is my son?" King Orfe asked. "In the water looking for her."

The coast was clear. There wasn't a guard in sight. Finora slowed. It was dark, but she managed to see some distance around her. The water was illuminated with small species that floated, swam and bounced around. Finora reached out to touch one. They didn't look edible. She feared the same sour taste she had the displeasure of experiencing when she went to the foreign land. Suddenly something large was in the distance. It appeared to be headed her way. Finora squinted. She couldn't make it out at first. Soon the familiar shape and colors came into focus. Finora gasped. Fear set in. It was a large whale. A Baika. And it had a young calf with it.

Finora dove deeper, in an attempt to move from its path. But the curious baby Baika followed her. Finora swam faster. The baby tried to keep up with her. Finora looked back. The mother was swimming as fast as she could, to keep up with her calf. But Baikas were not so skilled. Their size prevented such speeds. Suddenly she was surrounded by other whales. She swam down. She was at the bottom. She looked up. The whales were hovering above her. They let out a sound. Fear set in. They seemed nervous.

She suddenly remembered something. She had been in the company of fish before. Their humming reminded her of the sounds she made that day. Finora began to hum. The whales responded and made more sounds. She stopped. The young Baika calf swam to her. It got close. Fin reached out to touch it. She rubbed its nose as she tried not to show her fear. He was still massive. He could swallow her in one gulp. She continued humming. The baby whale floated motionless while she continued to rub it. Finora looked past the calk. Something was approaching. It's movements familiar. A Tetra.

"Oh no," she said, as the animal approached. Tetra's were one of the quickest and most dangerous predators in the water. It was twenty meters in length with large razor-sharp teeth. And would require an army of up to fifty men to kill it. The men were powerful in water. They were a formidable adversary against such water hunters. But Fin was alone. Her army was at Pearl Palace.

The Tetra headed straight for the calf. The large female Baika was quickly approaching to launch her own attack. She would die to protect her calf. And she would die in a battle against the Tetra, even though she was of much greater size. The mother whale started making sounds. Finora believed she was calling for reinforcements. Several Baika would be needed to be victorious.

The baby calf continued towards Finora, unaware of the danger headed its way. Finora feared for the young baby's life. She was faster than both animals. And she could have easily picked up speed and left the calf and saved her own life. But Finora felt bad for the infant Baika. She looked around. There was no protection. No guards. No one to help her. No one to help her save the calf.

Finora began to hum. The same as she had done when she was a child exploring for the first time. The nervous calf stayed with her. Finora could pick up on its fears. She touched its nose. Her humming seemed to calm it. The whining sounds it was making soon quieted. Finora was herself overcome with intense fears. She was treading on new territory. She hadn't a clue what her chanting would do. Her memory of that day she was not serving her well.

Numerous species of fish migrated quickly to the area. The large predator circled the calf. Its mother nearing. Finora continued her underwater vocal vibrations. It was melodic. She could see it was calling fish of all types. She was surprised. She had hoped to calm the predator. Get it to go away. But she had no effect on it. It was hungry. The calf, its meal.

Among the fish swimming near, was an arrowhead eel. Also deadly. Small yet lethal. Its electric current powerful enough to kill any fish. Including the Tetra. Its shape long and pointy. Used in the hunting of large fish. The eel was known to propel itself like a sword, lunging forward, while using electrical currents to stun its victim.

The Tetra charged, Finora floated in front of the calf, her humming increasing. Suddenly without warning, the arrow eel, charged past her, propelling itself, as the side of its body lit up. The eel spun in the water, at high speeds as it effortlessly entered the Tetra. The electricity from its body, jolting, causing the animal to jerk. The Tetra floated, stunned from the voltage. The animal went limp. Smaller predatory fish arrived and began feasting on its carcass.

The fish continued to feed. Finora floated backwards slowly, horrified, as the massive fish was devoured. She had never been so involved in sea life. Never witnessed how brutal life could be for them. It made since why no one lived in the sea. Some lived in lakes. Others in the deeper streams. But none lived in the vast oceans or seas.

Fin hurried away. She looked back. The mother whale united with her calf and the other sea life dispersed. She was shocked. She communicated with them. Her feelings channeled through sound and picked up by water animals not related to her. They protected her. Covered her. And one killed for her. Finora had a gift. One she'd just realized.

She smiled as she continued on towards home. It was a great feeling. She got a late start in water. Prohibited from entering it all her life. And now she was one with it. No other nermein possessed the ability to communicate with the creatures. Fin's gifts were a gift from the gods. She was a direct heir to the creators of Madaka. The granddaughter, many generations past, of the goddess of the ocean. A powerful ocean dweller named Contessa. The reason for Fin's strong attraction with water. And her ability to thrive in it.

Fin made it to home unscathed. She got out of the water and sat on the shores near her castle. She was within walking distance, but was not prepared to go home. She sat in the shallow water contemplating what to do. She had fled her engagement ceremony. She was sure her parents were upset with her. "I have to get away from here for a while. I have to," she said, as she threw stones in the water. Fin sat staring at the blue sky. She compared it to the sky of the land she encountered. It was similar but there were major differences. The sky of the other world was vast. It had white fluffy things floating. Not plain and clear, as the skies of Madaka. Finora hatched a plan. She could go there. Get away. No one would find her. She could take a moment for herself. Get her mind in order. And return home later. Hanging around, waiting for her upset parents to arrive and scold her for her hurried exit, would only add more strain. Fin stood up. She walked in further and then dove into the water. This time, headed for the dunes.

5

Something in the Water

"Uncle Lance!" Yasmine and Miles shouted, as they ran to hug him. Lance's family was in town to visit. Allan walked up. "Hey," he greeted. Lance was happy to see them. He missed being in Boston. He missed his family. He had a small family and they were close. And his brother Allan had worried about the move. It came on the heels of several devastating life events. But Lance was doing better. He had put his past behind him. Life was opening new doors. But Allan still worried. His younger brother had been dealt several blows, back to back. And he wondered how he was holding up.

"Hey," Lance said, bending down and swooping up Yasmine. She was his spunky, quick-witted six year old niece, who was as adorable as she was clever. "Uncle Lance. Why are you here? You don't like it back home?" she asked. Lance chuckled. "Of course I do. I had to come here and take over my father's business. Didn't daddy explain it to you," he said, giving his brother Allan a look.

"Yeah. She knows. She's just on a quest to compare stories. You know how she does," Allan joked. "Hey uncle Lance. Do you have another big house? I hope you didn't buy anything little. I'm going to need my own room again," his ten year old nephew Miles stated. "Yes. There's plenty of room. Let's get going," Lance said, as he put Yasmine down. The family headed towards the exit. Allan glanced at his younger brother.

"So… How is it here? You adjusting?" Allan asked. "Um. Yeah…About as well as I could hope. I miss Boston. But Cali is great. And Malibu is…Well, it's Malibu. What can I say," he said.

He hated to admit that he loved it. Allan was hoping he would sell the company and move back home. The brothers were used to seeing each other more often. Going out and enjoying the night life. The distance between them was extreme. Long flights to see one another would eventually be taxing. But Lance had been through a lot. A mentally ill mother. A failed engagement. The death of an unborn child.

Then the death of a father he longed to know and now would never get the chance. Allan imagined it all overwhelming. His reason for being there. He wanted to look his brother in the eyes. Lance was good at pushing past the pain. And Allan feared a nervous breakdown.

"Well, we're here. I can stay a few weeks. Catch up. You know I had to check on you," he said, as he pat his brother on the back.

$\mathcal{L}$ance awoke to the smell of bacon and the sound of children running through his home. He looked at the clock. He had slept past the morning news. It was the weekend. He had nowhere to be. His office manager, Lee Hiroshi, was supposed to drop off some files for Lance to go over. More projects that needed a second set of eyes. His expertise.

Lance got up and jumped in the shower. He could hear his brother on the phone. He closed his eyes and ran his hand over his face as the waters pulsated across his entire body. The special made shower, with shower heads positioned at every angle, was the best part of his day. Lance showered then got dressed and headed towards the smell of his second favorite part of the day. Breakfast.

"Good morning," his housekeeper greeted. "Good morning Anna," he replied, as he grabbed a piece of bacon and headed to the living room. He looked out at the water then walked closer to take in the complete view. Yasmine and

Miles were sitting on the plush throw rug watching cartoons. "Uncle Lance," Yasmine smiled. "Hey sweetheart," he said, as he plopped down on the couch. "Anna? Did they eat already?" he asked. It was late. He hoped she didn't make them wait until he was up.

"Yes Mr. Lance. They ate pancakes. They've been up since seven," she replied. Lance had asked Anna to stay as long as they would be there. She obliged him, taking up temporary residence in his 5,000 square foot multi-leveled home. It was an all-white stone and glass oceanfront home. The only entrance was off the private secluded road. A security gate gave the home a more private appearance but it didn't stop gawkers from trying. He still got a lot of visitors driving down to admire all the homes.

His home was the main attraction, which Lance hated. There was always a car driving by slowly to admire his homes' contemporary structure and unique detail. Lights all around gave it an elegant touch in the evenings. And to complete the look, a magnificent water fountain with a light show. Lance thought of removing the water fountain. He believed it added to the traffic. He had tried cutting off the lights to the fountain. But the traffic continued. So, he turned it back on. He did enjoy it himself. His father had exquisite taste.

"Can I go outside. I want to go to the water," Yasmine asked. Lance touched her cheek and smiled. There wasn't much of a front yard. His porch and lawn took up a lot of room. And his home sat close to the ocean, nestled on large rocks. They kids could take a small staircase down to the small sandy shore just a few feet from the water. It wasn't the safest set up. His home wasn't exactly child friendly. But he didn't want them to have to stay in-doors the entire visit either

The children would need to sit on the patio near the fireplace. Lance wasn't comfortable with them on the shoreline or on the dock. But Yasmine had a way with him. He had spoiled both his niece and nephew rotten. Yasmine was the daughter he never had. He never got a chance. His baby girl died in utero, and the devastation that resulted, ended his relationship.

"What little girl? And who's your escort?" he asked. "Miles," she bashfully replied, hoping to get a yes. "Miles! Can you swim Miles?" he asked. "Yep. Dad put me in class. I've been swimming since before I went to Edmond. And then I took more classes there. I can swim good Uncle," he proclaimed. Lance hesitated. "Alright. Just for a minute. Oh wait! I have something. A whistle to take with you in case something happens," he said.

Lance got up and went to his home office. He rummaged through his drawers looking for his old high school whistle, that he kept as memorabilia after the school was demolished. He used to be one of the volunteer lifeguards when he was a student there. He opened a second drawer, pulling out the items, frantically searching for the shiny metal whistle. "There," he said, pulling it from the back. It was still hanging from a purple rope. Now tattered and worn. Memories flooded in. The times he won awards for swimming. Times that his mother and brother sat in the audience cheering him on. Absent was his father. The father he hoped would surprise him one day and be there, sitting amongst the crowd. Lance stared at the whistle, in deep thought.

"Hey. You said they could go out?" Allan said, as he entered his brother's office. "Huh! Oh yeah. I was going to give Miles this whistle to blow for safety," he replied. "Alright. As long as you say it's ok. They've been asking me since this morning. I didn't want to say yes without checking that it was safe," Allan said. "They'll be fine. I told them it's just for a little while. I want them to stay on the patio though. I don't want them to enter the water."

Yasmine and Miles ran around the perimeter of the house. Lance watched closely. The home had a complete outdoor lounge area complete with a fireplace, tables, chairs, a retractable awning and an outdoor oven. Lance pushed a button and opened a metal sliding door than housed a theater sized television. He turned cartoons on. He hoped it would keep them close to the house. It was comfortable. Citronella candles and a bug zapper helped keep the bugs away. Lance saw Yasmine run straight to the rocks. "Hey Yaz. Get away from there. If you want to see the water, wait for Miles," Lance said. It was safe, but one careless move on the boulders and one could end up in the water.

Lance got nervous when Miles walked to the boulders and looked into the water. He started throwing small rocks into the water. His sister by his side. Lance watched from his huge picture window, as he drank a cup of coffee. "They will be fine Mr. Lance. Don't worry. The water is not deep right there," his housekeeper said. Lance nodded. He was worrying needlessly. But it was still better if they were supervised.

Allan had gone to the nearest store for items to cook his kids later. Lance had tons of food, but nothing the children would enjoy eating. Lance took another sip. He laughed as Miles tried to put Yasmine on his back. The two walked back to the patio. They asked if they could walk the dock. Lance agreed since the dock had railings.

Lance heard his door close. Allan sat the bags on the counter then walked over to his brother. "Where's the boat?" he asked. "Still in storage. I sold one. I guess I could have them deliver it. They offer delivery right to your dock. I just don't see myself on it yet. I have no time. I may have to store it all summer. Take it out next year," he replied. Allan was surprised. Lance liked boating.

"Well, after you get acclimated to this new company, you'll be more inclined to take up with your favorite activities. Just don't over work. Make time for fun," he urged. "I will. I just have to make sure Bandz does not fall apart. My father was a control freak. There are plenty of able minded, gifted people working there. He held the reins tight. There's a lot of projects that should be complete. I plan on running it a lot different. You have to let stars shine. That place has plenty of stars."

"Watch me daddy," Yasmine yelled, as she did a somersault. "Good job sweetheart," Allan yelled. Lance walked away from the window and grabbed his cell phone. He was still waiting on his office manager to bring what he asked for. He called him, then sat his phone down and walked back in the kitchen to make himself a bowl of fruit. Allan scaled the staircase, to retire to his room overlooking the water. He walked over to his window and opened it slightly so he could see and hear his children. His phone buzzed. It was his wife again. She was calling him constantly. She was angry that he had taken their kids without her permission. They were separated but reconciling. And Debra wanted her family back.

Her own mistake of having an affair with a coworker had cost her dearly. Her drinking and lack of self-control had always gotten her into compromising positions. And one night during after work drinks, she went too far in the parking lot of the Blue note Lounge. Allan sat in his car and watched it all unfold. And now they were taking baby steps to undo the damage. But Allan was having a hard time trusting her again.

"Hello," he answered. "Allan! Where were you? I've called you like a thousand times. How are my babies?" she asked. Allan sighed. He had answered this question already. "They're fine Debra. They were fine this morning and fine when you called two hours after that. Stop worrying. We'll be home soon. I'll bring them right to you. Ok?" he replied. Debra held the phone. Allan hoped she wasn't drinking. The main source of problems between them. Her behavior suggested she was falling apart. "Debra? Did you hear me?" he asked. "Yes," she said, in a low tone. The truth was she couldn't function without Allan. And it showed.

Miles picked up shells as Yasmine followed him. He slowly examined them. The detail. The faint lines. The rugged feel of the outside and the smooth shiny surface on the inside. He made his way to the dock. Lance watched more intensely since they were now going to be standing over deeper water. The dock had wood railings trimmed in white, slip resistant material. It was beautifully designed.

Miles walked the length of the dock, holding onto several shells as he looked out to the never-ending water line. The waves were perfect. Symmetrical. The view, breathtaking. He looked at the horizon. The sky and water seemed to meet. "It's so pretty," Yasmine said of the blue green water. Miles handed her a shell. "Oooww. I like this. Can I have it?" she asked. "Yep."

Miles sat on the edge. Lance got nervous. He was hoping they would go investigate and turn around. He wasn't sure if he trusted them not to get too excited or play too rough and go tumbling. The water at the end of the dock was at least six feet deep. Lance watched. He would give them a few more minutes. Then they would need to be called back to the house. Miles had rocks in his pocket. He took them out. He saw a fish. It was perfect. He threw a rock at it. "Yaz. Look! A fish," he said. Soon he threw more rocks. The fish swam quickly away.

"Dammit," he said. "Oooww. I'm telling. You said a bad word," Yasmine warned. Miles laughed. Suddenly he stopped and stared into the water. Something caught his eye. Soon it floated up and Miles jumped. He gasped and turn to run. Yasmine looked in the water and screamed then ran. Lance ran out onto the patio. Allan heard the commotion and hurriedly descended down the stairs. Lance ran down the long dock. No shoes. His feet stepping on small rocks. His nephew looked to be in shock. His eyes were wide. His mouth slightly open.

"What wrong?" he shouted. "I saw…I saw…" he said, still running towards his father and uncle. Lance reached Miles. Yasmine ran past Lance to her father. "What happened?" Lance asked again. Miles looked back at the end of the dock. "I…I.. Saw a woman. She was floating in the water," he said, trying to catch his breath, obviously shocked by what he'd seen. Lance stared intensely at him. "A woman? At the end of the dock?" he asked. Miles shook his head yes, slowly. Yasmine continued holding onto her father's leg. She was terrified.

"Yaz! Look at daddy. You alright? Did you see something?" Allan asked. Yasmine closed her eyes and held on tight. Allan and Lance looked at each other. "We should call the police," Allan suggested. "Wait. Let me have a look."

Lance walked slowly down the dock looking in the water as he walked close to the edge. He went to the end and looked in. He stood staring, trying to see as far into the water as he could. He could see some small fish and a few medium sized fish but nothing else. He shook his head. He wanted to get a closer look. If there was a body in his water, he wanted to see it. Lance sat down on the docks edge then turned around and stepped down to the next step. Steps that went far enough in for him to continue holding on for safety. Lance descended down. He heard his brother yell out. He continued into the water, looking around nervously. He was once a champion swimmer. He had won medals for both swimming and diving. He competed in swimming competitions, his whole four years of high school and even into college.

Lance descended the ladder into the water. He held onto each step carefully, as he went down further. The cool water hit his feet. He continued down each thick wood step.

He was soon submerged up to his chest. He took another few steps down. He went under the water. He stopped and looked around, holding his breath and scanning the area around him. The sun shone brightly and aided in his ability to see clearly. Something far out caught his attention. It didn't move like a fish yet it looked like it was moving. Fear set in and he came up out of the water. Allan walked his kids to the house and came back out. He stood on the edge. Lance popped his head above the water.

"What are you doing? A dead body is down there," he said. "No, it's not. There nothing down there but fish. There is no woman," he replied. "We still should call the cops," Allan said. "No. I don't want to be bothered with the cops. I'll check again later. And again tomorrow. There are plenty of large fish in these waters. No telling what they saw. I'm sure it was a fish."

Allan shook his head. His children were spooked. His son was still in shock. Miles was a smart kid. Well-travelled. Experienced with water and aquatic life. Allan was skeptical. If it had been just Yaz, he would question it since she was only six. But Miles was different. If he said he saw a woman then it was a woman. And the fact that both his children were in some type of shock had him concerned. Yasmine was still quiet and hadn't said a word. And Miles looked as though he'd seen a ghost.

Lance emerged from the water and climbed up the dock steps. He stood on the dock dripping wet. The brothers looked in the water again. "Nothing but fish," Lance said. Allan shook his head. He walked back to his children who were standing on the patio and took them back inside the house. Lance stood staring into the water. He saw something but it didn't look like a woman.

He looked out at the horizon. His mind ran through different scenarios. He was stumped as to what it could be. He wondered if someone weren't in the water with diving gear, scavenging across the bottom for souvenirs. A man had found several oysters with rare pearls inside. Maybe he was back. Lance looked down. He could see fish. Different groups of fish swimming together. Suddenly something appeared.

He adjusted his eyes. He tried to get a clear picture. It was at the bottom. It appeared to be a fish's tail. He followed the tail up. Soon he saw flesh. And soon the face of a woman. She appeared to be looking at him. And as suddenly as she appeared, she was gone. He gasped. Someone was in the water. They had to be on some underwater exploration. He didn't see a tank. He didn't see bubbles. But that didn't mean there weren't any. He believed his eyes were deceiving him. He wanted to get back in the water. Have another look. If it was a woman, diving near his dock, why not wave and make her presence known. Acknowledge the frightened children, so they won't be terrified.

Lance continued to look through the water. It was puzzling. His nephew was right. Someone was in the water. With some sort of apparatus on, that looked like the tail and fin of a fish. He wasn't sure what to make of it.

He walked swiftly back to his house. "What's wrong?" Allan asked. "Nothing," he replied, a bewildering look on his face. "Yes. It's something. You look as though you've seen a ghost," he replied. Lance paced. "To be honest, I don't know what I saw. Um…I saw something," he replied. "Did you see her Uncle Lance? See. I told you. It's a lady in the water," his nephew chimed in. Lance shook his head. He wasn't sure.

"Call the police!" Allan said. "What! For what? It's not illegal to go diving. I don't own the water. They are not trespassing," Lance replied. "Miles said she was floating. He said nothing about diving. She did not have on scuba gear. There is a body in the water Lance. A woman. Miles would never say something like that. He knows what he saw. Call the police," Allan urged. "Allan come on…She swam away. I saw her swim away," Lance assured. Allan sighed.

"Go upstairs. I'll be up shortly," he said to his children. He was concerned. There were two different accounts of what was seen in the water and he believed his ten year old son's version. His brother was stressed. And he could be processing things different. Lance wasn't the type of man to make stories up. But he had been through a lot. He didn't need any more traumatic events. It was obvious he was seeing things. A woman would not be able to just hold her breath and float at the bottom of the ocean. Not without scuba gear. And neither Lance nor Miles mentioned seeing gear. Allan watched as his kids walked up to their rooms. He walked over to his brother.

"This is a bad sign Lance. Can't you see. This type of thing never happens. You have been here, what, a few weeks. And now there's a woman, floating in the water. Near your home. My kids have witnessed this. You have seen this. You need to sell that company and come home. This place is bad news," he cautioned. Lance rubbed his neck. He continued to pace. "No. I can't do that. I'm ok. I know you think I may lose it. That I can't cope. But I can. I'm built for this. I will be ok. She swam away. There is no dead body. She swam!"

Fin went deeper in the water. She was still troubled by the children's reaction to her. She could still see the terrified looks on their faces. She felt like a monster. Their reaction to her, made her think. She had been swimming, discreetly, close to the shore. She wanted to get close. She wondered if this weren't a whole new race of nermeins, living in another land. She had been to the beach. She had gotten close to the swimmers. She could see that no one changed into their tail. And she realized that they were avoiding being submerged for long.

She saw they needed something in order to stay under water longer. She had witnessed a man near the rocks. He wore a black suit made of a strange material. He had fins for feet. Not a tail. She watched as he came out of the water and removed them. There was something on his back and face. It released bubbles periodically. Finora was shocked. She didn't know what to make of them. They were different. They obviously loved water. They laughed and splashed in it. It seemed to bring them joy. And she didn't understand why they didn't live in it. If they loved it so much, why not take full advantage of it. Swim far. Go down with the fishes. Explore the floor. It was a lot to take in. And then she realized something. And Miles and Yasmine's shocking reaction helped her figure it out. They couldn't.

Things were vastly different in the new land. But there were similarities. And it was all connected. They shared the water. The sky looked the same. The wind felt the same. The people looked the same. The only difference, was in their behaviors with one another. And in their connection to the water.

It was surprising to see the man place his hands on the boy's shoulders. The touch appeared to calm the boy. The man was animated as he spoke to him. It was intriguing. It made her want to see more. But these were things, that had her more doubtful that the people were like her.

In this new world, they engaged in physical contact. Even the little girl ran and grabbed her father's leg. Finora swam slowly across the ocean floor. Her mind raced trying to put all the pieces of the strange puzzle together. What were these people? How long had they been there? Were they peaceful? And who was the man, that was staring at her through the water?

She swam down towards the cliff. It reminded her of the one at home. She went to the base and entered a huge cavity in the side. An underwater cave. Small but large enough to accommodate her. She was in the Pacific Ocean. It reminded her of the Trojian and Palimora Sea, back home. She felt comfortable. She had good recall of how to get around. It didn't take long. This was her environment. Water. She could look at the ocean floor and make note of where she was. She had a natural sense of navigation and could easily get back to where she came from. But she wasn't ready to go. Not yet. Lance had her attention. She wanted to see the family again. But for now, she would stay comfortable inside the cave. It would be dark soon.

The sun shined through the clear ocean water. Like an array of spotlights coming through. Fin awoke and headed back towards Lance's home a short distance away. She wanted to see the man that stood on the end of the dock. The man who searched the waters for her. He was unforgettable. She was intrigued. He was handsome. Interesting looking. There was something about him that attracted her. His eyes. His voice. His physique. She was afraid to let him get close. He seemed bothered at her presence in the water. His demeanor changed at the sight of her. Something that troubled her.

She swam to the surface and looked to the sky. Something was coming. The clouds were thick. Finora liked this world. But not this new element. She could feel the power of a looming storm. She dipped back in the water and swam back inside the cave.

She sat back. Tired and ready to sleep. The stress was mentally exhausting. Her eyes closed slowly. A small flutter in the water caused her to open them again. She watched a fish swimming close. Fin stared at it. It reminded her of home. She realized she missed her parents, but she didn't really miss Madaka. There was something wonderful about this new place. Something that also felt like home. The feeling it gave her. The people. Their happiness and togetherness. It was deeper than what she witnessed in her world.

Her eyes tried closing again. And again, she opened them. Small friendly fish came close then scurried away. They didn't glow like the ones back home. But they were beautiful all the same. She thought of home. She wondered if her parents made it back to the castle. She was sure they were looking for her. That the prince probably had his men searching the sea. And she was certain that Lark too was worried. She could see the worry on his face when they made the journey to Eulachon. It was all a terrible mistake. Her parents believed they were doing what was best. Finora hoped they understood that she needed to get away.

She was thinking of returning home. But she feared being forced to marry Andreus. So, she decided to wait a little longer. If he thought she was dead, he would move on from the idea of her. Fin knew there was a chance he would always seek her for a wife. But she could not see herself being with him forever. Queen of a desolate land. Her plan was to stay long enough for him to marry someone else. If was rumored that his father was ill. It wouldn't be long before he would be crowned as Eulachon's new king.

Fin sat back against the hard rock. She tried to put her troubles behind her. She was safe for now. She closed her eyes. The water felt good. It was cool. Invigorating. It calmed her. She slowly fell asleep. She wasn't' ready to go home. She wasn't ready to face anyone. And she wanted to get close to the people of this world. Close to Lance. The handsome man on the dock.

*T*he rain came down hard. Thunder lit up the sky. The sound resonated across the sky. Finora peeked out from the cave then went back inside. She thought of swimming back to her land. The unknown world was getting creepy. A disturbing element she was unaware of. Suddenly a loud boom. The sharp crackling sound was heard, and felt, through the water. It made her jump. *What is this?* she thought. It sounded like the strange world was crumbling. Fin swam towards the surface, holding onto the rock for comfort. She could shield herself between its large crevices, if needed. Day had turned to another evening. She emerged and looked to the sky. A lightning strike startled her. She wished she could relax. She was tired. A good night's rest would suit her well after the long and difficult afternoon she'd had. But she was restless.

She held onto the large rock under the deck, close to Lance's home. Large man-made boulders placed in the water at the shoreline near the home for aesthetics. She looked around. She didn't want to be seen. She had already frightened one family. She looked at Lance's house. She could see him standing in his window. His house was well lit. Lights inside and out, had it illuminated brightly.

She stared at him, keeping herself hid. She watched him from behind one of the wood beams of the deck. He looked like he had a lot on his mind. The storm started to settle. The clouds were thinning. After an hour, the clouds dispersed. As quickly as the clouds arrived, they had disappeared. Hours went by. It was two in the morning. The sky had cleared, leaving a few scattered clouds.

The moonlight shone through. It lit up the ground and water below. Fin was still looking at Lance's house. She could see him laying across his bed and his brother talking to himself with an object up to his ear. Both men were watching people on screens. Fin stared in amazement. She could see the images. Lance walked back to his bedroom window. As if looking for something. Fin wondered why he appeared to long for something. Lance was himself wondering that same thing. Something had him curious. He was drawn to the water. It was magical. He didn't understand it.

He walked down the stairs and into his living room. Soon the living room television came on. Lance seemed restless. He walked to his sliding glass door and opened it slightly. He thought of going onto his porch. It was equipped for wet weather. The contemporary round chairs and table under a waterproof awning was perfect. Lance slid the door open and stepped out. He walked over to the chair and sat down. He placed the coffee he was drinking on a cup holder and sat back. He let out a deep sigh. He wondered what he would do. Was his brother right. Was this a good move for him. Everything was happening so fast. He hadn't had time to adjust. He hadn't mourned his losses. His baby would have been born by now. It would have been a month old.

"Hey," his brother said, as he slid open the door. He stepped out onto the patio with a cup of coffee. "Hey," Lance replied solemnly. "Can't even tell there was a storm not too long ago," Allan said, as he sat down. Lance put his feet up and got comfortable. "Yeah. The storm passed. The sky is clear now," he said. Allan hesitated. He tapped his cup. "Listen. Yasmine is distraught. She wants her mother. I'm leaving in the morning. Miles is ok. It's Yaz. She's only six. She won't sleep alone. I need to get her back so she can calm down," he said. Lance sat up. He felt bad.

"Of course. I'm sorry for all this. I should have never let them near the water. People swim, dive...I'm closer to the rock and so there are divers. A lot of clams and mollusk are near the rock. She's young. I just hate the thought that she will never want to visit. She'll always remember that. Talk to her. Help her understand what she saw," he said. "Yep. I will. We'll be back. She's just spooked."

Lance sat in his office with the door closed. It had been several weeks since his brother left. He had called to check on Yaz and spoke with her briefly. She had already put the incident behind her and was speaking of returning with the whole family. Lance believed she missed the comfort of her mother during the scary incident at his home and just wanted to be with her. He was glad she was not traumatized. Allan's kids were like his own. He would move somewhere less complicated and more child friendly, before he would allow something to affect them.

"Can you fax something for me?" he said, as he called his secretary. Maria got up and came to his office. "Yes Mr. Reed. What do you need faxed?" she asked, as she walked over to his desk. He handed her several documents and the number to send it to. "Knock, knock," one of his account executives said, as he lightly tapped on the partially opened door. "Hey," Lance smiled as he entered. "So, some of us are going to a lounge called Castille's. It's about five minutes away. We we're hoping you would come," he said. Drinks after work was tempting. But Lance was exhausted.

"No. Maybe next time. I'm not done with the Walden Project," he said. The men spoke for a few minutes about another project before Dave left the office. Lance completed the final points and had his project ready for specification by an engineer. It was a crowning moment. He was proud. His work was making a difference. "Mr. Reed. I'm leaving for the day. Do you need anything?" Maria asked. Lance looked at the papers on his desk. He checked that all faxes and important files went out to perspective clients. "No. I'm all set. Have a nice night."

The soulful sounds of Marvin Gaye's *Heard it Through The Grapevine* bellowed from Lance's speakers. He was fatigued. He planned a relaxing evening of dinner and a moment of tranquility while watching the sunset. It was still light out. He had over an hour before the sun would be lowering over the horizon. A steak and vegetables would be easy enough for him to prepare. He drove up to a light. A family in the car next to him caught his attention. It was a husband, wife and two kids in car seats. Lance smiled and turned his attention back to the light. It turned green. He took off. His mind now recalling the day Paula laid on an operating table with doctors carefully removing the dead fetus from her belly. Her blood pressure was dangerously low. They didn't have much time.

The doctors removed the baby successfully. A girl. Lance held his dead baby in his arms. He tried to get Paula involved. She turned her head. She couldn't take the sight of her baby in that condition. Doctors told her what she had feared. That they needed to remove her uterus. She would never have kids. It was devastating. They weren't prepared to be the parents of a dead child. Lance left the hospital and drunk himself to sleep. The next morning, he went to the hospital only to have nurses tell him his fiancé wanted no visitors including him. Paula kept her distance. Her tormented soul requiring medical intervention that she refused to get.

The garage door opened slowly. Lance pulled inside and hit the controller. He was glad to be home. The traffic was unpleasant and he desperately needed a shower. 3..3..7..5..3 disarmed the alarm. Lance dropped his head and sighed. He hadn't realized how tired he was. He glanced out the window as he walked into the kitchen. The waves were calmer. The sky was clearer. Boaters were enjoying themselves. He walked over to the window. A cup of coffee in his hand. A boater and his passengers decided to make his home a hang out. They were several feet out near his dock, laughing and joking. Lance hoped they didn't make themselves at home and walk right up his dock and to his door. It wouldn't be the first time. But he was used to traffic. There was always a gawker trying to get a look at his opulent living arrangement. The older gentleman and his three young female companions were obviously drunk. Really, Lance said, as he shook his head in disbelief. The man was fondling all three women as they laughed and giggled like school girls.

The women were scantily clad. Young. The man, well in his sixties. One of the women gave an enthusiastic wave. Lance nodded and raised his coffee cup. He hoped they moved along from their sight-seeing adventure parked right in front of his property. He planned to shower and walk naked to his dresser. The women whispered and stared. The man waved. Soon he gestured for Lance to join them. Lance shook his head *no*, then walked from the window. He was in no mood for their type of partying.

The shower was mildly successful at relaxing him. He wasn't sure why he was tense. The day had started off great. The company was great. His mother was doing better. And he'd heard Paula was doing better. There was nothing to be on edge about. Yet he was.

He slipped into a pair of linen pajama pants and a tee shirt. He was glad to see the boaters were gone. There was still some sun to enjoy before it would be dusk. Perfect time for a stroll to the end of the dock. He grabbed a sandwich bag and tossed fruit inside. His new favorite pastime was sitting on the dock eating his favorite fruit, and looking out at the horizon. The breeze always felt inviting. He needed it.

Lance sat down on the edge, letting his feet touch the water. It was a front row seat to a spectacular natural event. He sat his fruit down and made a call to a friend. A man named Barron, who lived back in his hometown of Boston. Fin was under his dock near the bottom. She could hear him on the phone. She slowly swam up, taking her time. His feet barely touching the water's surface. Fin got close. Lance became uneasy. And again, didn't understand why.

"B. What's up man," he said to his friend. "Lance. What the fuck man! You disappear. Don't answer your phone. What's good? How's Cali?" Barron asked. Lance chuckled. "What! Ok. You my father now. I've been busy man. When you coming? You would love it here. The weather. The..." he said, then removed the phone from his ear and looked down at his feet. "Lance! Lance!" Barron shouted. "Oh. Sorry man. I thought I saw something," he said. Lance continued staring into the deepest part. He could see a shadowy figure. "Hey man…I need to call you back. Somethings come up," he said. Barron responded in his usual long-winded way. Lance didn't hear a word of it. He sat the phone down. Something was in the water, floating motionless on the bottom. He couldn't make out what it was. But he had a sinking feeling it was a woman. He could hear Barron calling him again. "Hey. I need to call you back. Something's in this water man. I need to check it out. Give me a second," he said, before hanging up.

He took a deep breath and stood on the ladder. *What is in the water*, he thought, as he went down one step. His feet were in the water. He contemplated whether he wanted to enter and if so, how far. He had just gotten out of the shower. And whatever it was it was probably gone. He decided he would go in, if he saw something again. There were no predatory fish in the water. And if it was a fish, he was sure it would swim away. But he believed it was a diver. And he was determined to prove himself right.

"Did you find her?" King Orfe asked his son. "No. We weren't able to catch up with her. We will resume looking tomorrow. She is very fast. I've never seen anything swim like that," he replied. King Orfe was feeling better. He arose from his chair and walked up to his son. "What is on your mind? You seem troubled. She will be back. First time jitters. Her father stated she was nervous on the way here. That she is very sensitive and emotional. Give her time," he said. Prince Andreus didn't believe that description. The woman he had met in the waters that fateful day and now at his castle, was not some timid, emotional being. He knew better.

"No father. She is much stronger than that. I never told you but I'm going to tell you now," he said, looking at King Orfe. "What is it?" his father asked. "I met her before. I took soldiers and we swam to the waters off Mojarro," he said. He watched for a reaction. King Orfe didn't look too surprised. His son had always been aggressive and inquisitive. Always seeking answers. King Orfe always saw the good in his son. And his bold tendencies to break the rules, his way of self-expression. Harmless prying. His father nodded. Prince Andreus continued.

"She caught us as we were about to leave. I wanted to see the place for myself. It is as remarkable as we have heard," he said, as he walked to the window and looked down at the guards. King Orfe had never been there. He wasn't interested. As long as they continued to get what they wanted in trade, there was no benefit. "What were you looking for? You broke the laws of the land. You went without being invited there. And what if she decided to tell her father?" he asked. Prince Andreus smirked. "She won't father. Besides... What can he do about it? Our army outnumbers theirs. They wouldn't stand a chance if we decided to take what we wanted.

King Orfe looked swiftly at his son. "No Andreus! And besides...The other two cities will not support that. It would create panic. And without the trade from Panga and Piratchu, we would suffer. Our forefathers fought so we wouldn't have to. The land was divided into four. And laws were put in place to keep the peace. You mustn't think like that. Mojarro is generous. And you are to marry their princess," he urged. "She doesn't want to. I see it in her eyes. She never liked me. From that first day. Yet I have thought of nothing else. She is wonderful. I must have her. And I will. Or I will go... Take what is mine. Including the princess. You are ill father. I will be king soon. It should be my decision," he said.

The king paced slowly. His son was getting out of control. "You are not king yet. I still make the decisions. And I say no! We will not take anything from them. Her father has gone back to retrieve her. To convince her of what is best. She will be your queen. You will take the throne. And you will keep the peace between the lands," he replied. Prince Andreus walked to him. "And if she doesn't?" he asked. The king turned to his son. He hadn't thought of that. Part of the plan was to finally join the lands. Change history. He refused to consider the alternative. "She will."

"Look again," King Zander commanded, as he stared into the faces of his soldiers. Finora was not at the castle as he assumed. He immediately ordered his soldiers back in the waters of the Palimora Sea. Lark was instructed to go to the Trojian Sea and check everywhere, including the dunes.

Aterra looked at her husband. She worried about her daughter. She regretted not opening up to her. She blamed their talk or lack thereof, for Fin's difficulty in accepting her new life. "We will find her," Zander said to his wife. Aterra shook her head and quietly walked away. The king felt bad. Fin had never gone missing. And days had already passed. She should have been home. She was known to take a moment to herself. Usually on the grounds of the compound. He was troubled. Something told him she never left the water.

Days passed. Zander kept watch for any sign of his men returning from the waters. He saw one of his soldiers coming. He ran down the stairs and out the door. "Well," he said. "Sire. We cannot find a trace of her. Nothing! Should we go back in the waters towards Eulachon. Maybe she never made it here," he suggested. Zander thought of the dangers of those waters. It was filled with some of the most dangerous creatures around. "Yes. Send men back. I want two teams. Search here near the dunes. And send some men back to the Palimora Sea again. And don't come back until you find her," he said.

Day tuned to night, and the soldiers returned in large groups. The king watched out the window and his chief commander checked with each lead man, to get report of their progress. The men walked past Lark shaking their head as they headed to their quarters. They were exhausted. There was still one team not accounted for. Lark worried. He looked out into the distance. He could see no more men walking towards the castle.

He turned and looked up at Zander and shook his head in disappointment. King Zander let out a deep sigh. He would have to tell Aterra that her daughter would not be coming home that evening. The men planned to return to the waters and resume their search. Lark went to his personal room. He shut the door slowly and sat on his bed. He put his face in his hands and closed his eyes. If Fin had met a terrible fate, he would never forgive himself. He was supposed to watch her. He was Zanders personal guard. But the King always told him that Finora and his wife, were the priority if they were in a large gathering or on unfamiliar ground.

A knock on the door caused him to jump up. He ran to the door. He hoped it was the last team of men coming to tell him that they were delayed because they were chasing Finora. He snatched the door open. The king stood before him. A distraught look on his. A look that matched his. The king was well aware of Larks' affection for his daughter. "May I come in," he asked. "Yes sir," Lark replied. The king entered his room then turned to face him. "I want men in the water early. As soon as light allows," he said. "Yes sir. Of course," Lark said, trying not to look so affected. Efforts that fell flat.

"I know you are bothered by this. Probably as much as I am. I know that you care for my daughter," he said. Lark tried not to look shocked. He had believed his attempts at covering up his feelings had been well executed.

"Sir. She is like family. Yes… I want her safe. Yes…I am worried," he said. The king smirked. "And you love her. Yes?" he asked. Lark looked intensely at him. The acknowledgment of his feeling causing him to break down internally. "Um sir…I…," he stuttered. "You don't have to say. I've known for some time. The look on your face when we met Prince Andreus said it all. And I know you'd rather be in the water now. That you probably won't get much sleep tonight. But I need you to, because it is important that you lead the search for her. Because it is you, who will find her. You are compelled to do so."

Lark was speechless. King Zander was like a father to him. He had been a part of his army since he was a teenager. He was one of the youngest soldiers to join. His skill and in-depth knowledge of the waters and the land, made him a valuable asset.

"Get some sleep. You have a long day ahead. She doesn't want to be found. She is the fastest in all the waters. No creature could catch her. She is alive. She is angry because I tried to force her to do something she doesn't want to do," he said, as he walked to the window. He stared out at the beautiful dark blue sky. His emotions almost getting the best of him as he fought to keep control over himself. "That girl has always been a handful. Even as a kid. I should have known better than to try to follow some tradition with her. She is different. She can't be forced to do anything. She moves when she is ready. Just like now. Going after her is useless but I can't sit and do nothing. And I know you won't," he said, as he turned back to Lark. "Please find her," he said. "Yes, Your Highness."

"A message from Prince Andreus," the guard said, as he handed Zander a note. He read it then crushed it in his hand. His guards instantly became anxious. "Sire?" one said, hoping it wasn't bad news. King Zander rose from his throne and walked towards his wine case. He poured haku in a gold goblet and walked back to his chair. Fin was still missing, along with a group of soldiers who were unaccounted for. There were now, two search teams in the water.

"Is everything alright Your Highness?" he asked. "Yes," Zander said nervously. The king wished Lark were near. He only discussed his most crucial and secret information with him. And it was Lark's job to inform the troops. Lark was in the Palimora Sea with a crew he hand-selected. It was a dangerous task. They would need to go into Eulachon territory. They hoped to slip by the Uaru. The sea's soldiers would not allow them to cross past a certain point.

They lived in the waters. Appointed by a panel of citizens from each of the four cities. And it was their job to keep the soldiers and anyone else from entry into land they were not citizens in. It would keep trade fair. Keep down the temptation of treasure seekers. And above all, promote peace.

Each city elected fifty men. And once they entered the waters, they never came home. As an incentive, their families were greatly rewarded. It was a job many wanted but few were chosen for. It was noble. It was powerful. The men were regarded as heroes. It was an honor.

The king sent the guards out. He sat in his chambers, thinking of his daughter. He couldn't comfort his wife. Nothing could. Only the sound of her child's voice would do. And Aterra was not the only one missing Fin. The letter from Prince Andreus eluded to his cities disappointment at not having a queen. His letter claiming that the monarchy looked less stable without one. Prince Andreus was expected to marry and marry soon. His father was dying.

He wasn't sure how much time he had. And the letter was filled with words that sounded more like demands than suggestions. King Zander sat at his throne. The prince had revealed his hand. It was as King Nephrus had stated. He had warned Zander that Prince Andreus was trouble. And he wished he would have listened. Prince Andreus could marry anyone. A commoner, if he wanted. Queen Rasbora had two princesses to choose from. But he had his sights set on Fin and was now aggressively looking to seal the deal. With a letter that hinted at a possible war.

King Zander took a sip. He had to think of his options. He could see the prince was nothing like his father. A father who appeared too weak to care. Zander's mind raced. He played several scenarios out in his mind. Eulachon was three times the size of Mojarro. But there was comfort in knowing that Panga would be on his side. King Nephrus had already shown a dislike for Prince Andreus. It was Piratchu that he worried about.

If he could get the Queen to side with him, then a war would not be so easily won by Prince Andreus. The three cities combined would be more powerful. But Queen Rasbora was friendly with the neighboring city of Eulachon. She had high regards for King Orfe. And trade between then was easy and beneficial. Her city was joined to theirs. Land that was separated by volcanic land and abandoned arapaimas. She would be hard to convince. And informing her could backfire. If she betrayed his trust and warned them, it would send Eulachon charging his way. It was a lot to think about. And at the center of it all was Fin.

I'm not sure what's going to happen. But if Fin says no, then he will not be marrying my daughter!

6

Berries Oh Berries

"Allan! You get that mail?" Lance asked his brother, as he sat in the parking lot of the grocery store. "Yeah. That was generous. You didn't have to do that. He's turning eleven. That's a lot for a kid. I put it in his account. He's got a list of things he wants. Thanks! That meant something to him. I'll make sure Yaz gets something out of it as well," Allan said. Lance smiled. It was his nephew's birthday and he hated he couldn't hand him a gift. So, he sent a birthday card with a cashier's check inside. He had been there for every birthday. Every celebration. But he was now, miles away. He felt the burn. "Yeah, it's cool. As long as he gets what he wants," Lance replied.

After talking a few minutes, the brothers got off the phone. Lance cut off his car and took another minute to check his emails. He took his time to go in the store. He was working long hours trying to get caught up in his father's company. Everything was coming along. He hoped to redirect some of the work to the engineers and account executives, so he could work less hours. He was still healing from the trials of his life. The last year being filled with back to back tragedies. Lance sat his phone down. Simple task like grocery shopping had a way of forcing him to reflect on things he needed to forget. It was a quick run. He was in and out with a bag filled with fresh fruit.

The drive to Ellice Street was scenic. Lance carried the last of his groceries into the house and pushed his glass and metal door closed. His phone rang as he walked into the kitchen. He wondered who was calling him. Only his family had the house number. "Hello," he answered. The silence on the other end was deafening. "Hello," he repeated. He could hear the soft sounds of breathing. He closed his eyes and took a deep breath. It was Paula. He was sure. She was back to calling and holding the phone. "Say something," he said. The caller hung up. Lance held the phone for a second before hanging up. He called Allan.

"Hello," Allan answered. "Hey. Um. Listen…Did you give Paula my number?" he asked. Allan hesitated. He knew

Lance would not be happy. But he believed the two should work out their loss together. And get back together. They were good for one another. But the tragedy was too damaging. Allan hoped talks would help them recover.

"Yeah. She called a few days ago. Said she needed to talk to you. Why?" he asked. Lance sighed. "You know why. She doesn't want to talk. She wants to blame. She has unresolved anger over it. And I can't talk to her. I'm dealing with my own guilt. She needs therapy," he disclosed. "Of course she does," Allan replied. He held the phone. He hesitated. "But so do you," he said. Lance instantly became agitated.

"No. Actually I don't. I'm doing fine. I am mourning normally. It's going to take some time. But I'm good. I moved here for a reason. I need time away from Paula. Away from everything. You should have asked me first. I am not ready to talk to her. And until she gets the help she needs, I'm not sure what benefit I can be. Next time ask me Allan," he said. Allan agreed. Lance hated that Allan was so involved. He had no faith in his abilities to cope with tragedy. Allan himself had had a nervous breakdown. And he had a habit of projecting his own feelings onto the environment around him.

The truth was Lance was healing. He had come a long way. He was far from needing medical intervention. He didn't require talks with a psychiatrist although it would have been a benefit. Lance hung up. His brother had angered him again. Being a father instead of a brother. Over-stepping his bounds. Misjudging him. Another reason California was the best place for him.

*L*ance sat on the end of his dock. His linen pants legs rolled up. His feet in the warm blue water. He planned to sit until the sun set, then return to his patio and sit next to the sparkling rock, fire pit table. The large round outdoor fireplace gave the evening a nice ambiance. And as wonderful as his evenings were, something was missing. It was great. But Lance knew it could be better sharing such occasions with someone he loved. The sunset worked its magic again. He could shake the trials of his frustrating day. The view and fresh air were all he needed. Lance sat comfortably, a bowl of fruit, a mp3 player with earbuds and his cell phone at his side.

He ate strawberries, melon and blueberries as he watched his neighbor's boat go by. The boat coasted slowly. Small ripples hit his feet. The owner waved at Lance. He had wondered who the new owner of the home was. It was the boaters first time seeing Lance. They hadn't met yet, but Lance was nonetheless cordial. He knew his neighbors were anxious to meet him. The wife of the man on the opposite side, brought over a pie. She welcomed him to the neighborhood then asked if he would like to have dinner with her and her family. Lance declined and thanked the woman for the pie. It was a cherry pie that didn't last but a few days.

"Howdy," the man yelled. Lance waved back at the man, then continued to eat his fruit. He placed the earbuds in his ear and hit play. His playlist was full of old rhythm and blues, and music by some of his favorite artist like Gladys Knight, Elton John and Michael McDonald. Music he grew up listening to. Songs that always made him feel like his mother was right there. She would have approved of his playlist. It was her playlist. He got comfortable. He moved his feet around in the water. He took a deep breath in.

The voice of Anita Baker piping into his ears. He looked around. A slight uneasy feeling came over him. He looked around again. Unable to understand why he couldn't completely relax. He wondered if Paula's call had gotten to him. He didn't think so. He had received them before. She just wanted to hear his voice. It was nothing new. She was still having a hard time. And he understood. This was something else.

He looked into the water. He tried to focus his eyes. He tried looking deep down. But water, unless absolutely clear and unmoving, was difficult to see through. He thought he saw something. He looked again. It was a fish.

What is wrong with me? Am I still creeped out? There was no woman's body in this water, he thought. Lance's instincts were keen. He was right. There was something. Fin was under his feet. Down deep. Looking up at him. Watching him. Studying him. Her warmth and the vibrations of her tail picked up by him when she got close. Fin had returned. And he could sense her presence.

Suddenly something swam beneath his dock. Whatever it was, it was now underneath him. Lance looked around. He felt insane. It was just a fish. What else could move that swiftly in water. Lance jumped up. He tried to remain calm. He descended the ladder once again. Determine to put his curiosity to rest. If it was a fish, it was large. But something about it was strange. It had what looked like hair. Long, flowy hair.

Lance moved step to step, descending into the waters. The sun was setting. It wasn't dark but the dusk would make it difficult to see in front of him. He was trained in water. But his skill would be of little use with no visibility. Plus, it was dangerous. But Lance continued. He submerged into the unknown. He swam around, moving slowly past the dock's huge square shaped legs. He could see what looked like hair coming from behind one of the poles. *That's a woman*, he thought. He now believed a swimmer was embarrassed at being caught on his property. But he was correct in what he said to his brother. He did not own the water. And whoever was hiding, didn't understand they could be in the water near his house. Just not up on his land.

Lance went under. He could see her attempting to hide. He approached cautiously. He jerked back when Fin emerged from behind one of the docks' thick wood poles. He floated, staring intensely. She stared back. He was running out of air. He quickly swam to the surface to replenish himself and then returned. He looked around. He frantically turned his head side to side. She was gone. He swam out from the dock but then returned out of fear. Where did she go? he thought as he searched the water. She was beautiful. Breathtaking. He wondered who she was. Where she was from. Her beauty had him in a trance.

Lance continued his search. The sun was setting. Visibility was now down to a mere inch before him. Lance emerged from the water. He climbed the stairs. He stood on his dock, dripping wet and in shock. His mouth slightly open. His eyes scanning the surface hoping the woman popped up. She had no swim gear on. How was she able to stay under so long. Lance walked the perimeter of his property. He looked across the surface. She had to emerge at some point.

"Everything alright?" his neighbor shouted, noticing his behavior. "Yeah. Thanks," he replied, as he continued looking across the surface of the water. He never looked up. The neighbor looked at the water. "What did you lose?" the man asked. "Huh." Lance replied, finally realizing he was engaged in a conversation that he was not mentally tuned in on. "Oh. Sorry. I was looking for something. Sorry," he said, as he walked back and forth. Lance walked back to the end of his dock. He stood with his hands in his pockets.

Who is she? he thought. He was sure she was the one his nephew had seen in the water that day. He thought for a minute that it could be a neighbor. If it was, he wanted to meet her. He was intrigued. There was something in the way she looked at him. Even under water, he could see into her soul. Her eyes twinkled. She stared through him. She awakened something that was dormant for some time. And he wanted to know her.

But she could be someone's wife. He was new to the area. And it was a chance that this was what they did around those parts. And his biggest question was how she was able to stay under for so long.

"Have a good evening Mr. Reed," Maria said, as Lance walked past her. "Thanks Maria. See you in the morning," he replied. Lance was anxious to get home. The woman who appeared interested in the waters around his home could possibly there again. He would find out. He was prepared this time. In his trunk was the gear he would need to get in the water and stay in it. He had purchased a mask, goggles, a suit, cylinder and a regulator. He would not need to leave and go to the surface.

The ride home seemed longer. He was anxious. His curiosity was getting the best of him. He had left the office early. Cancelling two important meetings to go home and search when it would still be light out. He would see clearly. His mind raced. He wasn't sure why he cared. Why he needed to get another look at the mystery beauty who loved the water. Particularly, the waters around his home. He wondered why she looked so comfortable in it. Showing no stress at losing oxygen. No interest in popping up and getting more. How was it possible.

He thought maybe his eyes had deceived him. He asked the man at the supply shop, if new technology was out. Was it possible that the diver had something in her mouth delivering oxygen in a different manner. He told the man a woman was in the water and she had no obvious swimming gear on. That she never looked distressed. And never attempted to go to the surface. The man looked at him as if he had gone mad. Lance realized how crazy he must have sounded and quickly changed the subject. He questioned his sanity. He was under stress from the losses in his life. It could be his mind playing tricks on him. He discounted that theory. Nothing was wrong with him. He was fine. He saw what he saw. And he was going to see it again.

Lance geared up. He walked to the end of his dock. He was glad there weren't any neighbors looking. He felt ridiculous. He looked around. Then jumped in, feet first. His gear was working perfectly. Oxygen filled his mouth as he took a breath and checked that all was well before descending. He looked around and began swimming the long dock, checking near all the thick beams that held the dock in place. The muffled sound of bubbles, a reality check. He was in the water. Looking for a woman. He was sure Allan would have him committed. Lance swam slowly, pole to pole. He looked down and then out into the distance. She wasn't there. And after a half hour, he was ready to give up.

An hour passed. Lance emerged and pulled the mask off. He needed a break from the tightness of the rubber on his body. He held onto the stairs and climbed out. He sat down and slammed the mask down in frustration. *Damn*, he said, looking out into the water. Hours passed. Lance lost hope. She was a mystery that would stay a mystery. He stood up and walked slowly down the dock. Fin could see him in-between the cracks of the wood. She followed along, watching as his feet hit the wood, making an echoing sound. She got slightly ahead of him. He looked down, heavy in thought as he continued to his house.

He abruptly stopped. His eyes met Fin's. He fropped to his knees and peered through the small opening between the wood. He could see her. He ran to the edge and jumped in. She thought of running away. Lance entered the water. Fin went deeper under the wide dock. His oxygen tank and mask were where he'd left them. Sitting on the docks edge.

Fin swam back from him slowly. She had turned her tail back to legs. He was not half-man half-fish, and she was sure her tail would have frightened him. Lance stared in the eyes of the most beautiful women he had ever seen. Fin stared back. Lance abruptly swam up and took a breath. Before he could return, Fin stuck her head out of the water. "Hi," Lance said, unsure of what to say and hoping not to scare her away. He was as interesting up close as he was from far away. Fin analyzed him. Every inch. He looked like her. He sounded like her. The language was the same. But he needed help in the water. He wore the same suit she'd seen on another man.

"Hello," she said reluctantly. Lance smiled. He'd waited for this moment. She spoke. Her voice soft. Her eyes engaging. She looked deeply at him. As if she wondered things. He couldn't read her look. It was as though she was studying him. Absorbing him. Her in-depth interest in him was unique. She looked at his mouth as he talked. His eyes. She scanned his body. Taking him in. And afterwards, relaxing. As if he'd passed some test.

"What are you looking for? Shells? Fish?" he asked. Fin made a face. "No!" she replied. "Oh?" he said. "Then…Um…Why are you searching the water?" he asked. "I'm not searching," she said, her face crumbled. She looked displeased. "I have to go," she said, as she dove in the water. Lance dove right behind her. He could barely see her. She had swam so quickly, that all he could see was her long dark hair trailing behind her. He wished he could scream in water. He would yell out for her to come back. He didn't mean to interrogate her. She had done nothing wrong. *Damn!* he thought.

It was another beautiful sunny morning. Lance called in. There was no way he could go to work. It would be a useless day. He could think of nothing but Fin. She was bashful. Beautiful. Sexy. And mysterious. He sat on the end of the dock. A bag of fruit, his cell phone and his mp3 player. No gear. No oxygen. He would let her come to him. Maybe she would stop running and hiding.

Fin was there. Under his feet again. Deep enough not to be seen. She saw something small sinking. Something that had been discarded in the water. It was the stem of a strawberry. A small piece of the fruit still attached. She reached out and let it fall in her palm. She looked closely at it. She put it up to her nose. She looked up at him. He was eating them and discarding what was left, in the water. Fin put the strange looking soft thing in her mouth. The immediate sweetness was unlike anything she had ever tasted. Soon another floated down. She reached out, grabbed it and popped it in her mouth.

She got comfortable, as she eagerly anticipated each piece of strawberry and stem. The taste was heavenly. They had nothing like it in the world of Madaka. Only fish and plants. There were no berries. No grapes. No melons or bananas. Fin basked in the flavor. She floated under him and watched as he continually scanned the waters. She was sure he was looking for her. *I have to use my legs in these waters. Otherwise, he will be afraid*, she thought. She remembered the fear in the eyes of the child that saw her. The little girl who looked at her tail then screamed. Fin's tail was only really useful for helping her reach great speeds. It wasn't necessary. It was safe as it added to their ability to move from danger quickly. One never knew what they would encounter in the water. So, it was unheard of to be in the water without it.

Fin changed. The lack of body fat or gases in her lungs and bowel, keeping her from floating to the top. She floated motionless. Her body built for water. Courtesy of her ancestors, the gods and goddesses of the ocean. Fin had very little information to reference.

Their existence was centuries before her time. There was only legend. And legend spoke of a war that her ancestors won. But not before a rival goddess of the sea condemned their children to live under the ocean as fish. But human genetics were powerful. And so, it led to the mutation of humans, cast in Madaka, to live apart from the rest of the world. Their origin kept secret from them. The only existence known was their own. Until now. And Fin was surprised at her discovery. She wanted to know more. Much more.

She eased to the surface as dusk approached. She emerged and stayed hidden under the dock. It was like her second home. She had stopped swimming to the cave near Malibu. Lance sat, his earphones on, as he watched the sun lower. He sighed. An instrumental version of *Endless Love* playing on his mP3. He looked in the water. *She's there,* he thought. He reached without looking. The fruit was gone. He took the earbuds out and looked around. He narrowed his eyes. He was puzzled. It couldn't have fallen in the water. But then again, it had to. He stood up and looked around then glanced in the water. He saw something scurry away. It was her. Lance smiled. It was as he suspected. And he wondered if she had taken his fruit.

Fin sat near rocks off the coast. She opened the bag of fruit and pulled a whole strawberry out. There were just a few left. She looked closely at it then bit into it. "Mmm," she moaned, as she took another bite. Juice from the strawberry ran down her chin. "Mmmm," she moaned again, as she closed her eyes and enjoyed every bite. She wished she had more. She sat on the rock and watched boats go by. She was a few miles from Lance's home. Boaters pointed at her. She was in a strange place. There was nothing around her. The boaters were concerned that she may be stranded.

Several boats went by. Fin was attracting a small audience. Everyone wanted to know how she had gotten on the rocks in such a peculiar and hard to get to area. It was far from any reasonable land that one could walk on. It was off deep and dangerous water with heavy currents. Fin saw a boat coming closer. It was filled with a family taking a tour of the shoreline and the homes. They slowed down and asked if she was ok. Fin shook her head. She was nervous. She wanted to jump in the water and swim away but the boaters continued on. Soon another boat came close. "Are you alright?" the teenager asked. His father watched from the bridge as he tried to keep the boat from being pushed close to the rocks. "Yes," she yelled. The man smiled. Fin was attractive. "You want a ride?" he asked. "No."

Why are they so concerned? she said, as she thought about the boats that approached her. Fin got down off the rock and swam away. It would be dark soon. She was fatigued and she hadn't had a good night's sleep in days. The unfamiliar waters were difficult to get comfortable in. But as the weeks passed, she had begun to get more acclimated to the ocean. Its composition took some getting used to. But the similarities were close enough and her body had adjusted.

Fin swam back. She was now sleeping under his dock. She got comfortable. She settled at the bottom on top of rocks and went to sleep. It was 2:00 a.m. and Lance was asleep on his couch. By three, Fin was bored and suffering from insomnia. She popped up out of the water. She looked at his home. When she saw no movement, she decided to get a closer look.

"Fin this is the craziest thing you have ever done. What if he sees you," she said, as she walked down the dock towards his patio. The sound of a car had her jumpy. "What was that," she said. She stopped and looked around then continued towards the large window and sliding door. She could see Lance on the couch. His hand on his crotch. She instantly felt sexual tension at the sight of him gripping himself. He was fast asleep. A strange movie playing on his television. Fin was excited. It was the first time she was able to view closely what she was watching from the water.

It was images of people. Not people in present form. Fin marveled at the large flat board that was unlike anything she could have imagined. And the images were of naked people. It was shocking. Back in Madaka, they didn't show themselves to one another. Fin stared at the woman on the screen. She looked at the man a certain way. Her eyes danced. Her body swayed. She approached him then began to kiss him. Fin stood motionless. The man and woman were in an embrace. It was visually appealing. Fin began to feel hot. She began to feel that strange feeling she tried to describe to her mother. Soon the man and woman were on top of one another. And Fin's mouth fell slightly open, when the man entered the woman with his male part.

Fin was so fascinated that she didn't notice Lance had awakened. He stared at her. She was glued to the porn he had on. The look on her face was pure sexiness. Raw and enticing. Lance stood up. Fin gasped then turned and ran. She bolted down the dock and jumped into the water. "Hey!" Lance shouted. He ran to the water. She was gone. It was dark. He would never be able to see her, if he entered. Lance sighed. *Come back!*

Fin awoke from a quick nap. She wasn't prepared for what she was looking at. Lance was sitting next to her. She had fallen asleep on rocks, close to the surface, but completely submerged. She had mistakenly fallen asleep after tiring from a long swim to the cave to get away from him the night before. And Lance had gotten in the water after seeing her through a large gap in-between the planks of his dock. He could see her asleep on one of the large boulders in the water. The boulders were in a small area. Used as foundation when the home was built and extended out six feet from the house in water that was six feet deep.

Fin jolted up. "Wait!" he said, his arm extended. His hand open. Fin stopped. He looked desperate to talk to her. She came up out of the water keeping her distance from him. She sat back on the boulder. Lance slowly lowered his arm. He was shocked she was under his dock. He had only been sitting there a few minutes. He tried not to wake her. He just wanted to be close to her. He felt compelled. She was on his mind nonstop. So much so, that he had not been to work. All in a quest to find her.

"My name is Lance," he said. Fin stared. "Fin," she replied. "Fin. That a pretty name," he said, as his mind raced trying to think of what to say without causing her to swim away. Lance pulled something from his shirt pocket. A small cellophane bag. Fin lit up. Lance smiled. She reached out to take the bag of strawberries then pulled one out. "What are these called?" she asked. Lance narrowed his eyes. It was a strange question. Everyone knew what a strawberry looked like.

"They're strawberries," he said. Fin smiled again. She took a bite. Then put the rest in her mouth. "What is this?" she asked. "That's melon," he replied. Fin took a bite and moaned. Soon she had eaten every piece. "Would you like more?" he asked. "Yes." Lance walked then swam once he was away from the rock. "Don't leave. Please! I'll be right back."

"Fuck, fuck, fuck," Lance said, as he nervously entered his house. This was mind blowing. She was asleep in the water. He ran to his refrigerator and grabbed a hand full of sliced melon and whole strawberries. He grabbed his cell phone and called his brother. "Pick up, pick up," he said nervously, as he paced. He stopped to look out the window. He was anxious to get back to her. He hoped she wouldn't leave. He was sure she wanted the fruit. "Hello," Allan answered.

"You are not going to believe this. That woman in the water…She is here. I've spoken to her. She has been under my dock. Sleeping in the water under my dock," he said. The phone went silent. Lance thought maybe the call had been dropped.

"Hello," Lance said. Allan held the phone. Pausing before he spoke. "What? I don't understand," he replied, as he put his hand on his hip and closed his eyes.

"What do you mean you don't understand? A woman was asleep under my dock. In the water," Lance said, getting frustrated at Allan's attempts at trying to make sense of it. He was aware it wasn't typical. That it sounded crazy. But he was never one to imagine things or make up stories. And he was angry that Allan questioned what he was saying.

"Sleep in the water? Actually asleep in water?" he said. Lance stopped pacing.

"Allan. Listen again. I said in the water. Her head, submerged, in the water. Yes. And I want to know how that is possible? She had no equipment. She woke up when I was sitting next to her. I'm talking to her now. And she is gorgeous. You wouldn't believe... Fucking beautiful. She has dark hair. Her eyes are the brightest green I have ever seen. She has the most beautiful skin tone. It all started last night. She came to my door. But then she ran. I know this sounds crazy," he said. Allan paused. "Ok. Listen. Miles saw a woman in the water and now you have conjured up in your mind that there is a woman that lives in the water," he stated.

"What!" Lance shouted. "You're under a lot of stress. You need to come home. That place is driving you mad," Allan stated. Lance stared out the window. His energy changing. "I'll call you back," he said in a dry tone. "Lance. Wait! I hear you. I believe you. Maybe she has something new on the market. Humans cannot breathe under water. Do you hear what you are saying?"

Lance hung up on his brother and sighed. Allan called right back. Lance selected *decline,* forcing him into voice mail. Allan called back again. Then texted his brother;

Look man, I'm sorry. You are under a lot of stress and I am here for you. I apologize. Call me when you calm down. You sounded frantic. You need rest. Your taking on too much. First the baby and then your father. You should see that doctor I told you about. She could help you get things in order. Don't play around with mental health. Thoughts that don't make sense. Get out of your own head. You know people can't breathe under water. Come on. You know this. Talk to me. Call me back.

Lance sat his phone down. He knew he sounded crazy. But he expected more from his brother. They had grown up in the same household. They were both sane and rational men. "Crazy. He thinks I'm crazy," he scoffed. Lance walked through his sliding glass door out onto his patio and walked to the dock. He looked around to ensure no one was looking then jumped in the water and slowly moved under the dock. Fin popped up and sat back on the rock. Lance smiled.

"Here you go," he said, taking a seat next to her. He wanted to touch her flawless skin. It looked delicate. Beautiful. And it glowed with a translucency. She looked intensely at him as she ate the fruit. Her gaze hypnotic. He was taken with her. Curious about her. He hoped she would stay.

"You. um…Want to come in?" he asked. Fin hesitated at first. "Ok," she said.

Lance tried to contain his excitement. He was getting closer to the mystery woman. She was opening up. He reached his hand out. She stared at his hand. He wanted to touch her. Fin slowly raised her arm. She secretly yearned touch. It felt good. There was a connection that accompanied it.

Lance waited. His arm outstretched. Fin hesitated. "It's ok," he assured. Fin eased towards him slowly. She took his hand. Her delicate touch, soft as cotton. He rubbed her hand, and she felt something immediately. Lance guided her slowly out the water. They swam down to the end and emerged using the steps to get on the dock. He looked her up and down. The thin, strange silk-like material that covered the important parts and left little to the imagination, was sexy and would cause quite a stir if his neighbor saw. She looked naked. The color of the material looked similar to her skin and fit her curves perfectly. Lance couldn't help but stare in admiration. She was exotic. Luscious. And she had his full attention.

Lance walked with her back to his house. He slid the door open and Fin stepped in. She immediately raised her feet off the floor in a weird dancing motion. The floor felt cold. The material felt odd. The marble entryway unlike anything she had ever walked across. She quickly walked to the carpet. "You want some socks?" he asked. "What are those?" Fin replied. Lance chuckled then ran to his room to retrieve a pair.

Fin looked around. She was strangely quiet. She was normally much more talkative. Fearless. But this new world had her quiet and unsure. There were a lot of things she didn't recognize. This was a sophisticated society. The people were advanced. Their homes less bulky. More windows. Thin and elegant looking. There were trees. Lots of vegetation. The skies. The weather. The fish. The crafted items that floated on water and the metal ones that drove on land. She was overwhelmed. It was a lot. Her quietness was not a surrender. She was not afraid. It was an internal safety mechanism, designed to help her handle the bombardment of the new world. And it had done its job. She found herself feeling at home. She hated to admit it but there was something that felt natural about it. It *was* her world. But better.

It was remarkable that a society of people had things that seemed impossible to create. Madaka was a world of complacence. They were happy with their possessions. With their capabilities. With what they had at their disposal. No one sought inventions, improvements or new ways of doing things. But this world was obviously unsatisfied. Always striving for advancement. Fin understood. She too sought more. But there were no resources in Madaka. She made her own polish to apply to her nails. She made her own lamp out of a hemini plant. But here was a house brightly lit from something, and it was not a plant. It was fascinating.

The air inside his home was cold. He noticed her lips quivering. "Are you cold?" he asked. "Yes," she replied. Fin was still feeling Lance out. She was not ready to open up. She had many questions. And she knew he did as well. He was patient. He was gentle and kind. And there was something about him that she was drawn to.

"You can take a warm shower. I'll bring you clothes. I have jogging pants that will be a little big on you. But they should be ok. I have tee shirts and a hoodie to keep you warm. I'll be back," he said, as he ascended his staircase. Lance walked by his thermostat and turned the air off. He went into one of the spare bathrooms. His mind raced.

What am I doing? I don't know her. But she is sweet. And she is so beautiful, he thought. He worried about becoming involved. Wanting her. She was a stranger. He had just met her. Yet he was already thinking of a way to get closer. He was completely drawn to her. He had no real understanding of how she had him so engrossed. Her eyes were magnetic. He felt responsible for her. She was from a different place. He didn't care. He never saw her tail. Fin was careful not to show it. It would have frightened him. It would have prejudiced him. She looked like him. She talked like him. And other than breathing under water, there wasn't much else different.

He erased the doubts from his mind. He wanted her there. He had searched for her for weeks. And he had no plans to exit from his introduction and the chance to get to know her.

"I turned the shower on," he said. "The what?" she asked. "Oh. It's upstairs. Just warm water. I have clothes laid out for you in the spare room," he said. Fin smiled. "Great," she replied. Lance led her up the stairs and to his spare bedroom. "Right in here," he said. Fin walked to the bathroom and peeked in. She was in awe. Water was coming from metal. Back home, it wasn't carried in by soldiers and poured into a waiting small tub in the floor.

"Thanks," she said, as she waited for him to leave. Lance pulled the door closed. He stood on the other side. Fin could feel his presence. She walked to the door and touched it. She closed her eyes. She could feel him even more. Lance put his ear to the door. His heart fluttered. He let out a breath. Fin opened her eyes. She stepped away from the door and smiled. He was definitely there.

The loud high-pitched sound of the teapot snapped Lance out of his deep thoughts. He walked out the room and down the stairs. He wanted to surprise Fin with a cup of tea with strawberries. He removed the pot and poured half a cup over a few strawberries. A mild flavored grey tea to warm her from the inside out with the added touch of something he knew she loved. Strawberries.

Lance was still in disbelief. He was convinced she was either sheltered and confined from the world and had escaped. Or she was not from the modern world. And the latter sounded too far-fetched. So, his mind went with the sheltered theory.

Fin stepped into the huge glass shower. She kept her covering on. The warm water was soothing. It was the best feeling of water she had ever felt. She had never experienced it pulsating against her skin in such a calming way. "Mmm," she moaned. She had been in the Pacific Ocean for weeks. It was nice to get out of it and be on land. And even nicer to be under clean comfortable water. She opened her mouth and drank it. The taste was different. It tasted similar to the rivers and lakes of her world. The taste started her thoughts racing. Soon she was sad and missing her parents.

Fin! What are you doing? You can't stay here. You have to go home, she thought, as she pondered the thought. *No! Not yet,* she countered. She wasn't leaving until she learned what she could. And not until she got to know the handsome stranger that she was drawn to from the moment she saw him.

She closed her eyes, the steam opening her pores. Releasing some impurities. Fin felt more alive. She loved the way it felt against her body. Lance knocked on the door. She had been in the shower for an hour. "Yes," she said. "Are you hungry?" he asked. Fin paused. She wasn't sure she wanted to eat food. She had eaten crustaceans from the ocean floor. An experience that was not pleasant. "No. I'm fine."

Lance went back down to the kitchen. His heart raced. He was still anxious. Nervous. He was dying to ask her where she'd come from. How she was able to be under water for so long. He wondered if it weren't an elaborate trick. She didn't seem like the type. He was usually a good judge of character. And he didn't pick up any deceitful vibes from her. He planned to find out as much as he could about his visitor. He had questions. He was sure she had some questions too. "I won't overwhelm her with questions. We will take our time," he said to himself, as he waited for Fin to emerge from the room.

The King stood outside his castle. Guards flanked him. Lark and several other soldiers were walking towards them. Another day, another search, and Finora was not among them. Zander could tell by the look on Lark's face that he had become distraught over his failed attempts at finding her. He gave the king a look and walked past him. Zander sighed. "He's taking it really hard," one of the king's veteran soldiers stated. "Yes. I know. How far did you get?" the king asked. "All the way. We were almost at the shores of Eulachon. We killed two Baika and Lark killed a Tetra. By himself sir," the soldier said, as he cleared his throat. The King sighed. His men were facing great dangers. Finora's actions had cost several of them their lives and they were still coming into harm's way. The missing men were never recovered. Proof they met an untimely and devastating end.

"He wants to go again after we've eaten and regained out strength," the soldier stated. King Zander nodded. He desperately wanted Fin returned safely, and before Prince

Andreus located her. The note all but suggested he expected her to be delivered back to him. King Zander kept the contents of the note to himself. It would enrage his men. Change the morale. And possibly have the men ready to respond to the threat.

"You alright," the king said, as he entered Lark's room. "Yes, Your Highness," he said. The king didn't believe him. He gave his reply without looking up at him. "So, I hear you plan to go back in the water?" he asked. "Yes," Lark quickly replied. Looking the king in his eyes. "Alright. Take more men with you this time. The Tetra are night predators."

The men prepared to leave as ordered. Two senior guards looked at each other. They were weary. It seemed hopeless. But no one was willing to give up. Especially Lark. "He is taken with her," one soldier said to the other. "Of course. I noticed years ago. She is the most beautiful in all the land. And she is noticed wherever she goes. But he has always did more than notice her," he replied. The men agreed not to talk about it. It was forbidden for them to ogle, speak of, or desire the princess. And Lark was no exception. But he was closer to the king. He had special favor. He was the king's confidant. And there was no way of knowing if his actions would get him into trouble with the king. And so, it was important that their conversation stay between them.

Lark and his men prepared to leave. They unbound their legs and wore loose clothing. Lark looked to the sky. He took a deep breath and left his room. His men were waiting. He walked out and said nothing as he passed them. They followed closely behind him, looking at each other. It was understood. Lark loved Finora and they knew it. It was no longer a secret. His behavior was that of a man in love. The King and Queen watched out the window. Aterra looked at her husband. Her eyes bearing the pain of a mother missing her child. She looked away then turned and walked to her room. The king was also sad. He was unable to process the pain. Lark looked back. He glanced up at the king then continued bravely on, to the dark waters. It would be a long night.

"They are ready your highness," the soldier said to Prince Andreus. The men walked out of the compound towards the shores of the sea. Prince Andreus had seen King Zander's men searching the waters. He was puzzled at first. But then realized they would only risk their lives for one thing. The royal family. And the only royal unaccounted for, was Fin. Which meant they believed she was in the water. She was in the water. Probably the Palimora Sea. And he wanted to get to her first. Convince her to be his wife. It would save him the time of travelling to Mojarro. And it would keep him from flooding her compound with his men. Because she had no choice in the matter. He was prepared to play nice until his father was no longer in power. Andreus respected King Orfe. He loved his father deeply. And his loved for him was the only reason he was not planning a forced takeover.

Lark and his men searched from the bottom up. They searched as much of the vast waters as they could. They tried going in areas that they had not gone. After several hours and no luck, the men became discouraged. They tried to talk Lark into abandoning the difficult mission. The water was dark. Only illuminated in those areas where large schools of fish were. But Lark refused. The men forged ahead. They split off in groups of five. Lark was frantic. He realized too much time had passed. He feared the worst.

"Lark!" a soldier said, as he swam up to him. Lark looked intensely at him. "What!" he said, fearing the worst. "Prince Andreus and his men are in the waters. Why are they here? They too are looking for something. We saw them on the bottom. They are spread out. Hundreds. They are using small lit globes of some sort, to see their way."

Lark's mind raced. "Get the others. Signal to them to head back. She's not here. I don't think she's in the Palimora. She wouldn't hang out in these waters. I just don't believe she's here. And now, we have a bigger problem."

Lark and his men emerged from the water, solemn and frustrated at their lack of progress. And compounding their problems, and fears, was the presence of Andreus in the water. Lark walked with purpose. He entered the castle as his men continued past the door, towards the back of the property. Only Lark was allowed such freedoms. All other guards except the ones appointed to guard the inside, stayed outside.

"Where is the King?" he asked a soldier standing guard outside the king's chambers. "He is asleep. He was up all evening comforting the queen. She is distraught. She has been saying her daughter is dead. She had to be given something to help her rest," he said. Lark understood. He himself was exhausted. "I must see him," he said, as he walked past the soldier and entered. Lark walked slowly towards the kings' bed. "Sire," he said, as he approached. "Sire!" he repeated louder.

"Yes, yes," the king replied, as he sprung up. "Please Lark. No bad news. The queen is ill. She is making herself sick. I have to give her hope. Please," he said. Lark looked to the floor. He couldn't face the king. He had no good news. He had worse news. Fin was still missing. And Prince Andreus was spotted in the water.

"I'm sorry Your Highness. I have no good news. We searched. She is not there. And…We saw Prince Andreus and his men." The King jumped up. He threw the sheets off of his legs. "What!" he blurted, as he got out of bed. He entered into his privacy area. A small closet that was covered only by a privacy screen. Lark was heartbroken. And now he was angered. The king's reaction, other than showing some surprise, was not appropriate. Lark wondered what was going on.

"Sir! He was clearly looking for Fin. She is not his responsibility. There is no reason for him to be there," he huffed. The King reprimanded him with a stern look. "She is to be his wife. He has every right to try to locate her. We need all the help we can get." Lark simmered on the inside. A slow boil that erupted, as he tried to control his words. He had never gotten angry at the king.

"She doesn't want to marry him! That's why we're looking for her now! She was upset. I noticed it on the way there. It was all over her face. She knew she would be unhappy," he said. The king walked up to him. Lark was overstepping his boundaries.

"How dare you claim to know what my daughter wants. You have no right," he replied. Lark immediately regretted what he said. He didn't mean to upset the king. Tempers were high. Everyone was stressed. "Please forgive me Sire. I did not mean to offend," he said. Zander put his hand on Lark's shoulder. "You are just tired. You have been searching for her non-stop. I understand that she means a lot to you. She is like family to you. I want you to rest. Send others in the morning. You must take a break," he said. Lark shook his head no.

"I cannot do that Your Majesty. I must look until I find her. I will never stop looking. Sir"

7

Love and Loss

*K*ing Zander needed to address the citizens of Mojarro. He would speak to the masses and his words would be delivered to all who was unable to attend. Too much time had passed. Fin would not have stayed away, willingly, for that long. It was time for King Zander to face his reality. The princess was *dead at sea*. Lost forever. The future of the monarchy uncertain. King Zander walked in the middle of his men. He reached the entry to his compound. The massive wood doors opened. He stepped out and walked outside the gated walls. He and his men made their way just a few feet, to a stage made out of huge stone and wood. It was where he addressed the citizens. His words would be whispered among them. There were thousands in attendance.

And afterwards they talked amongst each other for those not close enough to hear;

Today we mourn the loss of my daughter. Princess Finora, the king said. The crowd gasped. Some whispered. The king had no answers and he was grief stricken. The queen was notably absent. She was inconsolable.

Princess Finora was lost at sea, on her way to meet the Prince of Eulachon. That is all I have. I have made no decision about how we move forward. She was my only child. This leaves a large void.

The faces of those in attendance said it all. The king looked around. He had nothing to say that would ease their stress. If there were no other heirs, then the future of the monarchy was threatened. He continued;

Mojarro is strong. We will go on. We will go into the future strong. There will always be a leader. That, I promise. But that's all I am prepared to say at this moment. I need time to accept what has happened and mourn my daughter properly. Thank you!

The crowd continued their whispers and talks among each other. The King turned and walked back through his gates. He glanced at Lark. The pain on his face was profound.

Zander acknowledged his pain with a nod. He was not completely sure she was dead. But they had to assume she was, and he needed to make the announcement, so that everyone would move on. Lark stood off to the side as the king passed him and the other soldiers. The men had heavy hearts. Their future was uncertain. They refused to give up. Fin was smart. She was not timid as the other women were. She was different. She was powerful. Fast. She was somewhere in the waters that surrounded Mojarro. And the men would continue looking. They would never stop. Finding her was their mission. She was their lifeline. Her children would be kings and queens. They looked at Lark. He didn't look like he was giving up. They were on the same page.

"Your Highness, Halacai would like a word with you," the guard said. Prince Andreus sat on the throne. His father wasn't expected to make it through the night. "I did not ask to speak with anyone. My father is dying. What does he want?" he shouted. The guard shook his head slowly. "Fine! Let him enter. If he says anything I don't like, he is to die in the waters of Palimora." The guard nodded. "He will see you now," the guard said. He escorted Halacai to the Prince's chambers.

"Your Highness," he greeted Andreus. "What do you want? Is this important? Now is not a good time?" he asked. "Yes Prince Andreus. I have news. It is about the princess. I was told you were supposed to marry her," the man said. Andreus sat up straight and leaned slightly forward. "Yes! What about her?" he asked. "She is dead sir. And the citizens are in a panic. The citizens are afraid to speak about their fears. Who will lead us if the King dies? She was to be our Queen. We seek answers," he said. Prince Andreus sat back. He had hoped she wasn't. And he had been patient. But if she were dead, then he had an answer to everyone's fears. Zander had no more heirs. Someone would need to rule Mojarro. He decided to tell Halacai enough in the hoped that he spread the news. He would give some detail of his plan. Enough to spark an interest.

"Yes... I was supposed to marry her. My heart aches for her. But life will go on. So will Mojarro. I will choose another bride. And Mojarro was chose another king. Go back. Talk amongst the citizens. Don't fear the future. Embrace it. Change is good. The citizens have more power than they realize. Choose your king. After he is gone, you will be free to choose your own king. Right? Our lands would have benefitted greatly after the union. It still can," he stated.

Halacai bowed and left out, escorted to sea by soldiers. He lived in the surrounding waters. An outcast, originally from Mojarro with strong ties to both cities. He had been living in fear of a takeover and used his connections with some of the uaru, to get closer to Prince Andreus. Word of a Mojarro citizen who wished asylum and a new place to stay soon reached Andreus' door. He was told the man was seeking refuge in Eulachon and the prince allowed him to speak. Prince Andreus did not trust Halacai and so he promised he would allow him entry into his land if he kept him informed of Fin. Halacai's intentions were good. He thought the information he delivered was for the betterment of everyone. It was a dangerous game he was playing. Pretending to want in on the desolate and isolated land was dangerous. If the prince agreed, he could be trapped there. The prince would never allow him to travel back and forth. It was unheard of for members of one society to move to another. If the prince allowed such a move, it would be the first in centuries.

But Halacai underestimated Andreus. He never saw his evil side. He hadn't been exposed to Andreus' manipulative behavior or his sometimes, vengeful thoughts. No one had. His father did a good job of keeping the beast in him settled. But King Orfe was succumbing to a rare illness. Something that neither salt water nor plants, could remove. He had slowly deteriorated. And by the following morning, he was dead.

"Long live the King," the men toasted. Horns blew and drums beat, to signal the new day. Eulachon had a new leader. Prince Andreus was now King Andreus. He smiled and raised his goblet. His men raised theirs. They took a sip of the bitter but potent wine as they celebrated his new position.

His father, King Orfe, was laid out to rest in the sea. Wrapped in binding and taken to the bottom of the deepest part, where he was buried. He was pushed into the soft sand where he would remain forever. His grave unmarked. As all graves were. The dead were not dead. They were thought of as gods and goddesses, reborn as fish and part of the sea forever.

Andreus was now free. No longer under the watchful eye of his father. He mourned him deeply. The toast was quick. Soon Andreus left the room. He felt strange cheering his new position when he missed his father. It was bittersweet. He walked down the halls to his meeting room. He walked over to the window and looked out. Several guards entered and shut the door. He had called for them.

"Yes Sire," the lead guard said. "Did you escort Halacai to the waters?" he asked. The soldiers, one of his most trusted confidants, nodded. "Good. Because I don't trust him," he said. "He speaks the truth. There is no harm there. He is our liason. Yes, he is originally from Mojarro and that makes him more loyal to their agenda. But he has no reputation for lying. There is value in using him to get your demands out to the other cities," the soldier said. Andreus agreed. "Yes. But still…He is more loyal to Mojarro, even though it is I who pays him handsomely. That worries me. He cannot be bought. Not in a way that is useful to me at this time."

There was now a lot to consider. Andreus paced the floor. He was feeling things he couldn't explain. The death of his mother was hard but his father's passing was unbearable. He sat on his opulent, special made throne. A gold chair with opals, emeralds and jadeite. A chair that was made and delivered as a gift from Mojarro, years earlier, for King Orfe. He pondered what to do. Fin had been missing for a while. It was not a stretch to assume she was dead. A blow for to the city of Mojarro. And it was showing. They were already unstable. King Zander was older, but he still had a lot of youth in him. He could reign for many years. He thought of taking the city. But if they were wrong and Fin was living at sea, then he may regret the move. And the people of her city could rise against him.

"What will we do about the princess, Your Highness? We have continued to search the waters. Is she really dead?" the soldier asked. Andreus weren't sure. He thought about that question. "I don't know. It is possible. But she is also stubborn. Just the type to stay away, in order to change the course of her life. I do not underestimate her. She wants me to re-marry. It is then, that she will emerge. Someone knows something. Find out. Go to the seas. Speak with the uaru," he replied. "What is your plan if we locate her?" the soldier asked.

"We look for her. If she is alive, she will be my bride and we will rule over Mojarro. The cities will unite. If not, then we will not wait. We will take them by force. And we will kill anyone not willing to submit."

The men talked in depth. They were not alone. They had company just beneath the window. He was cleverly hidden under the veil of darkness and covered by plants. "Say nothing. This conversation stays in this room. We look for her again at dawn."

Prince Andreus marched through the thin sparse vegetation. After several miles, his feet his the sands of the shoreline. He led his team towards the water. He was desperate to find Fin. There was no one else he saw himself married to. There were plenty of young and available eulachonians. But Andreus had his bride.

She had been the talk of Eulachon since she left. She was smart, beautiful and their king was smitten. And there was the added bonus of another land to call home. She would come bearing gifts in the form of trade. Opening the doors to the citizens having more goods at their disposal. The treasures of Mojarro would be theirs to share and enjoy, with the city's gold at the top of the list. They were using it in combinations with other metals. Shaping it into cups, pans, fasteners as well as using it to adorn themselves. They loved the highly malleable metal. It was easy to handle and highly sought after.

Andreus and his men reached the shores of the Palimora Sea and entered. The men looked straight ahead. Their strong legs thrashing through the pale blue water. Soon the water was up to their chest. And then over their heads. The closed flaps on the sides of their chest opened up. Their gills now aiding in their breaths. The men's mouths were slightly open. Taking in the water and with it, the life-giving oxygen.

The men pushed off the sand, kicking their feet then brining their legs together. They changed their legs to tails. A quick and painless transition, as their black tails formed from the fusing of a membrane. Andreus continued to lead, unaware that he would be met by King Zander and his army.

The sun settled. Lance stood in his window, holding a glass of red wine. He watched Fin as she took in the remarkable sight. She sat on his porch near the warmth of the fire pit after her long and comforting shower. His home now lit throughout. The perfect ambience for a talk. He slid the door to the side and stepped out. He was ready. She seemed comfortable. Relaxed. He sat down next to her. The light wind had the fire dancing. "That is remarkable. Really remarkable," Fin said, her voice soft, her demeanor easy and carefree. Gone were the tension and fear she originally had. Fin was comfortable but she was still feeling him out. He hesitated, then asked her what he really wanted to know.

"How are you able to breathe in water? Or were you using something. I don't understand," he said. Fin looked deep into his eyes. She knew more than he did. She had studied him. Studied the human race. She could see their strengths. Their limitations. And she hoped he wouldn't think she was a monster after she told him their differences.

"I have two ways to breathe. Where I'm from, we all have the ability to breathe in water. When I first came here, I was shocked that you couldn't. I discovered this place. Then I discovered you. Your kind. What are you called?" she asked. Lance furrowed his brow. "Um... People," he said. Fin looked down. She was sensitive to faces. Emotions. She could sense things about him and was much more adept at picking up cues than humans. His furrowed brow, let her know he was uncomfortable with thinking of her as different. So, she wasn't sure how much she should tell him.

"I'm different. I'm from the ocean. A similar world but not really. Does that scare you?" she said, looking over at him and gazing deeply into his eyes. She waited for his response. She wanted him to be honest. And he knew it. She may have been from another world, but her look wasn't. It was the look of a woman who wanted a man to be straight with her. And so, he was. "No."

Fin looked in his eyes, for what felt like an eternity. Her gaze instantly made him nervous. "Listen. I looked for you for weeks. I waited on the dock hoping you would come back. Deep down, I knew you were different. Maybe not from here. I wasn't sure what to make of it. But I continued looking. Because it didn't matter. Difference is ok," he said, holding the wine glass, as he looked back at her. Fin was relieved. She felt the same way. It didn't matter. Bonds mattered. What was shared, mattered. The rest were small details.

Fin looked back at the fire. She had questions. "Last night…What was that on the big thing that shows people?" she asked. Lance smirked. He swallowed hard. Then cleared his throat. Fin quickly noticed his hesitation. "What? Should I not ask that?" she said. "No, its fine. It was the way you said it," Lance noted. He took a minute. This was complicated.

"It's…um… called sex," he said, looking down at his hands. As much as he wanted to talk about it and show her, he believed it would be too soon. Especially for her. There was some apprehension about how much to tell her. She had seen the worst of it. A porn that included all types of sex, including BDSM, was a bit much. He was embarrassed that she saw it on his television. It did not represent his taste. He wasn't into rough sex. He just loved sex.

"How does it feel?" Fin asked. Lance's eyes widened. The topic had him feeling bashful yet intrigued. "You've never done it before?" he asked. Fin shook her head slowly.

"No," she said, pausing then asking more questions. "Why?" she asked. There was some slight embarrassment he felt explaining sex to a grown woman. But he was up for the challenge. "For different reasons. For fun. For pleasure. To make babies," he replied. Fin sat back. He had her attention. "And how does it feel?" she asked. Lance paused for what seem like an eternity. "Wonderful."

Talks of sex continued through the night. Soon Lance had questions of his own. By the time it was over, Fin was relaxed but feeling that familiar itch again. And Lance was completely turned on by her.

Tension between the two was thick. It was obvious they were into each other. Lance found her refreshing and different, in a good way. He wanted to know more. He wanted to give of himself more. Fin was fascinating. Her openness and honesty, a good break from all the pretentious women he had been exposed to over the years. And Fin loved everything about him. He had her ready to sample some of what she'd seen on the screen. And she wasn't alone. The attraction between them was powerful.

Soon the talk shifted to life in the ocean. Lance had his own curiosities about where she was from. The world of Madaka, the four cities and the mermaids that live there.

Lance listened closely. He was more than interested. She told him they lived in water. That they spent a majority of their life in water. She told him she could turn her legs into a tail. Lance flashed back to the first time he saw her. He remembered seeing a large tail and long hair obscuring her face and body. It was an amazing story. Lance believed in other species. Even the possibility of aliens. "That's amazing," he said. Fin grinned. The feeling was mutual. So was he.

"Are you okay?" he asked. Fin's mood had changed. Lance could tell there was something on her mind. Fin looked out at the water. "I have to return soon," she said. Words that Lance hoped he wouldn't hear. Not now. Not after meeting her. Talking with her. Engaging with her.

She listened. She spoke freely. She had a voice. And she had her own dreams. She was a woman of substance. And he wasn't ready to part with her. Returning meant it was possible he would never see her again. The rational part of him didn't know how to compartmentalize his feelings. She did something to him that had him captivated. Her heart commanded his.

He felt himself falling for her. Feelings that were way too strong. Like a spell cast from a beautiful maiden. And after a night under the moonlight, he felt out of control. It was way too soon to be so enamored. But he knew what love felt like. And this was the start of a deep and powerful love. He became worried about his heart. This was a first date. Yet she had him so involved. So interested.

"Stay," he said. Fin smiled. "Make yourself at home. I can show you around. There's so much you haven't seen. So much to know. Let me show you," he continued, pleading his case. Fin was quiet. Deep in thought. She was in no rush. Part of her was still angry at her parents. She was a woman now. Able to make her own decisions about her future. She thought about her troubles back home. And how comfortable she was with Lance. She was in a dilemma.

"I don't know. My family is probably worried," she said. "Worried? How long have you been gone? They don't know where you are?" he asked. Questions she was not ready to answer. It would bring back painful realizations. But it was her truth. "No, they know nothing about this place. I am the only one to have ever made it through the dunes. Through the opening called the lair. I was running. I ran from my responsibilities," she said as she became choked up. She continued, as Lance scoot closer to her. She seemed like she needed a hug. He wanted to hold her. Fin told him the rest as he intently listened.

"I was to marry Prince Andreus. I was taken to him. It just didn't feel right. I ran. I swam home. I was so angry. No one listens. In my world, you do as your parents tell you. Until you marry. And they decide who that will be. I couldn't. I knew they would return and make me go back. And that's when I came here," she said, her voice filled with emotion.

"You can stay here," he said, looking intensely at her. Fin gave a forced smile. A tear rolled down her cheek. Lance reached over and wiped it. Fin closed her eyes the minute his hand touched her skin. It was the first touch she'd felt in a long time. He kept his hand on her face. She leaned into it. "Stay Fin. Please!" he said.

"I must go. I'll come back," she said. Lance's mood changed. He worried for her. Being forced to marry someone you did not love was a horrid fate. It could end up being a poor choice and a lifetime of pain and misery. He could see she was heartbroken at the pending marriage. It was obvious she was not in love with the man. She described marrying him the way a person described getting a tooth pulled. She was affected by the events back home. He placed his hand over hers. "I'm here. I will always be here. If you must go, then go.

I'll be here if you want to return," he reluctantly said. It wasn't at all how he felt.

One hour went to the next. Fin yawned. She was exhausted. They stayed up until dawn, sitting in the same spot. They took turns sharing details. It was a lot to take in. They both had a million questions. And they both gave a million more answers. Fin got sleepy. Lance sat back and Fin laid her head on his shoulder. Soon she fell asleep. He sat still, as the dark skies turned light. He eased from her and grabbed an outdoor pillow. He placed it under her head.

Fin adjusted slightly, falling back asleep. Lance stood over her. She was beautiful. Even as she rested. He grabbed a black and white throw and laid it across her body. Fatigue had him sleepy but excitement about Fin had him restless. Lance laid next to her. His huge, oversized patio couch was wide to accommodate them with ease. He turned and faced her. Rubbing her face softly. Touching her hair. Fin moaned then took a deep breath in. Lance smiled. He could watch her sleep all morning.

He couldn't go to sleep. He was excited she was there. Happy to be in her presence. She exuded an energy that made him feel connected to her. It was her way. It was what their kind did. Their way of getting close. They possessed the ability to radiate their feeling outward. The ability to reach each other through their minds. Through smells. And through the eyes. Fin had him attached to her. It was an unconscious action. A result of her attraction to him.

Lance wasn't sure what had just happened. He was falling for her. It was the best date he'd ever had. He hoped when she awoke, that she wouldn't return to Madaka. His door was open. There was plenty of room. She was welcome to stay. Give him time to get to know her. A connection had been made. He felt strange about the idea of dating her. Something that should have repelled him, was pulling him close. She was from another world. He thought it should feel odd. But it didn't. She looked human. She felt human. The way she gazed into his eyes. How animated she was as she told her life story. And the tear she shed and how easily he comforted her. He was convinced it was more for him than thoughts of an unwelcomed marriage.

*D*ays went by. Soon weeks. Fin had become comfortable and Lance had returned to going into his office. He initially stayed home to help ease her stress. But Fin was relaxed. She understood everything in the house. Lance was teaching her about the world. He showed her everything from how crude oil helped the world, to how electricity lit homes. He talked about weapons. He showed her videos of past wars. He talked about man's lifelong battles over money, religion and even women. He showed her how to sword fight. And when she questioned him about cars, he educated her on the automobile industry using video to help explain the process.

Fin was smart. She caught on quick. She had become spoiled to the convenience and technology that made the new world such a great place to call home. She had outgrown Madaka. But she still needed to go back. She loved her parents and they deserved the right to know she was alright. Lance prepared for the inevitable. He never knew when Fin would announce the day had come, for her to leave. And until then, he counted his blessings and looked forward to the time he got to spend with her.

*F*in walked through Lance's impressive home. She was learning new things every day. The desire to return home had lessened. She missed her parents. But she hoped they would want to see her happy. There was still so much to see and learn. Things that would be of benefit back home. Fin was unaware of the troubles her absence was causing. Andreus was still searching. But he was now growing tired. And unknown to her, he wanted her land.

It was easy to forget her troubles. Lance was amazing. Helpful. He was taking her around the city. Around his neighborhood. She was curious about everything. And Lance tried to stay out of her way while she touched, smelled, and tested everything. Her delicate fingertips could feel the grooves of most fabrics. The fibers. And Lance indulged her every desire. He was making daily stops at a local store to buy items he felt she needed to experience. It was a journey of discovery for the both of them. And Lance loved every moment. He hoped she had given up wanting to return home. He feared for her safety. Her description of the aggressive prince that wanted her so badly gave him an uneasy feeling. Lance believed that if she left, she would not be returning.

"Mmm," she expressed, as she ate a spoonful of mayonnaise. Lance was due home soon. She walked over to the kitchen counter with a bag of fruit she pulled from the fridge. Lance had shown her how to use his juicer. Fin placed the berries and a banana inside and turned it on. She stared as the colorful array of fruit began to mix together. She stopped it and poured the contents into a glass.

"This is good," she said, as she walked to the patio door and slid it open. Fin walked to the dock. She walked to the end and stared at the water. She took another swallow of juice and closed her eyes. She was torn. It was a moment of clarity. She wanted to return and check on her parents. Then return to the man she had fallen in love with. I must go. I have to. I cannot do this to them. I will tell them about Lance. I will not marry the prince. If they try to make me, I will leave and never return. But I have to say goodbye. I have to, she thought. She fought back tears. She refused to be sad. This was her life and she was ready to live it. With Lance.

"Hey, I'm on my way," Lance said, as Fin took his call. She didn't like phones to close to her ears. She could feel the heat and the radio waves emitted. Lance had to teach her to answer using the speaker option. Fin hung up and smiled. She walked to the fridge and took out lettuce. She tore it apart and placed it in a bowl. She poured dressing on top and then placed, cranberries, tomatoes, sunflower seeds and parsley and wrapped it for him. Lance ate healthy on the days he went to the gym.

Fin knew him well. They had a routine. He was coming home and he would walk up to her, kiss her and then open the fridge. Today she planned on surprising him. She had watched him make his salad every other day and she wanted to make it for him. Because she had bad news. She needed to go home. Only for a brief moment and she was sure he would worry. Fin gave herself a few more days. Then she would need to leave. She was tormented about it. She didn't want to be apart from him. *I won't be gone long. Just a quick trip. It will be fine!*

8

A King's Demands

"I need to see the king," the hooded man said. The guard stepped to the side and let him in. The voice was well known. It was the king's secret advisor. No one was allowed to look upon his face. He moved as the king instructed. His job a mystery. No one, not even the queen, knew exactly what he did. King Zander was in a meeting with one of his lieutenants.

"Sire," the man said, as he walked over towards the king. "Excuse us," the king said to his lieutenant. He wanted a moment with the visitor. Zander waited until the door closed. He sat at his throne. "Did you find out anything?" he asked. Halacai looked like a man with information. Secret information. His eyes darted. He worried about a war. He worried about a lot of things that he had no control over. Mojarro was his original home. He was loyal to King Zander above all others. His special appointed position, began with Zander. He was indebted. He was sent to the other three cities to get close to their leaders. Play on their weaknesses. Pretend to be fed up with Mojarro. Give up information in order to get close enough to get information. It was a clever play. One Zander felt necessary as his forefathers predicted a war. His father King Zaire had warned him to stay ahead of the others.

But Halacai got in over his head. And decided to stay neutral. A self-appointed Prime Minister to all four cities. A peacekeeper. And Zander allowed it because he knew Halacai was well intended. But if Andreus knew he was playing for both sides, he would have him imprisoned or worst.

"The prince plans to move against Mojarro, if he does not get the princess. He and his men are in the waters looking for her right now. I had to swim low to avoid them. There are hundreds of them, Your Highness. I don't know how much time we have. Will you still deliver her to him? It will keep the peace Your Majesty," he said. Zander had no plans to. And he wasn't ready to disclose what he knew and what he would do. "The princess is still missing. Is that all?" the king asked. "Yes sir. That's all I know." Halacai said. Zander handed him a green jewel. Payment for his efforts. "Speak of this to no one," Zander cautioned. Halacai pulled his hood back over his head and walked out.

The King poured wine and sat down. It was as he feared. King Nephrus had not lied or exaggerated that day in his chambers, when he spoke negatively about the prince. He told him that he was dangerous. That he was a ticking timebomb. Nothing like his father. And he was untrustworthy. He wanted Mojarro. They were vulnerable.

The King sat his cup down and leaped from his chair. "Sparrow!" he called to his guard standing outside his door. Sparrow was second in command over the army when Lark was not around. But his main responsibility was that of protector to the king. Lark was still in the waters looking for Fin. So was Arfusei and other high-ranking soldiers.

"Yes. Your Highness," Sparrow said, as he entered. "Summon at least fifty men. Meet me in my meeting quarters at the end of the hall," Zander ordered. "Yes sir."

Sparrow rushed to gather soldiers. He ran up to a large group of them standing around a fire. "The king wishes to meet. Prepare everyone hortly," he ordered. The men ran in all directions. Some towards the sleeping quarters behind the castle. Some ran towards town. Others went around the property. All gathering soldiers for their emergency ~~journey to~~ meeting with the king. ~~men before they reach Mojarro.~~

The tension was thick. King Zander wasn't prepared to confront a Prince. ~~A future king.~~ He was unaware that Andreus, was in fact, a king. And that circumstances had changed. That a war was now possible. Madaka was civilized. There hadn't been war in over three hundred years. And there had only ever been one. The result was the formation of the four cities with their own unique settings, natural resources and valuables. What lacked in one city was acquired through trade with another. It was a system that worked. Peace between the citizens ~~s~~was maintained.

"I have to go into the waters of Palimora," he said, as he entered his queen's chambers. Aterra sat quietly. Fashioning jewels to a top she had received from the dressmaker. A local woman who was one of many tailors in town. Dresses were made specific to each woman body. ~~ally and tailored to their bodies.~~ It was a necessity. There were no mills. No manufacturers. Clothing was special. The thin dresses made was for ease in water. Short, sheer and completely absorbent. The fabric, imported from Piratchu. And as Aterra put on the finishing touches, she stopped to look up at her husband. She was angry. A feeling she had not felt in a long time. She blamed him. ~~Another rare reaction.~~

"Why? Are you still trying to locate my dead daughter?" she asked, the sting of her words not missed by the already emotionally wracked king. He sighed. "Lark continues to look for her. I have another duty. The prince is on his way here. Probably looking for her. I have to stop him. Our citizens will be uneasy with the arrival of hundreds of soldiers trekking through the town. I must meet with him, in the water," he said. Aterra turned her attention back to her sewing. She had no more words. She had no interest in anything other than the return of her daughter. Until then, what happened was of little interest. She nodded. Never looking back at him.

King Zander closed her door slowly. He stood outside it. He wanted to re-enter. Tell her how sorry he was. Tell her he had no way of knowing the outcome would be so devastating. But the truth was it was still in everyone's best interest that Finora marry Andreus. She could calm his uneasy spirit. He was sure of it. It was a power she possessed that he noticed early on. He knew his daughter was different. Special, strong and courageous. She had enchanting eyes that could render a spell. Her return was necessary. The town was in mourning. The citizens of Mojarro still held out hope. Lost as sea meant nothing to them. There was a chance she wasn't lost but hiding. She was rebellious. And until then, Prince Andreus would need to be patient. Zander would not allow his land to be taken by force. He could acquire it through marriage only. And would rule over it only after he and his wife passed on. Attempting a takeover would result in war. He would not tolerate it.

King Zander marched with his men through the city. The town folks stood along the side. They cheered the men on. Word had spread of a looming threat. In attendance, among the crowd, stood Halacai. He was nervous. He knew this was more than a looming threat. Prince Andreus was coming.

They walked on the white sand towards the water. Missing were Lark and his group. They were still in the Trojian Sea. Zanders wanted him to stay behind. He would need to run the castle if something happened to him. "Do you want Lark informed?" Sparrow asked. "No. Let him be. I need him to stay back. Just in case. Fin is not here. He will be my successor in Fin's absence," he said, as the they reached the water.

The waves calm. The water beautiful. What lie ahead a mystery. They would forge ahead regardless of consequences. It was inbred in them. Natural fighter who learned to live at peace. The men were resilient. Focused. They were the protectors.

King Zander entered the water. His men entered alongside of him. He said nothing. The water splashed around his strong, fabric bound legs. The fabric was loose enough to fall off when his tail tore through. Special made, lightly woven fabric. Made by the dressmaker. She was specially appointed. The best tailor in town. His men went to her in droves. She was the wealthiest citizen in town. Her creations made their lives easier.

The king started swimming, once the water was up to his chest. His tail bursting through. He looked at his men then picked up his speed. The men followed suit. They sped through the water. Their mouths slightly opened. Bubbles exiting their mouths, as their first set of lungs emptied. Their gills opened. Secondary breathing systems kicked in, to take on the water and process its rich oxygen content. The king thought briefly about Lark. He hoped Lark stayed in the other sea. It was not connected to Palimora, so there was no chance of bumping into him. Something that wouldn't play out well.

Lark would be furious. He would throw out all reason. Possibly be uncontrollable. His commitment to Mojarro and his undisclosed feelings for the princess, would cause him to act irrationally. The king hoped it was all a misunderstanding. "Where is Lark?" Arfusei asked. "Probably in the Trojian. I don't believe they are in the Palimora today," he said. The king looked ahead. He hoped not.

******

"How about some mophos and timb," the castle's cook asked the queen, as she stood outside her door. It was a favorite dish of the queen's, made from jellyfish and seaweed. The jellyfish was fresh, brought in from Eulachon. The queen opened her door. "Yes please," she said, as she exited. "Are you ok Your Highness," her life-long cook and personal assistant asked. Aterra didn't like to be formal with Basra. She was a loyal and committed servant. She had given up having any kind of normal life to serve the king and queen.

"I will be. I have made a huge mistake. She asked me things. I wasn't ready to talk. I was afraid. Ashamed of myself. She is like me. She feels like I do. And now she is confused. I let her down," she said. Her face filled with pain. Basra paused before speaking. She too felt the pain of a missing loved one. She had known and helped raise Fin. The wound cut deep.

"Fin is strong. She is not dead. I will never believe that. She is angry. Afraid. I could see she didn't want to marry that prince," Basra said. Aterra looked sharply at her. "What?" she said. "Yes, your Highness. I noticed. It was written all over her face the day you left. As she walked past me. She wouldn't look at me. She looked ahead. Trying to be brave. She was only doing it to please you and the king. But no…She did not want that," she replied.

Aterra looked off. She thought it was nerves. Marriages were arranged. All women waited to be married to the mate chosen by their family. Basra was one of the few who never married. She was orphaned. And so, there were no one to secure a mate for her. She lived off of the kindness of families in town until she was old enough to strike out on her own. The queen took her in as a servant. And Basra never left. "I should have paid her more attention. I don't know my own daughter."

The soldiers could see a large convoy of men swimming fast towards them. They were many miles from home, and they were fatigued. Everyone was exhausted from the constant search for Finora, and the weight of worry about their city's future. King Zander was front and center. Flanked by two of his strongest guards, Sparrow and Arfusei. The eulachon army was swimming fast. They were on a mission. The King could see Prince Andreus. He swam over to where he was. And the men slowed.

"Prince Andreus," he greeted. "KING Andreus," he corrected. The king looked piercingly at him. "King Orfe has passed?" he asked. "Yes. And he has been laid to rest," he informed.

"I am sorry for your loss. Were you traveling to Mojarro to inform me?" Zander asked. King Andreus gave a devilish grin. "No! I come for my bride. I am ready for my queen to be by my side. But I am hearing things. Rumors of her passing. Uaru soldiers remembered seeing her swimming through the waters alone. They say she can swim faster than any nermein. Any fish. So, it does not make sense, that she would have met with some terrible fate. Where is she?" he asked. The King could sense trouble.

"She is fine. Alive and well. She simply needed a moment to herself. She felt rushed. I will send her as soon as she gets herself ready to start a new life," Zander replied. The king's men stood ready. Zander was telling a lie. A sign of trouble. She was not fine and well. They knew nothing of the sort. And if the king was resorting to lying, it was because he feared something. They braced for an attack. Something was not right. King Zander did not lie. And he did not fear anyone.

King Zander's men were intimidating. They were unwavering in their fierce eye contact with King Andreus' soldiers. The Uaru's stood near. There had never been a meeting in the waters. One with such threatening tension. The Uaru soldiers floated nearby, ready to intervene. Their numbers not that great, but it was their job to keep the peace in the water. If an attack was wielded by either side, they would need to try to resolve it. Eulachon and Mojarro were breaking the laws their ancestors set in place. The waters were off limits for such meetings. But it was also known that a princess was missing. If the meeting was to discuss a plan, then it would be allowed. But it looked nothing like a cordial meeting to them.

"She has no time. I come to take her home. And nothing will stop me," Andreus said, as he stared into King Zanders eyes. He would not be deterred. He was authoritarian in his tone. King Zander looked to his left. Sparrow acknowledged the look and stared back into the eyes of his enemy. The king looked over at Arfusei. He snarled and looked back at the opposing force, the soldiers of Eulachon. "Atttaaack!" King Zander shouted.

Soon the force of men crashing into one another, made waves through the water. The vibrations, picked up by uaru's further away. Their sensitivity to the waters movements was honed perfectly. A skill that naturally became enhanced with time spent in the water. And they could detect changes, down to the faintest of ripples. The uaru's close enough to the men, tried to intervene. But the fighting was treacherous. Devastating. Men tore through the flesh of the man in front of them. Their nails sharp as spines. Their tails now massive pounds of flesh able to deliver a vicious blow.

King Zanders men were larger. But they were outnumbered. King Andreus grunted, then charged at him. He charged back. Swooshing his tail around, and slapping

Andreus hard in the chest. The blow, knocking Andreus back several meters. He shook the sting of the hit off, and charged the much older king. King Zander went to him, head on. Crashing into him. The shock of their weight combined, causing him to feel dazed. King Zander floated down. He had been knocked unconscious. King Andreus watched as he descended down. He smirked then continued in battle. He had defeated the king. As he raced toward one of Zander's soldiers, he was knocked back by the tail of Sparrow.

Sparrow snarled at him, then charged again. His hands extended. He growled as he neared. He tore into his flesh. King Andreus yelled out. Sparrow had his nails dug deep into his chest. Soldiers came to aid him. One tried pulling Sparrow off of their king. Soon another came. Sparrow was surrounded. A guard named Ithicus swam up. He was King Andreus' largest and most powerful fighter. He floated behind Sparrow. His nails sharp and long. His arms large and muscular. He grabbed Sparrow and dug his razor-sharp nails into the back of his neck. And with one powerful twist, pulled Sparrow's head off.

Soldiers continued to battle. Soon the water was teaming with floating bodies sinking to the bottom. The scent of their blood, calling predators from miles around. Uaru's had already picked up the frantic movements of Tetra coming. Baika were more like scavengers, feeding off dead fish and would consume anything not moving. But Tetra would attack. They were large, fast and skilled hunters.

The fighting ceased. The wounded prepared to leave the area. As large as their numbers were, they would be no match for Tetra's in large numbers. King Andreus and his men gathered their wounded and headed back to Eulachon. King Zander's motionless body was carried away by Arfusei and the saddened men that survive the battle. It was hard fought. There were no winners. Both sides had lost many men. And King Zanders was barely alive. His faithful and trusted guard Sparrow was dead along with countless others. It was all overwhelming. The men knew this was just part of a battle that would be fought again. The opposing king still had no queen. And now he would be vengeful and brutal in his quest to seize Mojarro and everything in it.

The men swam back to land. They exited the water to families hoping their loved ones were among them. The looks on their faces showing the relief they felt that their son was alive. But some families were distraught. A few mothers wept. It was a sad day for Mojarro. Ninety three soldiers did not return.

Lark had separated from his men. He swam near the dunes. He thought about that day, years ago, when Fin jumped into the lake at six years old. She had gone to the dune. Swam over it. The king spoke of how shocked he was, that she had been immune to its affects. Lark swam close. He stopped at the edge. He looked around. *Why would she come here. There is nothing special about this place,* he thought, as he tried to decide what to do. The clear blue water with low visibility over the dunes, due to the bubbles, had him curious. It was vast. No one had lived to talk about what was on the other side. Many had died attempting to travel over it and get to the other side. Some in hopes of riches. Others just looking to put facts with urban tales. It was said, that a beast lived in the mountains on the other side. A strange creature who devoured anything that got close enough to the lair. It was urban tales. Lark didn't believe in it. But he did believe that the purpose of the dunes was to protect the lair. He just wasn't sure why. Lark like many others, was unaware that the lair was the connection to the world that they came from. That

Madaka was land created by a cursed demigod named Hershiel and his lover the goddess Contessa, Queen of the Ocean.

Lark got close. Fin would go there to escape being caught. She would go knowing that no one else could cross it. Safe from discovery. Lark stared into the darkness. *She's there,* he thought. Suddenly Lark could feel something approaching. He turned swiftly around. Two of his men approached. "Why are you here? I thought this area was forbidden," one of the guards said. "It is. I am looking everywhere. I want every single area searched. Now keep looking. We'll end soon. It will be dark. But leave this area. If I am not back at the reef soon, go back without me," Lark said. The soldiers looked at one another. Neither thought it was a good idea. But Lark was in command. His orders were not to be questioned. The men swam away. Lark watched as they got further out of sight, disappearing into the water.

He turned back around. He wanted to try. He would hold his breath and go in. And if he was unable to reach the other side, he would turn around. He was skilled at not breathing under water. He was friends with a man who became a uaru. He taught him different tricks they learned in the water. Skills that only uaru's knew. It was part of their training. A necessity, in order to live in the waters safely when in areas where gases were seeping from the floor.

Lark took a deep breath. He held it, then swam over the dunes. He instinctively swam a little higher. To keep from close contact with the heat and gases. The cooled bubbles reached his body. He continued on. The water got murkier. Visibility was changing. Lark panicked. He was almost a half mile in. *This is crazy. I must turn around,* he thought, as he swam quickly back to the edge.

He took in water. He exhaled. He waited to see if he would get sick. The bubbles had touched his body. No one knew if the danger was in the touch of the bubbles against their delicate skin or if it was the inhalation of the gas that caused the demise of all that had tried. Lark felt nothing. He was impressed with himself. The training he'd had years before had worked. His return to the edge was from fear, not from lack of oxygen. If he didn't exert himself, he could use his oxygen reserve properly and get further. *I have to find a way to go further,* he thought. It was getting dark. Lark decided to return to the reef. He needed to plan another swim over the dune. He had a strong feeling she was on the other side.

The Queen walked the castle, deep in thought. Her daughter was gone with no word. No message. As if she had disappeared into thin air. Aterra believed she had to be dead. Fin would not stay away so long and not attempt contact. But then she thought of their last conversation. Fin was fed up. Angry. Disappointed. It was possible that her daughter went to live somewhere else. Maybe allowed to reside in Panga or Piratchu. She wondered if they were hiding her. Protecting her. Moving to another city was typically forbidden. But she was a princess. It would be allowed. Especially if she was living in Panga. It was well known that the King of Panga wanted Fin for his son. If she sought refuge there, they would welcome her with open arms.

Her reasons for leaving were irrelevant. The queen just wanted confirmation that she was alive. She walked the halls, saddened and trying to find a way to forgive herself. She had played a part in her daughter's unhappiness. But the reality of it, was hard to take.

Aterra walked aimlessly through her home, uneasy and on edge. She came upon the room that her husband locked and never opened. She wondered what secrets it held. Why it was off limits. She was an obedient wife. Her husband asked her to never enter. And she never did. But things were changing. A tragedy had befallen them. And she was no longer sure she could keep that promise. Something was on the other side of that door. Something that possibly held the answers.

There were changes around the castle. Fin's disappearance was beginning to affect everyone. The citizens were asking if the queen would address them in her husband's absence. They wanted answers. And Fin's longtime nanny and lady's maid Lillia, was away visiting family. She had been saddened since the girl she helped raise into a woman, went missing. Aterra could not help her get past her grief. She was too busy processing the pain herself. She was suffering in silence. She ran the conversation of that fateful day, over and over in her mind. Her lack of reply. Fin's lack of understanding. And she wished she could take it back.

Fin was not a baby any longer. There was no need to be so secretive. She would have questions. It was to be expected. She was different, just like her mother. But Fin had developed unexpectedly, and was able to live in water and form her tail. Aterra didn't understand why she was never able to change. Why water was her enemy. But she was glad her daughter could.

Aterra almost died when she tried to take water into her lungs as a child. A midwife and holistic doctor came running to the family's aid. He instincts and quick action breathed life back into Aterra's precious lungs. The woman examined her. She told her mother, Queen Phaedra, that she did not know why the child could not breathe water. That she was deformed. That she had no openings on her sides. No inner membrane between her legs as they all had. The membrane necessary to form one's tail.

King Zaire was away when the incident occurred. The Queen asked the woman to keep it secret. She told her that the king would not want such information spread about his only daughter. The woman, fearing for her safety, kept the remainder of what she found to herself. She concluded Aterra was deformed and was paid handsomely to keep it to herself. The woman then relocated. Queen Phaedra swore silence, and forced the few eyewitnesses to Aterra drowning, to secrecy. Even on her death bed, she spoke very little of that day. Even when asked.

Aterra had a vague recollection of a conversation she stumbled onto when she was a child, about her not being able to breathe water. A conversation between the king and queen. She remembered her father was uneasy. Defensive. As if he knew something. Phaedra always believed Aterra was orphaned and dropped at their doorstep. It was the story he told when he approached her holding the baby in his arms. Their son, the future king, young Prince Zander, at his side.

She stood up. She was in disbelief. Her husband held a baby. A girl. "She's beautiful. Where did she come from?" she asked, as she took held her in her arms. "She is orphaned. All alone. She is yours now," the King replied. Phaedra gushed over her new daughter. "Does she have a name?" she asked. "No. What shall we call her?" he asked. Phaedra looked into her daughter's eyes. She walked to the window and looked out. "We shall call her Aterra," she replied.

Little Prince Zander looked up at his mother. He was excited about having a new play mate. "You see the baby. This is Aterra," she said, looking down at her son as he stood close by her side. He had a new little sister. Phaedra bent down so he could see her closely. Zander smiled. It was a dream come true for the family. Phaedra had tried to have more children, with no luck. Aterra was the daughter she would never have. It was a blessing from the gods. The answer to her prayers. King Zaire smiled and turned to give her a moment. He shut the door to give her time to bond with the new baby.

"Let mommy be with her for a while. You can see the baby later. Would you like to go into town with me?" he asked his young son. Prince Zander nodded. The King took him by the hand. He could hear Phaedra talking to the baby. Telling her she was perfect. Beautiful. He walked away. He could never tell her the truth. Never say where the child came from because he did not know where he had been;

King Zaire swam near the dunes. He had heard that men were seen near it. Men not from Mojarro. He was there alone. His guards unaware that he had taken on the mission by himself. King Zaire wanted no one near the dune. He had heard things. Stories passed down from generation to generation. His grandfather told him a story that seemed implausible. That the dunes was put there to keep them from joining the free world. That their very existence was the result of a war between gods. And that a Demigod named Hershiel, was punished for the crime of adultery, and sent into the sea to live as a fish. He was said to be the son of Apollo, god of light. And a mortal named Talea.

He thrived and lived amongst the fish. And when his enemies sent a spy, a beautiful goddess of water named Contessa, they fell in love and she never returned. They hid deep in the Mariana Trench, and sought a place to live. Together they used their powers to blast a whole into the earth, leaving an opening that they would never reveal. And Madaka was created.

The new world expanded, as Hershiel and Contessa forged through the land. They saw the future. Generations of a race of half human, half fish people that could live freely amongst their own. Soon, Contessa left Madaka. She found other gods and goddesses who wanted freedom from persecution. Three other sets of families. All having power in water. Able to live in it. Thrive in it. They each took their own land. And the four cities were born.

But the gods found out and cursed them. They removed their desires and took away their sexual powers as punishment for their crimes. The new world was void of touch. Void of sex. Void of natural forms of love and intimacy. Only able to bond as close friends. Never feeling deep love and never experiencing sexual happiness. But the gods did not curse humans. And so, when Aterra was taken from the natural world and placed in Madaka, it set the stage for an awakening. And it opened the doors for a child to be born who would change their world as they knew it. A child who was the direct descendent of the original creator. The original goddess of the ocean.

King Zaire knew that he was the heir of Madaka's originators. That the dune was made by his ancestors. He wondered if that meant he would have immunities to the poison of its gases. The dunes that were home to the Dark Lair. It held the mysteries of their people. He swam over it. He inhaled a bit. He waited. Fears followed by feelings of foolishness set in. He questioned himself. He told himself it was insane. No one knew he was there. He would perish and be engulfed in the molten floor.

As the seconds passed, he felt no different. No ill feelings overcame him. His breathing was fine. His acuity, the same. His theories were precise. He could breathe in the gas that emitted from the ground. He was immune.

King Zaire swam over it. Finally coming to the Dark Lair. He looked around, puzzled at first. He entered the opening and soon emerged on the other side. He swam straight up, coming up from the water. His first entrance into earth's surface was met by tragedy. Something burning bright in the distance. He thrashed his powerful tail and swam to the source of the flames. It was a large object. A strange odd shaped vessel. It was engulfed in flames. Near it, a small round floating object. He swam over to it. He peeked inside. He was surprised to see a baby crying, right next to its obviously dead mother. Burned over a large part of her body and bleeding from every part of her skin. The baby appeared to be comforting her. Her small hand placed on her mother's back.

The king took the baby and the bags. He dove back into the water. The baby appeared to be in distress. There were no bubbles coming from her mouth. He raced back to the surface. The baby choked. She held onto him, terrified. He rubbed her back. It was what he saw her doing to her mother. The baby calmed down. She seemed exhausted. She laid her head on his shoulder as he floated.

The king looked around. He examined the baby. She had fallen asleep. He lifted her up out the water and looked at her legs. They appeared different. Missing was the fine, shiny, soft flesh that fused when the tail formed. He was confused. Her skin was not right. He pulled up her little top and looked at the side of her chest. She had no openings. The king soon realized that although she looked it, she was not nermein.

He thought long and hard about how to get her home with him. His handling of her, had not woke her. Her head still on his shoulder. He was in the middle of the ocean. No land visible. And it appeared her family had perished. The king thought about the best way to deliver oxygen to the child. He wondered if he covered her mouth, would she breathe the small amount of air he would leave in his lungs. It was dangerous. If he left too much, he could be crushed under the weight of the water. If he didn't leave enough, the baby would die. He had to try.

He entered the water, released some of the oxygen, put his mouth over the baby's airway and swam hurriedly back to Madaka.

9

Unimagined Love

Lance and Fin returned home from a day of shopping. He took her to six stores and purchased everything her heart desired. She purchased items typically not standard for normal everyday shopping. He delighted in being her personal tour guide. He enjoyed the look on her face as she discovered new things. A trip to the local mall was the best time he'd had. She gave him new found appreciation for items he normally took for granted. Like the nearly half-hour it took her to select a toothbrush as she excitedly looked at each one, remarking on the colors and shapes. And the nearly hour-long time it took for her to pick the nail polish she wanted. Lance chuckled as she tried on twenty colors, placing multiple colors right next to one another. Her fingers like rainbows. The colors too beautiful to leave any one of them behind.

Security came and Lance made the situation less awkward by telling him she was new to the store. Fin placed every polish inside the basket. Cleaning the shelf completely, as Lance looked on. He didn't care about the strange looks he got from people as they passed by. Fin was excited and eager to test every product. And he wanted her to enjoy the moment.

The money was no issue. And Lance found it refreshing that she lacked the awareness of the value placed on the dollar. He'd had his share of women wanting to date him for his wealth. Something that he was used to, but still annoyed by. He longed for a real connection. A deep and meaningful bond. It was easy to fall in love when certain things like money, was out of the way. He was glad to be in position to accommodate her.

He had deep pockets. He could buy their inventory. Fin's interest and intrigue was priceless. And Fin wasn't totally clueless. She believed that some sort of trade would occur at check out. She just wasn't sure what Lance had to trade. She was shocked that all he had was paper. Strange paper with writing. She looked at him. "I'll explain later," he said to her, as he turned his attention back to the cashier and smiled. "Thank you," he said, as he placed the bags in the cart.

The cashier glanced at Fin. She wondered why the woman seemed so out of place. So enthralled, with what she had in her basket. She wondered if Fin was an ex-con, returning home after years of being locked away. Or, had she awakened from a coma and was now being reintroduced to what she had missed. She didn't fit either scenario. But it was puzzling nonetheless.

The two left the store. Fin was thrilled. She caught the looks from the cashier. She didn't care. This was her journey. She *was* new to the things that were so generic and so random. She was excited. And she had no apologies. Lance loaded his SUV with more bags and it was off to another store. This time a clothing store. Fin was still in his clothes. An old pair of jogging pants and a tee shirt. She wore a pair of Nike flip flops. The one thing she struggled with. In Madaka, there were no shoes. Everyone walked barefoot.

They had a long drive ahead of them. Lance decided to take the scenic route to the mini mall near Glendale . He explained the currency. And how purchases were made. Fin told him about trade in Madaka. Their stories were similar. There was still an exchange of goods for goods. One thing they had in common. Lance turned on his radio. Fin got comfortable. Music was magical to her. All of it. She had no preference. Lance exposed her to all types. Jazz. Country. R&B. Rock. She liked it all.

The music had him emotional. The words of the song were reflective of how he felt. What he wanted. He looked at her hand. He grabbed it. He rubbed her ring. A symbol of their upcoming union. He had gotten comfortable having her around. His life was amazing. She hummed to the sounds of Gladys Knight. She stared out the window in her own world. She was utterly happy. She didn't see herself apart from him. She wanted to be a part of his world. But soon thoughts of her mother and father entered her mind. Her face changed. Her smile, replaced with a frown. She looked down. She began to cry.

Lance pulled over. "What's wrong?" he asked, leaning over, attempting to turn her face towards his. Fin shook her head. She didn't want to say that it was time. She dreaded telling him. He wanted to marry first. But she wanted their wedding to happen when she had a clear conscious. Not something rushed, on the heels of her trip back home.

She looked at Lance. He wiped her tear. He guessed her problem because he feared it. "You want to go home?" he asked, his voice taking on a lower tone. Fin could see he was disappointed. "Yes," she quickly replied. She grabbed his hand. She held it tight. "What about us getting married?" he asked. "We will. And it will be beautiful. And I will have no worries because I would have said my goodbyes," she replied. "They won't let you return," he said. "I am coming back. It is not up to them. But I must go," she replied. Lance turned from her. He sat back in his seat. She could hear him exhale sharply.

"I know you miss your family. But I love you. I don't want you to marry him," he said. His words caused a flood of tears from Fin. "Oh Lance. I love you too. I will not marry him. I can't. But I have to see them. Tell them how I feel. When I tell them I am in love, they will let me return. In our land, when you marry someone, you are expected to honor your husband. Stay with him. Even if it means living in another land. They will let me go," she said. Lance looked intensely at her. "Then marry me now?" he asked. She looked straight ahead. It would be rushed. "Did you hear me Fin. Marry me. I love you. You love me. You make me happy. I want to be everything to you," he said, as he leaned across the seat and kissed her. Fin closed her eyes. He kissed her passionately. And she reluctantly gave in. "Alright."

*F*in walked in his closet. She touched and smelled his clothes. She could smell him. His cologne. It was erotic. Their romantic nights of kissing and touching had her desiring him. Lance talked to her about sex again. She was intrigued. He didn't think she was ready and so he held back. But she was. She had waited. She had yearned for intimacy without knowing what it was. And now that she knew. She wanted him totally.

She daydreamed about their evening before. The way they cuddled throughout the night, naked and kissing on one another. Fin was ready to go further. She didn't have long before she would be leaving. She lusted for him. But she was a virgin. And Lance wanted to take her slow. He wanted to wait until their marriage just a few days away. Their closeness reminded her of the conversation with Aterra. These were the feelings she tried to describe to her mother. And now they were ten-fold. Her body longed for Lance. It confused her at first. Until she tied the feelings to the sight and smell of him.

Lance told her all about sexual attraction. About the male and female anatomy. About pheromones. And visual stimulation. It was a relief. She had always thought something was wrong with her.

He was surprised that her people did not engage in sex where she was from. That they had a strange way of procreating. That they used water as a way to fertilize eggs inside them. Like fish. It was odd. He found it strange that her people seemed to be fine without such intimacies. But what neither of them knew was the lack of sexual intimacy in Madaka was the result of the war between the gods. And as punishment, their forefathers stripped of his sexual desires. Forced to be as fish. Sperm secreted in stagnate water for the woman to then enter, was the way they procreated. Fin had sexual desires because she was more human. A result of the union between Aterra, a human and Zander. A nermein.

But Fin understood her body now. Lance helped her make sense of her desires. And now she understood what it was. She wondered if other nermein women felt it. Fin was watching porn daily. Sometimes as Lance explained what she was looking at. It was thrilling. She wondered if it would soothe the intensity of the sexual energy she felt between her legs. Touched made it worse. And Lance's kisses, drove her mad.

It was still light out. It was late afternoon and Lance would be home soon. Fin popped strawberries in her mouth, as she descended the staircase. A delicate three karat ring adorned her ring finger. She was used to diamonds. Mojarro had them in abundance. But this diamond was special. Humans used them to express love. To show their commitment to one another. And they were to be married soon.

She hadn't been in water in days. She was becoming less inclined to do so. She wanted to be more like Lance. She wanted to be more human. Experience what he experienced. They were obsessed. The sexual tension between them was building. Lance wanted to take her. He envisioned being with her. Feeling her. He wondered how she felt. If she would feel the same. Or would there be something slightly different about her vagina. It looked the same. Beautiful, delicate and covered in a fine soft hair. He was ready. He had called her three times since leaving. He anticipated every moan. Every warm part of her. This was their night.

Fin could tell he was planning something. He was coming home a little earlier than normal. He seemed anxious.

He seemed nervous. He told her he was bringing dinner. They usually cooked together. He also told her he had something special. Fin wondered what it was. Suddenly her feelings overwhelmed her. She wished he was there. She would make him make love to her. She was tired of waiting. She missed him when he was gone. But Fin was unaware that Lance was ready. That he was coming home to make love to her. She wouldn't have to wait any longer. He was hers. And she was his.

The family next to them came out and sat on their porch. Fin walked to the window and stared at them. An older man and woman along with another younger couple and three small children. The family made her think of her own. She wondered about her father and mother. She had been gone a long time. It had been a several months since she showed up in the waters outside his home. She was sure her parents were mourning her.

Fin walked away and over to the kitchen sink. She wasn't sure why she was so uneasy. She poured herself a glass of water. She thought about Lance. She wondered if he was near. She looked out. She could see down the street. She watched as a little boy played ball with his father kicking it with his feet towards him. She chuckled. Her smile quickly changing to a look of worry. She felt a need to return to Madaka immediately.

Why am I so anxious suddenly? Something must be wrong. I can feel it, she said. She could not wait to tell Lance. He wouldn't want her to go. The look on his face would compel her to stay. And she wouldn't want to hurt him. She took a deep breath and convinced herself to just leave. "He'll wait for me. I'll be back soon. The marriage must wait," she said.

Fin put her thin sheath dress on and headed to the water. She sat on the docks edge and looked around. The sun was going down. She inhaled slowly. She was returning to a life of limitations. To a city that pushed for a marriage of confinement to a horrible man. But something was looming. She felt danger ahead.

I'm sorry Lance. My sweetheart. I will return to you. I love you. And if the worst should happen, know that you were my one true love, she said, as she dangled her feet in the water. A tear fell. She wiped her cheek. She pushed her body off the docks edge and landed in the water. She thought about Lance. He would be confused when he got home. He would look for her. *I will be back my love,* she said, as she looked at his home one last time before swimming towards Madaka.

Lance walked to the window. She gasped. He was home. He ran to the glass off the patio and ran out. It was turning dark. He ran down the dock. "Fin!" he shouted, as he frantically tried to reach her. "I have to go back," she cried. Lance jumped in the water. Fin swam back to him. Her legs now a tail. He looked in the water. It was the first time he saw her changed. Fin wasn't sure she wanted him to see it and changed back to her legs. They stared at one another. Lance was in shock. Not over her tail. She told him about it. He could care less. He was in shock that she was leaving and hadn't said bye. It was a cruel way to leave. He had tried to get mentally prepared for it. But this was wrong. Leaving this way, was wrong. And before they marriage.

"You're leaving?" he said, his face filled with pain. Fin shook her head slowly. "I have to go see them. I will be back," she said. "No. They will make you stay. Force you to marry. You said so yourself," he said. "But I won't. I promise. You have to trust me," she pleaded. Fin swam closer to him and put her arms around his neck. "Take me with you. I want to make sure you're alright," he said. Fin had thought of that. But there was no guarantee he would survive the decent into the trenches or the atmosphere on Madaka if he did.

"I can't. How? You will drown. I will be back. I promise," she said, trying to ease his fears. She smiled to keep from crying. She wasn't sure she would return. It depended on things not in her control. She needed to see Madaka. See home. Find out what happened in her absence. Then say her goodbyes and return to him.

"Fin. This doesn't feel right. Please stay," he begged. Fin gazed into his eyes. His love was powerful. She pushed him backwards, under the dock. The dusk of the early evening shielding them from prying eyes. She wrapped her legs around him and kissed him passionately. Lance pulled her closer to him. He looked around. No one was close. No boats floating near. No neighbors on their porches. It was as though they were the only ones around. Lance thought it was ironic.

She could feel his manhood. Lance didn't want her like this. But he wanted her to never forget him. Never forget what they had. He pushed her closer to the rocks. He turned around and put her back to the beam. He removed himself and entered her. Fin closed her eyes as he slowly made his way deep inside her. She didn't expect it to feel so good. It was beautiful. She moved on him. Naturally. Effortlessly.

Lance dove his tongue in her mouth. Fin moaned then let out small sounds he never heard. They turned him on. He held her bottom as he moved in and out of her. Fin's ability to float effortlessly allowed him to be held by her arms while he did what he wanted to her body. Fin dropped her head back. He kissed her neck. She kept her eyes closed. She concentrated on him. His body, as it mixed with hers. Soon Lance lets out a loud grunt. Fin opened her eyes. She continued moving up and down on him. Her vagina warm and tight, as she gripped him snuggly before she came. Fin moaned as she came, keeping her eyes closed as she felt something warm from him shoot out into her. Lance grunted and jerked. It was the greatest felling he had ever experienced. Fin looked at him. She was out of breath. She kissed him once more. A fierce kiss as she held onto his face. "Again," she said as she moved on him again. Lance smiled as he became hard again. Fin bounced on him, as she threw her head back once again. She stopped suddenly and looked him intensely in his eyes. The fire in his eyes, she would never forget. She would take the look he had on his face at that moment, with her. Engrained in her mind.

"I'll be back. I promise," she said. "You better. Or I'm coming to get you," he said. Fin smiled. Her lips anxious to feel his again. Lance looked at her mouth. He kissed her lips. Fin opened her mouth then moved her body vigorously up and down. The combinations of her moans and passionate kisses, had Lance ready to come again. "Uhhh," he grunted, as he released inside her once more. He held onto her. His eyes closed as his head touched hers. Fins stared at him. She kissed his forehead. Then his lips.

Fin laid her head on his shoulder. "I love you," she whispered, as she released her legs from around his waist and swam away from him. If she stayed any longer, she would never go back. Lance swam the short distance to the boulders and climbed up to the top. He walked quickly down the dock to catch a last glimpse of her. It was a beautiful way to let her go. But the pain was still deep. It was real. It hurt like hell. And he would suffer a broken heart until she returned.

He watched as she ducked beneath the water and disappeared into the night. He stood there motionless. He never felt so helplessly in love. He had never made love to a woman and felt one with her. It took him a minute. She felt wonderful. She had his heart body and mind. She *had* to return.

"Your Highness," Arfusei said. Queen Aterra stood from her chair. "Yes," she said, feeling uneasy. His demeanor was off. Their long-time personal guard Arfusei seemed stressed. He was normally calm. Nothing frazzled him. "What is it Arfusei," she said. "It is the King Your Highness," he said. Aterra gasped. "Take me to him. Now!"

Arfusei walked the long hall to his chambers. Aterra walked hurriedly behind him. Her head down. Her heart racing. Arfusei opened the door slowly and looked at Aterra. She walked past him. His soldiers stood around him. Saddened. Quiet. And totally grief stricken. Aterra was confused. He looked sleep. She looked around at the soldiers. They nodded and bowed their heads. Aterra approached his bed slowly. She began to see signs that he was battered. His eyes closed in an unnatural way. His body damp and cold.

"What happened?" she said in a barely audible voice. "We went to war Your Highness. Right in the middle of the sea. The Prince made demands. And the King ordered the attack."

Aterra touched her husband's hand. The men looked at each other. Touch was rare. It was shocking to see. She closed her eyes. She held his hand tighter. The men tried to pretend they were unaffected by it. But their minds raced. They wondered what she was doing. It was forbidden and not welcomed. Only children were touched. Babies. The youngest of their society.

But Aterra was not like them. She desired touch. She was not condemned as they were. She came there as a baby. She was ten months old when she arrived. She came from a doting mother and father who filled her world full of love, affection and physical displays of love. She didn't remember them. But touch was familiar. She had moments she shared with the King that no one knew. No one saw.

She taught him how to touch. She taught him how to kiss. She awakened things in him. It was a source of their deep love and affection for one another. And when Fin expressed sexual feeling, she panicked. But she knew what it was. She had them herself. Because she was human. And so was Fin. More so than her nermein bloodline. The reason for her differences. Physically and emotionally.

"Can I have a moment with my husband please?" she asked. Aterra realized the soldiers had seen more than they should have. The men left, one by one, as Aterra took in a deep breath and exhaled. Her husband, the love of her life, was gone. Fin was gone. There was nothing else. She had no desire to run Mojarro. She felt bad for them. She wanted to be with her husband and daughter. The city would need to find a way.

Aterra laid next to her husband. She kissed him and held his face. "You can't leave me here. You can't," she cried, her voice trembling. She sighed. She raised up and looked on his table. She looked around. She saw his ornate, jewel and gold encrusted shawl that the dressmaker made for him. She eased out of bed, grabbed it and got back into bed. She pulled a gold brooch from it. She laid the shawl over him. She wasn't sure how to proceed. It was a dull ornament with square corners. She had never heard of someone hurting themselves. Only one another. And only in battle.

She could see the bruises on her husband's neck. She touched hers. She felt her pulse. Her lifeline. It was where she would strike. She pulled her arm back. She leaned her head to the side. She closed her eyes and held the brooch at an angle. Aterra swung towards herself. The metal ornament entered her neck. She muffled her own cries as blood squirted from her onto the King. She dropped her hand. Shock set in. The room spun. She could feel herself becoming lightheaded. She laid her head on him and closed her eyes. She would be with him soon.

Aterra slowly slipped away. Her life no longer a mystery. She had gone into the room. The locked area that was forbidden. She found things that were not of their world. A bag full of items she had never seen before. A bottle. A pacifier. A woman's wallet. Baby clothes. And a picture of a child that looked eerily similar to her. Same red hair and freckles. A child sitting on the lap of a woman who looked a lot like her and a man standing over them. A family. Wearing heavy duty clothing that looked of another world. Aterra could see herself in the child. It was her.

She had some answers although there were still a lot of questions. She was from another place. A world unknown. The picture showed a background that included a house and landscaping. It was unlike anything Madaka had. This was not Madaka. Aterra knew she was orphaned. But she did not know she was from another world altogether. It was a relief. She was not deformed. Where she was from, this was how they looked. She thought of her husband as she took her last breath. She was proud to have been his wife. Theirs was a great love story. They had done things they had no idea their bodies would do. It was in Aterra naturally. And she taught him. They were as one. And they would continue to be as one.

10

Longing

*F*in swam through the brine, down through the dark lair and out into the Trojian Sea. She stopped and looked back. Her pain at leaving Lance behind was immense. "Lance," she wept, as she pictured his face. She hoped to get back to him quickly. Her heart was crushed. She had left him devastated. He didn't deserve such pain. He had told her only a few nights prior about the premature daughter that he still mourned. And the devastating effects of some recent tragedies in his life. He looked Fin in her eyes. And told her she was helping erase the pain. That he wasn't sure he could feel again. Love again. But he did. And he told her he would never love another the way he loved her.

Fin gathered her composure and swam towards the castle. She neared the familiar rock and emerged from the waters. She looked around. Madaka was eerily quiet. No one was on the shore. Her castle was on the top of the cliff. She couldn't see it from her vantage point. But it was there. And she had to face the music.

The waves crashed against the rock. She could scale them to the top. Or swim to the beach and then ascend up the hill to the castle. Fin decided to scale the rocky cliff, with its large grooves, perfect for climbing. She reached the top and look over the land. She could see a few guards deep in conversation. Their demeanor solemn. Their faces carrying a sadness she hadn't seen. Fin walked slowly. One of the guards looked off. His eyes squinting as he tried to see her clearly. Soon his eyes bulged. He couldn't believe it was her. He pointed. Then excitedly shouted. "The Princess!"

The men ran towards her. "Princess! Princess Fin!" they yelled. Guards exited the servant's quarters and ran towards her. Fin smiled. Over one hundred men were running her way. She felt missed. It felt good to be so wanted. She always felt nothing but love and protection from the soldiers who once protected her father. Fin was overwhelmed. The faces of men she hadn't seen in months were approaching. Clem, Casio, Arfusei and Ziege. Soon the other guards circled around her.

"Princess! Where have you been? We have searched for you. We never stopped." Fin teared up. She couldn't look them in the eyes. She didn't mean to be such a burden. But her life there, was going in the wrong direction. She didn't have the heart to tell them how she feared marriage to Prince Andreus. They would blame him. Get defensive about it. And she needed them to keep the peace with him. They still needed to trade goods with Eulachon. It wouldn't be good for them to start off despising him.

"I just needed time. A lot of time," she said. "Yes. You were gone so long. We all thought you were dead," Arfusei confessed. "I know. I'm sorry. It was necessary. I have so much to share with you. So much to tell you." Fin looked around. There was no way her father wouldn't have noticed his men gone. He should be running to greet her. And she wondered about Sparrow and Lark. They should be standing there as well.

"Where's dad?" she said. The soldiers and guards looked at one another. Fin's smile faded from her face. "Arfusei!" she asked, looking to him for an answer. Arfusei hesitated.

He stepped closer to her. She took a step back. "Princess...I'm sorry to have to tell you this," he said. Fin grabbed her mouth. Her eyes bulged.

"Don't...Don't you say it. Where is he. I want to see him now," she demanded. He is still in his room. We were waiting to find Lark. He is gone," he said. Fin fell to her knees and sobbed. The men looked intensely at each other. They weren't sure how to console her.

"Show me him. Now!" she said as she stood up and ran to the castle. "Wait Princess!" Arfusei shouted, as he ran behind her. She picked up speed then ran through the front door. She shot up the stairs and down the hall. Her eyes so filled with tears, that her vision was blurred. She got to his door and turned the knob. Arfusei grabbed her arm.

"Wait Your Highness," he said. "What? Why did you say that? I am not the Queen. You address me as Princess," she said, as her heart sank. He had never called her that before. It was not a mistake. "Why did you call me that?" she shouted, afraid of the answer. "The Queen...," he said. Fin let out a blood curdling scream. She opened the door. Arfusei entered with her. She ran to the bed. Aterra and Zander lay side by side. As if asleep.

"No... No... No...," she said, her voice loud and powerful. She was broken. She was saddened. And she was angry. "Leave me. Get out. Please get out," she said, pushing him towards the door.

"Ahhh," she wailed. Arfusei stood motionless. Afraid to leave her side. It was the same thing the queen had said. And he felt to blame because he stood outside the door as she ripped her throat open with a gold ornament. "Your Highness please. Come sit down. Let us help you," he said. Fin didn't budge. "No! I said leave me."

Arfusei closed the door slowly. He was terrified of what she would do. She could hear Arfusei call to the other guards. She dragged her feet across the floor. She was weak. Her head light. The pain of the moment, unbearable. She was afraid to touch them. This wasn't real. They were asleep. Nothing more. She touched her father's hand. "Oh," she whispered, as she felt the cold of his flesh. "Dad... Mom... I'm so sorry," she said.

Unable to stand any longer, she fell to her knees. She pulled his shawl off and smelled it. It was all she would have of him. A shawl that still smelled of his scent. His favorite covering. Fin cried hysterically, as she clung to the edge of the bed. She was heartbroken. She blamed herself for their deaths. She didn't have the whole story. But she knew somehow, it was all about her.

She wailed loudly. The guards were shaken. She was their new queen. Their safety was in jeopardy. The citizens were doing everything they could to keep word of the king and queens passing, a secret. But now there was hope. They had their queen. A new leader. And even though the town knew nothing of Fin, she was still respected. She was the daughter of King Zander. Who was the son of King Zaire. All powerful. Strong and resilient. And both were great leaders.

"Find Lark," Arfusei said to one of the soldiers. "But he isn't coming back. He's in the sea," he replied. "I know that. Find him! Now! He will return for Fin."

"Your Highness...Are you ok?" Arfusei said, as he knocked on the door. He hadn't heard a peep from her in two days. He slowly opened the door. She lay on the edge of the bed. The same spot she was in when he checked several days earlier. "Um...Your Highness. Can you come sit down and eat? Basra cooked you a nice meal. Your favorite. I can get her to bring it to you, if you prefer," he said. "No. Please leave," she whispered. Arfusei cleared his throat. He had something else to say. It was important but he could see she wasn't ready. But he needed to inform her anyway.

"Um...Well...We need to get the bodies in the sea. They are beginning to crumble," he said. Fin looked at him. "Decompose," she said. "What?" he asked. He hadn't heard the word. "Nothing. Just please," she said, as she laid her head back down. Arfusei let out a long exhale. He turned and shut the door behind him.

"They found Lark," the soldier said, a glow on his face. Lark was possibly the answer to their prayers. He knew Fin well. They were closer than anyone. Had been since they were young. They needed him.

Arfusei smiled when he saw Lark's face. Lark had been gone just as long as Fin. He had turned to the sea and never came back. His sole mission, to look for Fin. And after the death of the king and queen, he vowed to never return. He became an uaru. A water soldier. But Arfusei knew better. Lark loved Fin. And he would return to see her.

"Lark!" he exclaimed, as he bowed. He couldn't be happier to see him. Lark was their top commanding soldier at one time. He still received the same respect that he always got from his comrades. Other soldiers entered, smiling and greeted him respectfully. He was missed. He was their backbone. Afraid of nothing. The kings most trusted guard of all.

"Where is she?" he asked. Arfusei stepped aside. Lark looked at the door. He looked around at the happy but emotionally drained and scared soldiers. He knew they feared an uncertain future. They had no real leader. No plan. And Prince Andreus could only be held back for so long. He still had a strong army. He still wanted Mojarro. And he still wanted Fin.

Lark opened the door slowly. His heart dropped as he laid eyes on her. She was alive. She was before him.

"I said leave me," she cried. "I will. But first we have to burry your parents," he said, his voice deep and powerful. Fin raised her head. She knew that voice. She turned around.

"Lark!" she said breathlessly, as she jumped up and ran to him. He was not prepared for the touchy, feely and emotionally woke Fin. She hugged him. His body hard and frigid. He touched her back. She laid her head on his chest. Lark was surprised. Her touch made him feel a way he had never experienced. Fin put her face in his chest and continued crying. Soon Lark relaxed and started holding her. "It's called a hug," she said, as she wept on him. "A what?" he asked.

Fin chuckled. She could feel the wide range of emotions from him. His original apprehension, to his now open and welcoming embrace. Fin stepped back from him and wiped her eyes. He stared intensely at her. Something was different. More sensual. More magnetic. He wasn't sure what it was. "Where did you get that from?" he asked. "What? The hug? A friend," she replied. Lark looked puzzled. "I'll explain later."

The guards stood around. They couldn't make out the muffled sounds that came from the room. Fin and Lark were heavy in conversation. And Arfusei was happy he was there. Things would move forward now.

After an hour, Fin emerged from her father's chambers, with Lark right behind her. "Arfusei. Gather the rest of the men. We need to bury them tonight. Under the darkness. Lark will throw off the uarus. We have to move fast." Arfusei looked at his men. He expected them to do whatever she said. Without question. And his fierce body language was understood. It was not officially announced, but she was their queen.

"Casio! I need you to travel to Panga. Tell the King I wish to meet with him," she ordered. "Yes, Your Highness." Fin looked at Ziege. He was one of their best swimmers. He could go long distances and was powerful enough to fight off most predators. "Ziege! I need you to travel to Piratchu. Tell Queen Rasbora that we need to meet. Arrange a way for her to get here safely. Tell her it's a matter of life and death." Ziege bowed then hurried down the hall. Arfusei was proud. This was the Fin he knew and loved. Tough. Smart. Capable. Fin turned to Lark.

"Thank you. I will see you soon," she said. The guards could see they had a stronger bond. Fin was never that open with any of them. She never looked at them the way she was looking at Lark. "Ok. See you soon," Lark said, getting one last look before moving swiftly past the guards. Fin watched him walk away. She believed in him. He was loyal. He was fierce. And she needed him. Arfusei looked at her. Your arrival must be witnessed. You are queen. We must go into town. Make your presence felt. Give the citizens hope," he said. Fin agreed.

******

Queen Finora walked through the town. The citizens came out and stood outside the castle. Some were lined along the streets. They were happy to see her. They had renewed faith. She looked powerful. She was their new queen. They hoped she would address them soon. Tell them of her future plans. "The Queen," the voices whispered, as citizens bowed. The sounds of gasps and whimpers could be heard as her parents' bodies were carried through the streets. Finora fought back tears. She looked ahead. Her eyes focused on the sea. Her heart with her loved ones who had perished. And she was now responsible for thousands of citizens. Mojarro was the second largest city in Madaka. And Fin had a plan. She had been informed that Prince Andreus was responsible for her father's death and in turn also responsible for her mother's. Her thoughts turned to Lance, as she made her way to Palimora. He had taught her a lot. And his teachings would aid them greatly.

The white soft sand gave way to the warm blue water. The long rows of men led by Finora was a powerful sight. No one spoke a word. The somber occasion was heart felt. Water splashed as the large group entered. Finora was their beautiful and elegant queen and they would die in the waters to save her. They were proud of her. She addressed them elegantly before they left. They needed to be uplifted. Their leaders were gone. Men had perished.

Fin mentioned their bravery and dedication. How honored she was to have them as her faithful protectors. How lucky Mojarro was to be under that same protection. The men came alive. Their faces showing signs of being renewed. This burial at sea was a celebration of life. Not a symbol of their death. And Fin spoke of how they would be remembered and honored through continued dedication to the city they died for.

Lark was already there waiting. He was accompanied by several uaru. He had already checked the surrounding area for eulachonians. Fin felt safe knowing that. She could see he was worried about her safety. And she could see that he loved her. She was experienced with men. With feelings. Her time with Lance was eye opening.

As the water made it way up her body, she settled on one thought. That it was possible she would never see Lance again. It was painful. She promised him she would. She left him in tears. But a nation needed her. She had no idea she was coming home to two dead parents. This was a severe blow to her people. Her heart would have to take a back seat.

The water was up to her neck. She pushed off the sand. Her soldiers followed. The bodies of her parents wrapped in special silk wraps made by the dressmaker. Queen Aterra was in gold colored silk adorned with large emeralds and rubies and fastened with gold metal pins. King Zander was wrapped in a dark blue silk fabric adorned with diamonds and rubies and fastened with pins and blue silk ties. Their bodies carried by three soldiers each. One at the head. One in the middle. And one at the feet.

Finora swished her tail then increased her pace. She looked back to check on the soldiers who had her parents. They were situated in the water and were comfortably carrying her precious cargo. She continued on. Her spirit still crushed after losing not one but both of them. They would never see her marry. Never meet their grandchildren. She would never have the conversation she so desperately wanted to have with her mother. She would never get a chance to tell her father she knew he meant well. That she could have never married Prince Andreus. Arfusei had told her about the battle. And how her father decided to attack the man who stated he would just take her. Fin couldn't be prouder. Her father died fighting for her honor. Fighting for their city.

They reached the middle of the sea where the ground was softest. It was a common burial area. The water was dark. Their way lit by special lights made from the brightly lit creatures on the Trojian Sea housed in small glass containers. Lark approached. Fin was relieved. She wanted him by her side. He had a way of calming her with just a look. It was something they shared since they were young.

He swam up and joined them. Arfusei nodded at him and looked ahead. Lark glanced at Fin. The last time he swam beside her in these waters she was on her way to marry Prince Andreus. But not this time. They were there to say goodbye to her parents. Her father, was like a father to him. Her mother, his caregiver. A woman who accepted him with open arms. He was devastated. He eased his hand to hers, trying to keep the soldiers from seeing him. Fin spread her hand open. She took his hand into hers. He held it the rest of the way. He had abandoned his fears of being caught.

King Zander and Queen Aterra were laid to rest deep in the sand of the sea floor. Finora kissed their covered faces and floated backward, allowing the men to push them deep into the soft sand. Their graves unmarked to prevent trophy seekers. Fin swam away. It was hard for her to see them go into the ground. Soon the soldiers joined, swimming back to land. Lark swam after her. He followed her back. She stayed a few meters in front of him. She was inconsolable. He understood. But he could not take his eyes off of her. The last time he did. She disappeared.

$\mathcal{F}$in awoke after a restless night of tossing and turning. She had slept in her mother chambers. The largest of all the rooms. Sleeping in Aterra's room made her feel safe. Closer to her. She rose out of bed and walked to her dresser. Stained cherry colored wood with gold inlay and diamonds along the edges. She touched it. It had a beauty that the new world's furniture did not. It was made from a labor of love and gifted to the queen. Finora looked around. She missed the amenities of the new world. She missed Lance's house. She missed him. But Fin refused to think of him. And she pushed thoughts of him and the comforts of the new world out of her mind. She could live without the vices that had human's spoiled. This was her life. Her home. Finora was determined to forget. If it were that simple.

Fin opened her door. "Can you have Lillia draw me a bath?" she asked. "Yes, Your Highness," the soldier said. "Listen. Call me Fin please. And spread the word. I am only to be called queen or your highness in front of the citizens," she urged. "Yes your…I mean, yes Fin," he said, as he walked off to get her request to Lillia. Fin shut her door. She had a meeting shortly. The Queen of Piratchu was on her way. And King Nephrus of Panga would be arriving shortly. Fin was strangely calm. She would deliver a message. She would get them to hear her out. And they had a small window. There was one other person she would need to meet with. She had not seen him around. He usually visited the castle whenever he thought he could get a moment with the king.

Fin was moody. She couldn't stop thinking of her parents. And she was unable to think of anything but Lance. She sighed. His face was a constant image in her mind. It had been a week since she had buried the king and queen. Since she left him. She hoped her days would get easier.

"Fin," the soft voice said. "Come in," she replied. Lillia entered with three guards carrying a large, thin, gold bathing tub filled with water. "Sit it over in the corner," she asked. The men placed the tub as Finora asked and left her room. "I made you a snack," Lillia said, as she sat a small plate of mussels and karra beans on her table. Fin looked at the food. She wished she had strawberries to go with it. She immediately thought of Lance. The image of his face soothed her. She could see his laugh. His eyes. His smile. He loved sea food and oysters were his favorite. But something wasn't right. She leaned forward.

"Fin," Lillia called to her. "Fin," she called again. Fin grabbed her stomach, then threw up on the floor. She looked dazed. "Oh my. Come and sit down. Lark!" she called. Fin made her way to the bed. "Get that plate out of here. Take it away," she asked. Lillia grabbed the plate. Lark ran into the room.

"What's wrong," he asked, as he touched her back. "I don't know. I suddenly felt ill," she replied. "You need to rest. I will see to it that the Queen and King have comfortable accommodations until you can meet with them," he said. "No! I must speak with them. Just get me over to that water. I will get myself together."

Lark helped Fin to the tub. "Help me with my clothes," she said. Lark swallowed hard. He would see her naked. "Alright," he said. Fin turned slowly and raised her arms. Lark pulled her dress over her head. He looked at her. She kept her back to him. She stepped in the tub and slowly sat in the warm water. "Oh yesss," she said. Lark was speechless. Fin was stunning. Her body was magnificent. Toned and perfect. Her breasts were larger than normal. Her hips rounder than other women. She was curvaceous. Her hair, long thick and flowy. Lark was mesmerized. Fin closed her eyes The water felt good. She opened them and looked up at him. Her tender smile melting his heart. "Are you ok now?" he asked. Fin nodded. "Well, I'll be close if you need me," he said. "Ok."

Queen Rasbora was due to hit land at any moment. Fin had her soldiers travel to the shores of the Trojian Sea, to wait for her arrival. She had to travel the long way to avoid going through Eulachon. She was worried. Rumors of war in the waters had reached as far as Piratchu and had all of her citizens fearful.

"Your Highness," the guard greeted Rasbora, as she exited the water in a long green silk and taffeta gown. Her head adorned with a fabulous gold and pearl crown. She was accompanied by one of her two daughters, Princess Darbee.

The women walked to their awaiting chariot. A small step was placed on the outside, for their convenience. The Queen was regal. She commanded respect without uttering a word. She sat, straightening her dress as she waited on her daughter. The men closed the door and whisked them off to the castle. King Nephrus was already there. She looked at her daughter. Her famous look of entitlement worn elegantly.

Queen Rasbora was as snobby as she was generous. She believed she had the best of Madaka. And although Mojarro was covered in jewels, she had everything else. One could not eat jewels. And one could not grow the best herbs from a land not heavily covered in nutrient rich soil. Piratchu had clean lakes. Its waters teaming with the best their world had to offer. And Piratchu itself, unlike its neighbor Eulachon, was beautiful. Second only to Mojarro in visual appeal. Their cone like mountains scattered throughout and covered in green or blue moss, were spectacular.

The queen looked around. She was impressed. It was everything she remembered. "This ought to be interesting. How old is the princess?" she asked her daughter. Darbee was a shy and timid twenty-one-year-old woman. Nothing at all like her independent and strong-willed mother. "I think she is in her late twenties. Not sure mom," she replied. Queen Rasbora rolled her eyes. "A child. What could she possibly have to say to me. And where is the king. He must be ill," she complained.

The chariot ran through town. Citizens saw the Queen. Her presence meant something major was happening. She never visited. The last time she was in Mojarro was years prior. She looked out her window. "Slower please," she shouted, as her chariot rocked. The soldiers pulling them along on a brick paved road. The commotion causing citizens to exit their homes. They were getting concerned. No one knew anything other than the king and queen were dead and that Fin had taken over.

The chariot arrived at the front door of the castle. "I forget how gorgeous this place is. Reminds me of my first home," she smugly said. Princess Darbee snickered. It was typical of her mother. To hurl insults. The women were shown inside and escorted to the meeting chambers. The queen sat down at a fabulous gold and red satin chair encrusted with rubies. She smiled and took her seat, noting how fabulous the throne was. "It was the queen's," King Nephrus commented. "King Nephrus," Rasbora greeted. He walked up to her and bowed then sat at a gold and green silk cushioned throne with green emeralds placed perfectly along the sides and head rail.

Fin entered and sat at her father's throne. A combination of rubies and emeralds. The most luxurious of the chairs. She wore a fabulous bright gold gown adorned with emeralds. Her head, adorned with a head piece made of the same gold silk and emeralds. The dress fit her shapely body. The Queen took notice. She was instantly jealous of the beautiful and exotic looking woman. The green colors picking up the striking color of her eyes. The last time she'd seen Fin, she was a young girl. She was now, anything but.

"Your Highness," Fin said, as she sat back in her chair. She had the guards place their chairs in a small circle, facing each other. The soldiers for each leader stood behind them. King Nephrus was impressed. He still harbored resentment that she was not given to his son as a wife. But he wasn't there to open old wounds. Neither was Queen Rasbora. And she was the first to speak.

"What is this meeting about? Where is the king? I assume this is about the fighting in the waters of Palimora. A war that neither myself nor King Nephrus had knowledge of, until after the fact. I was not aware there was a problem," she said as she looked for confirmation from King Nephrus. He nodded, as she continued.

"I am fatigued. I have travelled a long way. This must be very important. Why not send the information by messenger? And why am I not meeting with the king? Have you been appointed to some position that I am not aware of?" she complained. Fin looked intensely at her. Her youth possibly causing a miscalculation in the queens' judgement.

She was neither inexperienced or fearful. Her quick response, setting the record straight.

"Because I am queen. My father and my mother are dead. And because you are in danger," she replied, her voice strong. King Nephrus sat straight. Adjusting himself in his chair. He was now on edge. "You too, Your Highness," she said to King Nephrus. Fin glanced at Lark. He stood in the corner. His job was to read their reactions. Gage whether they would be for or against Fin. He was clever. He was gifted in reading people. "What! I am in no danger. From who? What threat?" Rasbora exclaimed. "What threat do you speak of?" King Nephrus chimed in, a look of worry on his face.

Fin paused. This was a onetime shot. If they did not believe her, join her in battle, it could spell trouble. "I need all the guards out! Everyone, except Lark," she ordered. The men stood waiting for their orders to come from their own leader. Queen Rasbora waved her men away. Soon, King Nephrus nodded to his men, who turned and followed the queens guards out the door. Fin felt safe to continue. This was top secret. She couldn't take any chances.

Fin paused. She examined the demeanors of both leaders. If they rejected what she said, it could pose a risk of exposure. One or both could inform King Andreus thwarting any element of surprise from her men. Fin had good instincts. She had paid attention to her father. He taught her to use body language and words, to sway non-believers. Fin was ready. She realized that it was her war now, and could be their war later. One successful takeover would open the door to others.

"Eulachon is looking to take Mojarro over. My father died at sea after discovering they were headed here to take me and the city, by force. The now King, Andreus, retreated. He didn't expect my father's soldiers to be so skilled. The war was brutal. He lost a lot of men. So did we. But it is not over," Fin informed.

"So… This war is between you and them. It has nothing to do with Piratchu," the Queen said. "Or Panga," King Nephrus added. Fin looked between the both of them. Her demeanor changed. She sat up. She crossed her legs.

"If he is successful, and takes us over, what stops him from coming after you, Your Highness," she said, looking at Rasbora. "You are closest to him. You have pearls. You have soil. Plants that don't grow on their spoiled land. And you, King Nephrus. Panga is the smallest city in Madaka. It would be an easy win for him. You have even more soil. Your land is rich in nutrients. You have oil. You have coal. You have resources he would surely want. Don't you find it strange, that all this has come about, after his father's death. Which means, he had this planned the whole time. He was just waiting for his father to pass away. King Orfe was a good man. He would have never allowed this," Fin said.

The Queen looked terrified. As if she had seen a ghost. King Nephrus became anxious. He never thought of it. He had taken the trades for granted. And even though he knew the prince was not a good person, he never imagined him to be brutal. And they hadn't had a war in centuries. So war, was never considered possible. The cities got along.

"Listen! His land is ruined. The gases have all but destroyed Eulachon. Have you seen the land lately? Nothing grows there. No moss. No algae. No plants. Nothing! I believe they want out. And I believe they want to take over all of Madaka because they believe they can."

King Nephrus' mind raced. "If this is true, then we don't stand a chance. His army is larger than the three of ours put together. We can't win," he said.

Fin stood up and walked closer to them. "What if I told you there was a way. That I know things. How to make things. That the old days of fighting hand to hand, will be their downfall," she said. King Nephrus looked at Queen

Rasbora. She stared back at him. "Go on. I'm listening," he said. Fin looked at Lark. He nodded. She continued.

I know how to fashion what are called weapons. It provides the user with an advantage over their opponent. Made from materials we have here. All I need is branches from the trees on both of your lands. Go back. Tell no one about this conversation. Get your men to tear as many branches as you can. Get them delivered here. Preferably in the dark. My men will meet your men half way, and take it from there. Once the weapons have been formed, I will need your permission to command your army. Release them to me. I will prepare them for battle. I will train them. And we will keep a close eye on Eulachon. We will not strike until we are ready. We will not harm their citizens. This is soldier to soldier. Fighter to fighter," she said, sitting back at her throne.

Fin's eyes appeared glassy. Rasbora watched attentively. Fin sat forward and grabbed her stomach. "Are you alright Queen Fin?" King Nephrus said. "Yes. I think so. My stomach," she uttered. Queen Rasbora watched her. She looked her up and down. Suddenly a thought. Fin's movements and complaints were familiar. The color of her skin and the way she was breathing was telling. "No! You are not alright. You are with child," she blurted. Fin stopped abruptly. She wasn't sure she heard the queen correctly.

"What did you say?" she asked. "You are going to have a baby. I noticed it as soon as I saw you. But I wasn't sure. You have all the signs. You will feel it move soon. And you will have the baby shortly. You are further along. The reason you look reddened," she said, smiling, as if to congratulate the new mom to be. Fin looked over at Lark. His face was full of pain. He looked away. Fin was embarrassed. She had no idea. And she wasn't sure the queen was right.

"Well. You have the support of Panga. I will get you the wood you need. We will begin collecting it and it will be delivered to you soon," King Nephrus stated. "And what about you, Your Highness?" Fin asked. Rasbora rubbed her lip softly. It was a risk. She was the closest city to Eulachon. All they had to do was cross one small body of water and they would be on her land. "We join you. He is in a slump right now. His father's death and whatever else is on his mind, has taken its toll on him. We have time. They cannot get him to leave his room, let alone go into battle. This will give us time to prepare. Time to strike," she said.

Rasbora was connected to Eulachon. She and King Orfe had a friendship. She felt something was off about his son but never thought much about it. She was not surprise to hear he was planning to do such horrible things. She knew him better than anyone. And she had gotten word of his depression since losing his father. But she also knew that he would mourn and then emerge, mad at the world. And so, it all made sense to her. He had to be stopped.

Fin smiled and stood. She bowed her head as she had seen her father do countless times. "What about King Andreus? He will be at the forefront of any battle. Are we capturing him or killing him?" Rasbora asked. The question sent Fin's heart racing. She was furious at his actions. At his gall. And his inability to control himself which resulted in her father's and mother's death. She looked at Rasbora. The answer to her question was clear. Fin was unsympathetic. Her words, frank and to the point.

"He is my enemy. He killed my father. Since all of this started over me, it will end with me. He chose to kill. He will be killed."

"Mr. Reed you have a call on line two," the voice said through the intercom. Lance was preparing to go home. Bandz was doing well. He had hired a few new recruits and the company was growing, despite having a dismal first few quarters. "I can't take it. Please put them in my voice mail," he said. "But it's your brother. He called yesterday too," she replied. Lance sighed. "Alright. Send him through."

Lance picked up the phone. He stood and walked over to his window and looked down at the traffic. "Hello," he said. "Hey," Allan replied. He was in no mood to talk to his brother. He wasn't in the mood for much of anything since Fin never returned. He was heartbroken. Life for him was a daily routine of work, followed by a stop at the store or gas station. And then his grueling ride home to an empty house where everything reminded him of Fin. Where he watched out of windows or went down to the dock, to wait for her.

Some of his neighbors had noticed his daily walks on the dock. And had watched as he sat for hours, taking occasional breaks and then returning. He seemed to be waiting on something. Months had gone by. Each day harder than the one before. It was clear he would never see her again. And he still had not processed his loss.

His neighbor George drove by on his boat often and had commented to his wife, his curiosity about their neighbor's strange behavior. Sometimes he would sit on the edge of his dock in the middle of the night. He did it for weeks until one day he abruptly stopped. His next-door neighbors noticed the same thing and had invited him over, as a way to cheer the seemingly sad bachelor up. But he never accepted their invite. And now he was avoiding his brother's calls.

"Hey. Wanted to see if you're in the mood for some company. I got some time off. I was going to come stay with you for a few days," he said. Lance could stand the distraction. He was having a hard time. But this was Allan. His sometimes-well-intentioned brother who could be overbearing at times. Lance thought hard. And without much hesitation, said yes. Allan was ready to leave. He was overdue for a much-needed break.

He was still the main caretaker of his children. But they were miles away visiting their maternal grandparents and

Allan wanted his own vacation. He wasn't sure his brother would allow a visit. He could tell something was on his mind. His mood had drastically changed. For the first time in a long time, his brother appeared happy. And then suddenly, his demeanor changed. He had become withdrawn and quiet. "Ok. I will see you Thursday. I'm on line now, and I see a flight I can catch. I'll book it."

******

"Allan," Lance said, waving to his brother as he exited the terminal. Allan smiled and grabbed his brother for a hug. "You ok," he said. "Yeah. What else you bring?" Lance asked. "Nothing. This is it," Allan replied. The men turned and walked towards the exit, grabbing coffee at a stand on their way out.

"How was your flight?" Lance asked, as he grabbed his brother's bag and tossed it in the back seat. "Good. I got in a good nap. I feel refreshed actually. How was your day. Did you go to work this morning?" Allan asked. "Naw. I stayed home today. Worked from my office. I turned that large spare room into a full working office. I go in pretty much every day but Bandz can run without me. Dave is phenomenal. And Ashley in accounting, is top notch. Between the two of them, there's really no need for me to be there. But of course, I'm the owner. So I have to go in," he replied.

The success of Bandz had become his mission. It was his new baby. He was working hard to keep the company thriving. A job that wasn't easy. He had a new found respect for his father. It was a tough market. Many small unknown companies with similar technology was hitting big. Being a larger sized company was no guarantee of success. One wrong move, or getting too comfortable and not keeping up with trends, could cost you. Lance knew what it took.

He was constantly reinventing the wheel. New marketing strategies. The best hiring practices. Incentives to get and keep the best engineers and tech whizzes. It was quite taxing. But he loved it. He lived for it. His life was good, despite his brother's doubts. He had gotten over his lost child. He had moved on from the failed relationship. And he was over his missed opportunity to know his father. What he wasn't over was Fin. And he hoped it didn't show.

Allan got in the car and took a sip of coffee. The weather was great. His kids were having a good time with their grandparents. And Lance appeared to be ok. He could relax. Lance tipped the valet for allowing him to leave his vehicle unattended. He walked up to his door and inhaled deeply. He was hiding his broken heart. His pain over a lost love. It seemed he was always losing something or someone. And Allan was his biggest supporter as well as his toughest critic. Allan wanted him ok. He wanted his brother to get back to the strong, *force of a man,* he knew him to be.

Lance wasn't sure when the tables had turned. When Allan viewed him as needy and in a weakened state. He was crushed. But he was dealing. And he hoped Allan got the confirmation, he was sure his brother was there for.

"Had to tip that man. He watched my car while I came inside to get you," Lance said, as he made small talk. Allan reached over and turned the radio on. He scanned the channels as Lance pulled off. "I'm starving," he said, as he stopped on a familiar song. Allan sat back. He relaxed. California was beautiful. He could see why Lance was unwilling to return to Boston. "Man. One thing for certain. This place is beautiful," he said, as they pulled away from LAX.

*A*lan stood in the window. He loved the view. It had been three days since he touched down. This trip was a stark contrast to the one before. He went with Lance to work every day, learning the marketing side of the business. His way of preparing for inclusion, in case he decided to relocate. He was getting *California Fever*.

Malibu was spectacular. The homes were grand. The views breathtaking. His wife wanted a divorce. The separation that was originally meant to help them take a break and get their minds in order, had opened the doors to something unexpected. She started dating. She was in love. And now she wanted to end what they had. Allan was hurt. He hoped she would get herself together. He believed they would repair their broken marriage. But requests for help through a marriage counselor fell on deaf ears. Allan found himself thinking of his next move.

He was leaving in two more days. Lance seemed good until this day. Lance sat on the dock. There was something in his manner. Something in his posture. He looked like a man longing. Waiting. But for what.

Allan sat his drink down and slid the door open. The nice breeze was an instant refresher. He walked slowly across the patio and over to the dock. Lance could hear him coming. "I swear you have to be the luckiest man I know. Your home. And this view…" he said. Lance chuckled. "Yeah. I guess. It seems like heaven. It's all in how you look at it," he said, as Allan approached and sat down next to him.

The wind picked up slightly. Allan let his bare feet in the water. He knew the look. The mood. He had felt it himself, several times before. The look of a man in love. Missing someone. Thinking of someone. He no longer believed it was Paula. She was back in Boston asking about him. He could get her back if he wanted. This was something else. He wondered what Californian had managed to capture his brothers' heart.

"Who is she?" he asked. Lance looked swiftly at his brother. A part of him was ready to open up. He paused. He thought of how he would sound. The truth was hard to believe. Hard to picture. But it was his truth.

"I met someone. Someone phenomenal," he said. Allan smiled then placed his arm around his brother's shoulders. "What! Is that all. I could feel something was going on. Congratulations man. That is awesome news. You deserve it. Who is she? Where is she?" he asked. Lance looked down at the water. Allan felt the mood change. "What's up?" he asked. Lance shook his head back and forth. There was no easy way to tell him. He wasn't sure he should. But Allan was all he had. Their mother was not lucid. She struggled with her mental functions. Her mind was deteriorating. She was enjoying her senior years at a nursing home courtesy of Lance and Allan.

"It will be hard for you to believe. I have told no one. Not a soul. No one would ever believe me," Lance said. Allan dropped his arm down. Things sounded serious. "I will. I know you. You don't make up stuff. What is it?" he said, as his mind raced. He wondered if she was too young. Or was it a woman with a complicated life from the wrong side of the tracks. Or, was she married. Whoever she was, he believed she was a controversial lover. Or else he wouldn't hide their relationship. Allan waited. Lance paused. "She lives in the water."

Allan's eyes narrowed. "What? What are you talking about Lance?" he asked. "That's the unbelievable part. She is from another place. Another world. She is able to live in water," he said, watching Allan carefully to gage his reaction. Allan stood up. He put his hands over his face then paced the dock. "You have got to leave here. You're coming home with me," he said. Lance stood up.

"This is why I hadn't told you. This reaction right here...The one where you doubt me. Think I'm losing it. Exactly, what I should have expected," he said, as he walked back toward his home. Allan walked behind him.

"Do you hear yourself? A woman in the water. Let me guess...The same woman my son thought he saw. Well, I asked him when we got home, and he said it was too blurry to see clearly. He could have been wrong. He wasn't sure what he saw. People can't live in water Lance," he argued. Lance felt betrayed. He was not insane. And he didn't understand why his brother couldn't take his word for it no matter how unbelievable it sounded.

"And what about Yaz?" he asked. Allan snickered. "What about her?" he replied. "So, what she saw gets discounted because she's only six. They saw the woman. And you believed them. That's why you're here. To see if it's true. You're puzzled. Curious. Your children are not insane and neither am I. Miles is changing his story probably from pressure from you to do so. And so now he is saying *maybe* he didn't see anything."

Lance was furious as he continued to his door. Allan stopped and watched as Lance continued on. He stood speechless on the dock. "What is going on? Maybe I'm losing it," he said, as he slowly made his way back to the house. Lance immediately retreated up the stairs. He could not convince Allan. He needed him to believe in him. Believe what his children saw.

The sound of boats could be heard. It was the weekend and boaters were out early. Lance kicked the covers off of his legs. He grabbed himself. He adjusted his manhood then closed his eyes again. He opened them. The chime of his doorbell could be faintly heard. Lance rose up. He looked out at the water then waited to see if the bell would chime again. Whoever it was, was not welcomed. He glanced at the clock. The sound of the bell rang again. Then the sound of his front door opening. "What the fuck," he complained, as he walked to the top of the staircase. He could hear Allan talking to someone.

"He's been through a lot. Our mother isn't well. And just last year he lost his baby and then broke up with his fiancé within months of each other. Then his father died recently. I thought he was handling everything. But I don't know," he said to the visitor. Lance descended the steps slowly. He walked then turned the corner and entered the great room. Allan looked nervously at him. A woman stood in a skirt and blouse. She wore a smile like a uniform. It didn't look genuine. And Lance wondered what was going on.

"Lance. This is Dr. Karpowski," he said. Lance stared at Allan. He looked at the doctor. "Hi Lance. I'm Dr. Karpowski. But you can call me Helen," she said, as she extended her hand. Lance turned from her and walked into the kitchen. Just as he bent the corner, he called his brother for a side bar. "Let me see you in private," Lance requested. "Excuse me," Allan said, as he walked into the kitchen.

"Exactly why is she here? What kind of doctor is she?" he asked. "I called a buddy of mine. He reached out to his friends and they got you an appointment with her. Just to talk. Nothing major. Just clear your mind. Help you sort out your feelings," he said. Lance chuckled. "Oh! She's a shrink," he said, smiling to hide the anger he felt inside. Allan didn't find it funny. He thought Lance had gone mad.

"You need help Lance. Please. Talk to her. House calls this fast aren't easy to get. In fact, no one hardly does them anymore," he said. Lance took a sip of water as his eyes seemed to pierce his brother's soul. "I have no need to talk to her. And soon, I will have no need or desire to talk to you. This is, the ultimate fucking betrayal," he stated. Allan's heart sank. This was not going as planned. "Come on Lance. Don't say that. I love you man. I'm looking out for you. Let's just sit and talk," he urged. Talk about what's bothering you. I'm trying to help. You know I love you. I want you good. Please man. Do it for me."

******

Lance sat across from Dr. Karpowski. He looked at her. He looked at Allan. If she was there to analyze him, then he would give her a glimpse of what he felt. Allan was right about one thing. It could possibly help. He could relive it by recounting the events. It was a peek into an extraordinary experience. And he was ready for the ride. He needed to talk about Fin. He needed her to be real. She was. And holding it in, like some scandalous secret, was maddening.

"Ok Lance. This is your session. I want you to talk about the most important thing in your life right now. It's always good to lead with the important things. Whatever you are mentally and spiritually connected to at this moment. That thing you can't escape. If you were to pick one thing to talk about, what would that be?" she said, as she crossed her legs. Allan sat on a chair not too far away. Lance wanted him to listen in. And Helen asked that he do it from a distance. To give his brother a chance to speak without distraction. Allan sat behind Lance. He listened closely. He wondered what Lance would want to talk about. There was so much history. He had lived a fabulous life until the last few years. He was smart. He excelled at everything. Women adored him. He was envied by his friends. And he was unstoppable. Would he talk about the good things. Or would he reflect on the loss.

"Do you know where you want to begin?" she asked. "Yes. I want to talk about Fin."

Allan was perplexed. He had never heard the name. He was aware of all of Lance's loves and his conquest. He was never shy about talking about his love life. "Ok. Is she your girlfriend? Your wife?" the doctor asked. "Yes," he replied. "Ok. Which is she?" she asked. "She's everything." Lance said, being facetious. He knew they would never believe him. It would only do him good to hear himself talk about her. Not actually tell them about her. He needed the therapy. But for other reasons.

"Ok. Listen. I have to speak. Uninterrupted. And after I'm done, I don't wish to answer questions. Or elaborate on anything you feel confused about. Are we clear?" he asked. "Sure. Can I take notes?" she asked. "Yes."

Lance spent three hours telling Dr. Karpowski about the love of his life, the way they met and how devastated he had been since she left him. The doctor took notes as she sat completely absorbed, listening to him recall every day he spent with her. She kicked off her shoes and got comfortable. Lance had eased his posture. He was comfortable. And his memory was remarkable. The story of the woman from the sea was fascinating. His profound expressions and body language added intrigue to an already engrossing love story. He allowed himself to escape into his conscious and subconscious mind. It was noteworthy. And Helen didn't believe she was in the presence of a crazed lunatic.

She in fact, saw no signs of mental illness at all. His recall was detailed. And when he returned to a specific detail he'd already mentioned, he would recount the details precisely as he'd stated before. She had no doubts he had met a woman who was in his water. What she couldn't believe was that the woman could breathe water. The doctor believed as Allan did. That a woman diving around the docks, for tokens and treasures, had reluctantly made an introduction. It explained the reason it took him weeks from the first time he saw her, to finally meeting her. Allan himself was intrigued. Lance wrapped up his amazing story. Allan sat dumfounded. He believed his brother. He had no reason not to. The story was incredible. But Allan had to think back to the practicality of his brother. Lance liked simple. Plain. He was not a drama seeker. And he was right. Allan's son told a similar story. A woman in the water with no diving gear, looking up at him. He described her the same way Lance described Fin. He believed she was otherworldly. And he believed she existed.

Dr. Karpowski closed her notepad. She wiped a tear from her eye. "I'm sorry. I don't usually get emotional. That was just so beautiful. That was the greatest love story I have ever heard. Ever!" she said. Lance smiled. It was the greatest love story he'd ever lived. The shortest but the most powerful. The most loving. The closest he'd ever felt to a woman.

Helen stood up. "I want to thank you for sharing. I hope you find her. You must find her. That kind of love is rare. Hard to find. I want to give you my card. Call me anytime you want to talk. I would love a follow up if you find her. Please," she said, handing him a tan colored card with shiny red lettering on it. "Thank you so much. I needed that," he said. Allan stood up and walked her to the door. Lance sat reflecting on his words. He was emotional. She had to come back. He had so much more to show her. So much more love to give. It wasn't over.

"He's fine Mr. Grant. He has no signs of delirium or mental illness. None! The only thing I don't understand is his confusion on her ability to stay underwater. It's probably some new scuba gear. Maybe she wanted to enchant him. I don't know. I would love to talk to her. But anyway, I need to get going. He's fine," she spoke in a low tone, as she touched his arm. "Thanks doctor. He's not confused. She lives in the water. I didn't disclose what else I knew but my son saw her too," Allan said. "Oh wow. Then I have no explanation. All I know is the man I just had a session with is not hallucinating. He is a normal thinking, mentally healthy human being," she replied. Allan closed the door. He was no longer worried. Lance spoke nothing about his past. He had moved on from it. Healed from it. Allan smiled then walked towards the living room. He sat next to Lance. "There's something I need to tell you," he said. Lance looked at him. He wondered what Allan would say now. It didn't matter. He was done proving himself.

"Miles said the same thing. Described her the same way. And I doubted him. The same way I doubted you. But I don't anymore. Miles doesn't lie and neither do you. I will never question you about her again. I really hope she returns. I would love to meet her someday."

Lance hugged his brother. It meant a lot to him that Allan believed him. "Thanks man. That means a lot. But it doesn't matter. She's gone," he said. His mood changing as the words left his lips. Allan sighed. He hoped she wasn't. His brother was incredible. She had to come back. She was missing out on a great man. "She'll be back."

******

"Hi. I have reservation for three for Doctor Karpowski," Helen said, as she entered the lobby of *Ocean Grill*. "This way please," the man said, as he led her to a table with a great view. "I am expecting a colleague," she alerted. "Sure Doctor Karpowski. I will show them back," he nodded. Helen pulled her cell phone from her Chanel clutch and scanned the call log. "Damn," she said, as she noticed she missed a few calls. She checked her texts then her emails. She looked up and saw her friend walking towards the table. Helen lit up. She was glad her busy friend of ten years, was able to make it. She wasn't sure she would.

"Susan," Helen said, as she stood up and kissed both cheeks. "Helen," she replied, as she kissed her left then right cheek, making sure not to get her bright red lipstick on her. The respectful greeting of the elite. Susan was at the top of their field. She had been in practice for fifteen years and hailed from a family of behavioral specialist and psychiatrist. The women sat and placed their napkins over their laps. Helen put her phone away. She wanted to talk to Susan undistracted.

"So, what was so important?" Susan asked Helen. Helen smiled. "A strange case that fell in my lap. And I find myself questioning my own analysis and conclusion about it. I have to be careful. I know with patient confidentiality and the laws, I'm not supposed to discuss the case," she said, hoping Susan wouldn't view her as untrustworthy with patient information.

"Well…As long as you don't disclose names. And it is just one professional to another. You know, for help in diagnosing and such. There are no laws being broken. How about you tell me the specifics. I can help you categorize the behavior."

Helen spent an hour telling Susan as she sat speechless and totally absorbed in the story. Helen noticed Susan's fascination. She had the same look on her face when Lance told of a woman from the ocean. A woman whose enchanting ways and loving heart, capture him totally and had him spellbound. Susan listened, intently, her mouth slightly opened, hanging on every word. So completely engrossed, that she hadn't touched a morsel on her plate.

"I don't know Susan. He is incredibly gorgeous. I found myself attracted to him. And I wondered if that was hindering me from diagnosing him with an illness. I mean, I have Tom. I'm not looking to date him. But there was something about him. And I must admit, I was jealous of his affection for her. I have never witnessed a man so consumed. A man with that look in his eye. When he spoke of her it was almost like he was hypnotized. I wanted to meet her so badly. To see how she was able to get his heart so completely in such a short time. A rich, handsome and powerful man like him. He must get a dozen offers. Women must fall at his feet," she said.

Susan leaned on her hands. "You know this story is from ancient times. Greek mythology. A story about a woman of the sea. They called them merfolk. Mermaids. Some people fantasize about the reality of them. There is a story about a woman who thought she was one. She spent a lot of time in water with her own self-made tail. She taught herself how to hold her breath for extended times. She would be seen on rock and near shores and would disappear. Then one day she was never seen again. Some people think she drowned. That she pushed the envelope and tragically died as a result. Maybe this is a copy-cat. Someone looking to get to him. You say he is rich. Maybe they want his money. I don't know. The way you describe him…I see no signs. But clearly, someone has been successful in having him doubt his own reality. There are no mermaids. But he is a very interesting case. See if he'll let you write his story. It is fascinating."

Helen and Susan left the dinner. The women held onto one another, arm in arm, as they laughed and waited for valet to bring their cars. "It was great to see you Susan. Thanks for having lunch with me. I'll call you soon. We have to have lunch again soon," Helen said, as she walked around her car and entered. Susan blew her a kiss then climbed into her two-seater sports car and pulled off. Helen was relieved. If Susan could see no behavioral issues from the description provided, then she felt good about her conclusion about him. If he needed help, she was doing him a terrible disservice by skating over his symptoms;

Susan said he sounded stable. Clear in his thinking. And she saw no signs. Ok. I can move on to my next case. I'm closing this out. Nothing is wrong with him. But there is still the question of the woman. And who believes in mermaids. That is folklore. Tales. That is not real!

11

Anointed

*K*ing Nephrus' men waited at the agreed meeting point. Their strong bodies carrying wood, wrapped and bound together, across their backs. The men could see the soldiers of Mojarro coming. Over a hundred men swimming in rows of ten, from top to bottom. Their standard water formation.

"This is all we could gather. Every tree in Panga has been cut. We only left the branches at the top to preserve the trees life," the soldier informed. Lark nodded and ordered his men to take the piles of wood. His tail switching slowly back and forth to keep him suspended in the water. He took a strap fashioned from dead whale flesh and placed the bundled branches on his back as another soldier tied the strap. The men made the exchange, carrying thousands of branches of varying sizes, on their bodies to return to Mojarro. Lark bowed in the water then turned and led his men back to their city.

"We have more wood Your Highness," Lark said, as Fin sat with her hands on her face. She appeared stressed. "Ok. Thanks Lark. I just need a minute," she said. Lark stood over her, looking down at the top of her head. He wanted to know. But it would be disrespectful to ask a queen her personal business.

But she was more than a queen to him. And he wondered who she had fallen in love with. A baby meant someone had her heart. Babies were planned. It took time. Their creation was intentional. And he wondered when that could have possibly happened when he'd known her all her life. No one was that close to her. No male. She had one friend. A female. And she did not spend a lot of time with Rae. It was troubling. He was angry. Jealous. But he needed to keep his cool.

Fin peeked through her hands. Her eyes, blood shot red. She was unable to pull herself together as thoughts of Lance consumed her. "Yes? Is there something else?" she asked him. In all her worries and obsessive thoughts about her lover on the other side of the dark lair, she had forgotten that

Lark loved her first. Something she'd known her whole life. "No Your Highness," he said, as he turned and walked away. "What is his problem?" Fin said, then sighed. The look on his confusing at first. Then she remembered something. He was there when Queen Rasbora blurted she was pregnant.

"Oh...Lark!" she said, realizing he must have been devastated. Fin jumped up and ran to her door. She opened it but it was too late. Lark had left the castle and retreated to the quarters where his men waited instruction.

"Lillia!" Fin yelled. Lillia ran through the halls. The walls were covered in a beautifully woven silk wallpaper. The stark green and gold colors were magnificent. She walked past a housekeeper, who washed the walls with warm water. "Please do the kitchen next. I cooked mophos and timb. The smell is in the walls. Please clean it before the queen enters. She has been ill lately. Smells affect her," Lillia said, as she continued on to the queen's chambers.

"Yes, Your Highness," Lillia said, as she entered. Fin looked flushed. He beautiful caramel colored skin pink and spotty. "Please bring me herbs. I must get well so I can meet with my men. We have to construct the weapons. I must be at my best. My strongest," she said, as she held her stomach.

"Right away," she said, as she rushed from the room to search the garden for something to ease Fin symptoms.

The herbs were a gift from Queen Rasbora. Seed planted in soil from King Nephrus had yielded a garden of exquisite and exotic plants for consumption. It was a small garden. Its contents specially grown for Fin. "Here you go. Drink this," Lillia said, as she placed the teacup to Fin's mouth. Fin sat up and took a big gulp then laid back down. "Tell Lark I need a minute. Please wake me soon. I just need to rest."

No one said a word as Fin slept for two days. Lark asked that no one wake her and he and Arfusei went about making the weapons that they would use in battle. Fin had already shown Lark and he in turn showed Arfusei and Ziege. On the third day, Fin felt better. She called the day a moment of reflection. Some of the men were allowed to leave and spend time with family before they left for battle. Word of Prince Andreus being seen in the waters had the citizens on edge. War was coming. And no one knew the outcome.

𝓕in walked the halls confidently. Her belly protruding. She could feel the baby moving. The time to give birth was near. The herbs were working. The queasy feelings and accompanying emesis had subsided. She wore a version of her father's shawl to cover herself. Her legs were bound as the men's legs were. Her belly was wrapped to protect her baby. She looked prepared to go into battle. Something done to relax her soldiers. She wasn't quite ready. She had somewhere to be.

Fin was under enormous pressure. Halacai had delivered bad news. The uaru's mentioned Eulachon men in the waters. They appeared to be checking for uaru's positioning. To see if their numbers had increased. Maybe checking to whether they were policing the waters closer to Eulachon, or just scattered and relaxed in their duties. Fin thought of the burdens of war. How the thought of it stressed the families to no end. She walked the halls with heavy burdens of her own. Soon she passed the secret room. "I am opening that room if it's the last thing I do," she said. It was next on her agenda. It would be a room of secrets no more.

Fin exited the door. Her long wavy hair flowing behind her, swaying as she moved. She walked past several guards. They stood to attention. She embodied the spirit of her father. She carried her head high as he did. The respect of her soldiers already earned. They were well aware of her fearlessness. She was going with them. A move unheard of. What they knew, of the battles that formed the lands of Madaka, did not include any mention of a female fighter. But Fin could not be deterred. Lark was nervous. He now had three people to protect and fight for. Himself, Fin and her unborn child.

"Your Highness," the soldier said, as he opened the door to the quarters. Fin walked into a large room. Forty of her strongest men stood around. Ready for their commanding leader to give the word. Lark looked her up and down. Fin ignored him. She knew he wanted her to stay back. But she couldn't.

"Did you make them? As I showed you?" she asked Arfusei. "Yes Queen," he said, as he walked towards a huge wicker basket and dumped its contents onto a table. The small spears made from melted and hammered gold, were perfect. Fin was proud of Arfusei. He labored for hours, over the last few days. And when he was done with the metal spears, he and Lark turned their attention to the branches, carving them into spears. Dozens of pointed spears, the size of a hand, came tumbling out. The men looked in awe.

"What are we supposed to do with these Your Highness," one soldier said. Fin walked over to the table and picked one up. She walked to the soldier. "Touch it! There! On the tip," she said. "Ahh," the soldier said, after touching the spear and quickly withdrawing his hand. "That is what it does. It will kill your enemy in half the time. Why waste time in hand to hand battle. It is nothing but a long and tortuous death. This is quick. And it leaves you with enough energy to take down several others. Hand to hand is tiring. Makes you tire quickly. But even better are the longer spears. Stand over there," she said, as she grabbed a wood-carved spear. Arfusei and Lark had been up all night following her instructions.

"Now. Come towards me," she instructed. The soldier looked around. He felt strange being instructed to approach the queen. "Come to me. Its ok," she said. The young male walked towards her. Fin swung the spear around. The soldier watched in awe. Fin advanced towards him, then put the spear to his belly. He gasped. Fin grinned.

"You feel that?" she asked. "Yes," he said, his eyes wide. Fin retracted the spear and took a step back. Her legs straight. Her back, lean and tall. "Again," she said. Fin did the move repeatedly as Lance showed her. She twirled it then swung it around, precisely landing it exactly where she wanted it. At the soldiers abdomen. He nodded. He understood. So did the rest of her men. Fin walked to the middle of the crowd. The men surrounded her. They were committed to the fight. To the cause. She had successfully gotten to the heart of why they were embarking on the mission. It was more than saving the individual cities. Even the people of Eulachon deserved as much. This was not a war against the people. It was army to army. No civilians would be harmed. The men stood valiantly. It was an honor to be close to her. She was more than a standard of beauty. She was the face of a new era.

"You will have two weapons at your disposal. Everyone gets a long spear and a short one. Start with the long one. It keeps your enemies at a distance. But if it becomes lodged in their bodies, or if they grab it, you will have the smaller knife to continue your attack with. You can't depend on either weapon alone. And don't waste time trying to get it back. Once you wound them, take them out. Or they will gather themselves and use your own weapon against you. Do not allow them to do that," she commanded.

Fin walked among them looking the men directly in the eyes. Something she grew up watching her father do. It came naturally to her. She was a leader. She was brave. And now she was a skilled and formidable enemy of King Andreus. "I want you to practice. And just when you think you have mastered it, go another round. Water is more dense than air. Once you have mastered the air, go into the Trojian Sea. Practice handling yourselves in water. Go in groups of a hundred or more," she said, as she smiled at Ziege. He and Arfusei would need to oversee the soldiers progress. Fin was sure they would be triumphant. The men looked ready. And their confidence was showing.

Fin continued with her speech of encouragement. She told the men they were brave and that their families were proud. She lifted the morale of everyone there. It was something her father did well. And they could see King Zander's spirit in Fin. She was now their beloved queen. They thought it was brave for her to want to go into battle with them. They preferred if she didn't. But if she did, they would protect her fiercely.

Each man vowed to die defending her. Fin was brought to tears as the men expressed gratitude for her inventive solution to help ensure victory. Fin thanked them and then asked that they visit their families once again. She understood the value of words and encouragements from loved ones. She herself had somewhere to be. She winced in pain but tried to keep from appearing weak. The confidence they had ready to fight alongside of her, was what she wanted. If they looked at her as vulnerable, it could cost them their lives. Especially if they spent time worried about her when she needed them to focus on the enemy before them.

"Fin!" Lark shouted, as he tried to catch up with her. The skies were dusk. It would be dark soon. Fin turned around and waited for him. "Where are you going?" he asked, as he neared. Fin bit her lip. His interest in her every move was unwanted. His timing was bad. She was pregnant. A small protruding belly that hardly anyone noticed but Lark. She would deliver soon. And she didn't feel like sharing the moment with him.

"Lark. I have to go. My baby is coming. Please. I will explain to you later. It is no one you know. Don't concern yourself with it. I need you to stay focused," she said. Lark became emotional. Fin's heart ached. She was torn. He loved her. Perhaps even more than Lance. But theirs was a bond built on a lasting friendship. He was family. She loved him, but it wasn't enough. There could never be. Not with Lance taking up the entire space of her heart. She belonged to Lance. And she didn't expect Lark to understand. She was connected to him mentally and spiritually. She had been with him sexually. They had done things that Lark could not fathom. Nermeins were virgins. Unable to visualize sex and lacked any desire for it. Their sexual parts were void of nerve endings. Or so it seemed.

Fin turned and walked towards the Trojian Sea. She wasn't sure how much time she had. Her baby was moving more aggressively. The feeling of twisted knots in her belly, was increasing. The baby wanted out. Fin touched her stomach. "Ok baby. Calm down. I have to take you home. You cannot stay here. I may not survive this battle. Your daddy will want you. He will love you, like I love you," she said, as she wiped a tear.

She walked to the cliffs edge. Lark stood in the same spot, watching her. He wondered where she was going. Was it someone in Panga. Maybe King Nephrus' son Osiris. Panga was on the other side of the Trojian Sea. Eulachon and Piratchu were off of the Palimora Sea. Fin looked back. She couldn't soothe him. He wanted things she couldn't give him. She stared at him. There was great distance between them. She could see enough to note the look of longing on his face. She turned and walked back. He ran to her.

"Lark. I love you. But I love him more. Please...I hope you understand. You are such a wonderful man. You are going to make someone an awesome husband," she said. Fin went towards him. She leaned into him and kissed him on the mouth. He took in the strange yet sensual touch of her lips on his, instinctively closing his eyes. She pulled away and smiled as he kept his eyes closed then slowly opened them. Fin took a few steps from him then returned to the cliffs edge. She waved then turned and leaped into the water. Lark exhaled sharply. He was shocked at his immense feelings. Fin affected him in a strange way. She could elicit feelings from him that were from a deep place inside his spirit. It was why he loved her. She awakened things in him. He was sure there was more.

The people of Eulachon lined the streets. King Andreus walked among them, surrounded by guards as he greeted his people. He needed their support. Their understanding. He was going to force the hand of their neighbor. A former ally. And it could backfire on him. But the people of Eulachon had faith in the decisions of their beloved former King Orfe's only son. And even though many of them were not in support of taking Mojarro, many stood by him and their army. Members of their family. They had to support them. It would help ensure they returned home.

"King," the woman said, as she bowed. King Andreus smiled as he walked past. Everyone he approached bowed as he passed. It was an affirmation of his rule. His way of claiming the land as its new king. Andreus saw a familiar face. A woman named Mayat who stayed on the edge of town near the sea. He walked over to her. She was in the city visiting her ailing mother. Her daughter and son looked on from the window.

"Ma'am," he greeted Mayat. She was an excellent seamstress and he hoped to get her to fashion him new attire. "Your Highness," she greeted and bowed.

Andreus looked over her shoulder. In the window stood a beautiful young woman. He wasn't sure he had ever seen her before. He was good with faces. He would have remembered. He turned his attention back to Mayat. "Would it trouble you to come to the castle tomorrow. I would like you to consider being my personal clothier," he said. Mayat was honored.

"Why yes, Your Highness. I would gladly fashion your wardrobe," she said. Andreus nodded in approval. "And who is that in the window?" he asked. "Oh. That's my daughter Guida," she said. Andreus looked over at Guida once more. He was smitten. "Great. I have a party tonight. Please attend. And bring your family with you," he said. "Of course Your Majesty," she replied.

Andreus glanced at Guida. She blushed at the attention she was receiving. He saluted her and walked away. Mayat turned and smiled at her daughter. Guida walked from the window. The king wanted her at his party. His look told her he wanted something more. Guida was anxious. She had heard about him. He was dangerous. Unpredictable. But he was handsome. And he was their king. She was going. He had her intrigued.

The king entertained Mayat and her family. She was surprised. She was unaware the attention would be on them. It turned out that they were the guest of honor. Mayat sat next to the king. Guida and her brother Shalam, on the other side. Guida clapped at the entertainment, as she and Andreus made eyes at each other most of the evening. The king rose from his chair. "Madame," he said, as he extended his hand. Guida looked at her mother. Mayat nodded and smiled. It was tradition to ask the father when a man wanted to speak with an unmarried woman. But Guida's father was not present. Andreus assumed he was dead. A man would never miss an outing with his family. And especially one where the king extended the invitation.

Guida took his hand and stood from her chair. She walked with the king. She was nervous. It was a bit overwhelming. They were followed by a few of his guards. The king gave them a visual warning. One that they knew well. They were to stay back. Give him space. And especially since he was in the company of a woman.

He took her outside to walk in his garden. One of the few viable gardens in Eulachon. He wanted to impress her. Guida was quiet. Hard to read. She looked beautiful in a thin lavender and gold dress. Her golden hair long and wavy. She favored Fin, but without the dark hair and green eyes. And there was an ethereal quality that made her stand out. He hated to admit it to himself, but she was a lot like Fin. It was the reason he was initially drawn to her. But there was also something about her that spoke to his heart. The same adoring feeling he had when he met Fin. But Fin despised him. He saw it in her eyes. He felt it in his heart that day. And there would be no changing it. So he was moving on. And Guida would be his bride.

*F*in swam up the lair and back into the now familiar waters of the Pacific Ocean. She picked up speed once she was close to the surface. Sturgeon fish and whales swam past her as she kept a steadied and fast pace towards Malibu. Suddenly a sharp pain in her lower abdomen, slowed her. Fin grabbed her belly. A whale got close and she took off again. She looked back, trying to put distance between them. Fin knew nothing about the new world's sea life. She was pregnant and refused to take any chance. But the whale seemed to be following her.

Another piercing sharp pain went through her stomach and her back. Fin once again, slowed down and grabbed her belly. She bit her lip. She panicked. She wasn't going to make it at the rate she was swimming. Fin looked back. The whale was quickly approaching. Fin hummed to calm the whale. Her melodic underwater vibrations that had a soothing effect quickly calmed the whale. She used her throat to create the vibrations that resonated with the aquatic life around her. Soon the whale slowed.

Fin put her arm out to thwart an attack. The whale touched her with the tip of its baleen, in a gesture similar to the baby Baika. Fin touched its nose. The animal seemed to be aware that she was in distress. Fin felt herself get lightheaded. *Oh no*, she thought, as her eyes became heavy and hard to keep open. She could feel herself losing consciousness. The whale began to push her. Her body wrapping naturally against its mouth as the animal swam towards land. Fin rubbed its nose as she continued to feel her strength fading. She continued to make clicking and pulsing sounds. Suddenly everything went dark.

The currents moved across Fin, taking her slowing towards the shoreline. Her limp body floated on the ocean floor near Lance's home. A mackerel got close and picked at her fingertips. Fin jolted awake and looked around. She was home. She smiled at the kindness of the whale and wondered how it knew where she was going. She was followed by all types of fish. She guessed the animal recognize her from her travels deep in the ocean. Or the times she swam around taking in the scenery between Lance's home and the area surrounding him.

Her pain was immense. She felt she couldn't move. The baby was coming. She feared passing out again, and carefully made her way to the boulders under his dock. It was dark and cold. She climbed to the top of her favorite spot. The boulders were positioned perfectly for relaxing. Stacked in a way where she could sit comfortably. She changed from her tail. It felt more natural to deliver the baby from between her legs. Although it was not the traditional way the women delivered babies.

Fin let out a yelp, as she cliched her teeth together. The pain was unbearable. Soon she heard a neighbor open his door. She could see him with a flashlight coming to investigate the noise. She submerged herself. The water would muffle her screams. Soon the man went back inside, but she could see him standing by his window.

I can't be seen. I can't...Oh no, she thought, as she opened her mouth. The water muffling the otherwise high-pitched scream she was emitting. She instinctively pushed, barely able to catch her breath. She pushed again then dropped her head back. Her legs open. Her body immersed over her head in water as she held onto the rock and pushed her baby out. Her legs wide, floating apart. She screamed another muffled sound as she laid across a large rock. Blood seeping from her vagina as the baby's head began to emerge. Fin worried the blood would attract unwanted sea animals.

She looked around. She tried to pick up on the vibrations of the water. She didn't detect any fine movements. She pushed again. She screamed Lance's name. She wondered if he was inside. Asleep. It had been a long time. She wondered if he still thought of her. Or if he'd given up on the love they shared.

Fin opened her mouth and took water into her special lungs. Her eyes closed tight, as she continued pushing. Soon her baby's head popped out. There was some relief, but then another contraction had her clawing the rocks. She looked down. All she could see was the silhouette of her baby and smiled. The dark skies and even darker waters, prevented her from viewing her precious bundle. She laid back on the rock. There was still more. It was taking too long and she feared the unknown. If the baby had more human characteristics, then it would not survive being submerged. And her screams would alert others, is she emerged from the water. It was risky. And Fin was getting weaker.

Come on baby. Come on, she said, as she prepared to bear down and push her child out. Fin bit her lip and with all her strength pushed her baby out then grabbed it. She climbed up the rocks and sat partially exposed. She held the baby on her shoulder and rubbed its back. Soon the baby let out a low muffled cry. Fin burst into tears. It wasn't how she envisioned having her first child. She was supposed to be at home with her mother and midwife by her side. She cried for Aterra.

"I wish you were here mom," she said, as she held her baby tight, frightened and unsure. She had no mothering skills. No information on how to take care of a baby. Aterra was gone. And with her, any advice she could have given. Aterra was private. Not forthcoming with a lot of things. But Fin was sure she would have helped her raise her child. She missed her mother.

The moon was bright enough to illuminate her surroundings. Fin could finally see her daughters face, once the clouds movement allowed the light to come through. She looked her baby over. It was a girl. "I'm going to call you Isla," she whispered.

Isla was a smaller version of Fin. Beautiful olive complexioned skin and a head full of dark curly hair. Her eyes the same stand out bright green color as her mothers. But under the veil of darkness, it was hard to see her clearly. Fin cried as she kissed Isla's small clinched hands. She checked her toes. Her fingers. She smelled her. It was overwhelming. But the feel and sound of her baby brought her the greatest joy. The clouds dispersed. The light of the moon gave Fin the chance to look into her baby's eyes. She smiled when she saw her baby had her hair color and eyes. They were the only ones. It was a trait that no other nermein had. It was a trait Fin felt was her own. "You are so beautiful," she said, as she continued inspecting her daughter, now that she had more light.

She could see the baby had no gills and no soft flesh between her legs. She checked again. Her baby was human. And life would have been hard for her in Madaka. The thought saddened Fin. No matter what happened, she would always need to leave Isla with Lance. There was no other option. "I can never take you back. No matter my fate, you will always be here. This is where you belong my little princess," she said to Isla.

"Shh," she whispered, as the baby became fussy. The baby began sucking on Fin's skin. She quieted. But then cried when Fin tried to adjust her and place her over her shoulder. "Why do you want to suck on my skin?" she asked, chuckling at Isla's mini sized outburst.

Fin sighed. *She's hungry already*, she thought. She remembered the time, as a child, when she saw a nermein woman covering a newborn with a cloth close to her breast. Fin allowed Isla to suck her skin. But the baby kicked and screamed out of frustration. Soon Isla made her way to Fin's breast. She stopped crying. Fin looked down at her. She squeezed her other breast and was surprised when something came out. Fin instinctively understood. She laid back Isla nursed as Fin closed her eyes. She hoped to get enough energy to climb the rocks and knock on the door. She needed Lance now more than ever. He would know what to do. And he would have wanted to be a part of the delivery. But Isla had her own schedule. She came when she was ready. An unfortunate fact of childbirth that Fin had not anticipated.

She laid her head back and held onto her baby, too weak to move. She had loss blood. She hadn't eaten. Soon her weakness took over and she closed her eyes. Isla squirmed. The coolness of the water and wind was causing her discomfort. The baby tried suckling again, but became frustrated. Fin wasn't holding her in position and she was unable to reach her breast. Her cries became louder. Fin awoke disorientated. The loss of blood affecting her. She closed her eyes again and fell fast asleep as her body began replenishing what it had lost.

Lance moaned then turned on his left side. He had to be up early. A meeting was scheduled for six in the morning. He would need to be up by four. He tossed then flipped to the other side. Soon his eyes opened. "Huh? What was that," he said. He sat up and looked out the window. It sounded like a wounded bird. Or perhaps some small mammal. Lance removed the covers and sat on the edge of his bed. The sounds continued and he became irritated. *What is that?*

It was a beautiful night. Lance had just a few hours to rest. He stood up and walked to his window. The lights along the water line were dim. He looked over at his neighbor's house. The property was dark, with only scattered exterior lights on. He remembered seeing them with large bags, leaving in a Mini Van. He assumed they were going on vacation. And he hoped the sound was not someone snooping around the property. The man had complained about someone gaining entry while he was on vacation before. Lance was prepared to go investigate.

He opened the door and stepped onto the porch off the master bedroom. The low-pitched whining noise was closer to his property. He looked down. Whatever it was, in was under his dock. Lance wiped his tired eyes and went back inside.

"What the fuck? I have to get some sleep," he complained, as he searched for a flashlight. Lance grabbed a small flashlight and exited through his patio door. He headed towards the dock and turned the flashlight on. He checked around, flashing the light onto his property as he walked towards the dock. He could hear the sound getting closer. His eyes narrowed. He hoped it wasn't an injured animal. That would mean it could die under his dock and leave a foul smell for months.

Lance stood over the sound. He flashed the light between the spaces. He could see something. *What is that?* he thought, as he got down on his knees and shined the light through the space in between the planks.

"Fin!" he shouted, as he ran to the edge and jumped into the water. He moved quickly towards her. He was excited, anxious but he also feared the worst. He hoped she wasn't injured and unable to call out. His mind couldn't make sense of why she didn't come inside. Knock on the door.

"Fin! Fin," he said, his emotions on high, as he drew closer. He didn't see the baby right away. He assumed the noise was Fin. He approached her. She looked asleep. She was holding something. Something small.

Lance got close. His eyes widened from the sight before him. It was a baby laying on her chest. Fin held her close. Her instinctive and strong motherly grip keeping Isla safe. "Fin?" Lance said, as he kissed her. He touched her cheek. Then rubbed the side of her face. The cramped position between the rocks made it hard to get to her and lift her. Lance took the baby from her. Fin woke up slightly. "Lance," she mumbled, her voice shaky.

"Fin. You came back," he said, kissing her. He looked deep into her eyes. Fin cupped her hand on his face. "She's yours," she said. Lance looked at the baby. His eyes wide. He was in shock. Tears fell from his face. "Don't cry," Fin said, as she wiped them. Lance gently touched the baby. He kissed the top of the baby's head as she suckled her mother's breast. Fin was surprised. He instincts kicked in. It suddenly made sense. "Oh. That's what she wanted," she said softly. Fin rubbed the baby's head, as she leaned against the rock. "I named her Isla," she said. Lance smiled. "She's perfect," he replied, as he took her in his arms. Fin was relieved. She was getting weaker. She had lost blood during the delivery. She needed rest.

Lance carried the baby into the house. He laid her on the couch and then returned to Fin and picked her up. "Everything's gonna be alright," he said. Fin put her arms around his neck and held on tight. She was never more sure of anything else. She would be alright. He was her hero. He always was.

Lance carried Fin to the room and laid her next to Isla. Finn immediately fell back asleep. He pulled the covers over her and then moved Isla over and placed pillows around her body to protect her. He stood, staring at his family. He was still reeling from the excitement and shock of it all. He bent down and kissed his baby. He touched her curly hair and smiled, then kissed Fin. It was all overwhelming. He had a family. New responsibilities that he looked forward to.

"I love you," he whispered, as he turned and walked out of the room, gently closing the door. He stood against it. Unable to move. *A baby*, he thought. He would have never imagined. He was a father. His dream had come true. And there was still one more dream to fulfil. But he had time. He needed Fin back healthy and strong. And then they could build a life together.

Lance took several days off while he tended to Fin. Isla had turned out to be quite a handful. She was feeding every two hours. And to give Fin rest from the demanding feeding schedule, he purchased a breast pump so he could help out with the baby's feeding. Lance didn't know much about childcare. Everything he found out was a result of Allan's input and suggestions. Allan was instrumental in his own children's care. He knew a thing or two about it. And he was happy for his brother. Lance sent him pictures of his family. Allan promised to come and visit. He helped Lance and Fin understand the baby's needs and they were grateful for him. Lance began video chatting with his brother and soon Fin joined in. She too learned a lot from Allan.

Lance sat in his home office waiting on a fax. He was helping Dave pull together the important points for an upcoming meeting. "Hey," Fin said, as she peeked in. "Come on in," he said, happy to see her up and around. It had been over a week since she had given birth to Isla. Fin has something on her mind. She didn't imagine it would take that long to heal. But now that she was back feeling her normal self, they needed to talk.

"Am I disturbing you?" she asked. "No," he said, as he closed his laptop so he could give her his undivided attention. He could feel the tension. It was in her eyes. In her voice. Something had her nervous.

Lance suddenly felt uncomfortable. His stomach was in knots. She was leaving. He could tell. She had returned to bring the baby. To give birth near him. He could see it. It was clear. And she hadn't said a word.

"You're leaving?" he asked, staring her directly in her eyes. Fin looked down. She felt guilty. She would be hurting him all over again. She knew he didn't understand. She had people dependent on her. She knew things and she needed to relay that information to her army. It was stuff he taught her. Things in regular conversation that expanded her thinking. He was instrumental in the preparedness of an army. In her world's future. And she loved him for it.

"Yes. I have to return," she said, her eyes begging him to release her again. Lance stood up. "No. No Fin," he said, as he shook his head slowly at her. "You have a life here. A family. We are a family now. You are not responsible for a whole civilization," he shouted. Fin's eyes teared. "I am! You don't understand. I am their leader now. My parents are gone. Yes Lance! Gone! I returned home to dead parents. And now it is up to me. They are lost. I have to lead the army. I have to reassure the future of my people. Please," she said, getting close in his face. She touched his chest. Her eyes staring deeply into his. It was a journey she did not want to make. But Madaka was dependent on them winning the war.

Lance stepped away from her. He sighed then rolled his eyes and walked away. It was more than his heart could take. "And what about Isla?" he asked, as he stood in the doorway. He hoped she had no plans of taking his daughter. "She's yours. She's more human. She cannot live in water.

She will always be with you. No matter what," she said. Lance 's heart tore in half. Her words sounded final. As if she wasn't sure she would be able to return. War was dangerous and unpredictable. There was no guarantee. Lance turned and walked away. His head down. Fin cried. She closed her eyes as the tears came streaming out. She couldn't leave things this way. She would be useless in Madaka. Fin wiped her face and gathered her composure. She needed to go to him. He needed her.

Lance sat on the porch off of his master bedroom. He looked out at the rocky pier that separated him from the ocean. He held his head down. His hands balled in a fist out of the frustration he felt. He thought of Isla. Fin was a wild card. She had other responsibilities. He wondered if she was in it for the long haul. If she would ever be able to separate herself from her life in the ocean.

Fin paused, then walked out onto the porch. Lance could hear her approaching from behind. She walked over to him. She got down on her knees and held his hands. Lance tried to avoid looking at her. But his love for her was too powerful.

"Tell me what to do? How can I fix this? Don't make me choose between you and thousands of people whose lives depend on me. You helped me learn things the things that I must pass on to them so we can be victorious. You did that. We are in this together. I must save them. Do you want them to perish?" she asked. "Of course not," he said, looking out at the water. It was the only thing he could say. He couldn't say he didn't care. But if he had to choose between the two, he chose her.

Lance knew that was a cruel way to think. And even crueler to say. She loved Madaka. He would have to have faith once again. And as difficult as that was, it was what he needed to do. The truth was he wasn't sure her presence was needed there. She was one person. He believed Madaka would survive somehow. That her citizens would adjust. People had a way of surviving the worst of circumstances.

"I need you to trust me," she said, as she tried to muster up a smile. He had a right to be selfish when it came to her. Their love was a selfish kind of love. No outsiders allowed. Him and her against the world. She wasn't sure she would want him leaving to fight a war he may not return from. It was an understandable feeling. "What do you want?" she asked. Lance squeezed her hand gently. She was going regardless. And so he had a few requests.

"I want to make love to you," he said. Fin chuckled. "What? Ok. What else?" she asked. Lance paused. "And I want you to marry me. Today. Now. After we make love," he said. Fin grabbed her heart. She threw her arms around him and kissed him passionately. "Yes. Yes. Yes," she said, planting kisses on him with each word. Lance was overcome with joy. He and Fin would finally seal their love with a ceremony and a promised commitment to one another.

Fin took Lance by the hand and guided him into their bedroom. Isla was still sound asleep in the spare room. Her quick paced breathing and occasional whimpers could be heard clearly on the baby monitor. Fin undressed slowly and approached him. Lance instantly reacted to the sight of her. She was sexy. Her body was phenomenal. Toned and curvaceous. Every inch of her glowing. Her smooth and supple skin felt like butter. Lance pulled her to him and kissed her passionately. He had wanted her since she'd returned. But he could tell she was too weak and hadn't completely healed from giving birth to Isla.

"Are you ok?" he asked. "Yes. I'm fine. Don't take it easy on me," she chuckled. This was his moment. She was the sexiest new mom he'd ever seen. Her body bore no trace of having been pregnant. Her stomach was flat and toned. The only sign was slightly larger breast that complimented her already superb figure. And Lance was eager to be inside her.

"We have to go. It's getting late," Fin said, as she walked into the master bathroom. Lance was fixing his bow tie. He smiled at Fin. She wore a long silk white dress that he ran to pick up after she selected it online. The department store was a forty-minute drive away. Lance made a point to grab small onesies for his newborn. The woman helped him find an all-white onesie, perfect for the occasion. He always envisioned a huge wedding with family and friends but this would have to do. They could have a second ceremony after she returned.

"You look beautiful," he said, as he kissed her. "And you look handsome my king," Fin replied. Lance put his cuff links on as Fin walked to Isla's room to check on her. She smiled at her sleeping baby. Isla looked beautiful in a white onesie and a white skull cap with flower appliques. The family was ready for the biggest day of their life.

Lance carried Isla to the car. Fin grabbed her clutch then looked herself over. She smiled at her reflection. She had mixed feelings. She was marrying the man of her dreams. But when she returned, she would need to leave him and her newborn. It was bittersweet. Her only solace was the fact that Madaka would be better. They couldn't win the war without her. And time was of the essence. She wasn't sure how much time she had before Andreus would make his way to Mojarro. She needed to leave soon. If she returned to a devastated land and no army, it would be too late. And Madaka would be under his control. Panga and Piratchu didn't stand a chance once Mojarro was taken over.

It was time. Fin's confidence was in the fact that Lance was everything. Her child had the best father. A solid man who would love and protect her. *Everything will be fine,* she thought, as she slid into her white and pearl ballet flats and walked to the car. Lance looked back. He was still securing the new car seat and making sure Isla was comfortable.

His wife was breathtaking. Her hair had turned out good. She had watched a video at least a dozen times, in order to perfect putting her hair in a bun on top of her head. She attached a rhinestone hairpin in it to dress it up. Lance was amazed. Fin picked up things from their world quickly. As if she'd always been a resident. It was hard to tell she wasn't actually from their world.

"She's good. I think I was moving her around too much," he said. "Why do you say that?" she asked. "Because she's awake," he replied, giving Fin a devilish grin. Fin asked him to be gentle. She wanted Isla asleep for the ride. "That's just great honey. Now I have to ride in the back with her just to keep her quiet," she said, as she walked around to the other side. Lance shut the door and got in. He started the car and slowly backed out of his driveway. Headed to the courthouse to get married.

******

Fin and Lance hugged for what seemed like an eternity. They laid staring into each other's eyes, no words exchanged, as they took each other in. He wasn't ready to let go. Fin touched him gently. She needed to feel him. She wanted to remembered what he felt like. What he smelled like. She'd spent the last two hours holding Isla and rubbing the soft ringlets on her head as she laid in a fetal position with Lance behind her. She needed more time.

Lance watched television as Fin lay on his chest. He tried to remain calm. To show Fin he supported her. It was important that she go back home knowing he was standing behind her. She needed to have a clear mind. She needed to focus on what she was doing. Lance knew that guilting her to stay would only weigh on her. Make her weak. And mistakes could be made.

"I'm ready to go now. Keep our baby safe. I will be back soon," she said. Lance kissed her forehead. "I will. We will be fine. You just make sure you come back to me," he said. Fin knew it was hard for him. She raised out of the bed and walked to the bathroom. She closed the door and cried, away from sight. A quick sprint of tears that she quickly wiped away and then found her strength within.

"Ok. Time to go," she said to herself. Fin opened the door. Lance was standing on the other side holding Isla. Fin kissed the baby then him. She walked out the room and down the stairs. *Don't look back. Just go,* she thought, as she walked to the door. She slid the glass door open and walked out onto the dock. Lance followed close behind. Fin got to the end and without hesitation, jumped into the water. She swam out a short distance then turned around. Lance waved. He could see her under the moonlight. Fin got one last look at her family and then dipped into the water and headed back to Madaka. Fierce and strong as ever.

Fin swam hurriedly, close to the ocean's floor. A journey she could now do with her eyes closed. She knew every landmark. Every sunken ship. This world was now her home. But before she could make it her permanent residence, Madaka needed her guidance. Fin was near the lair. She pushed onward. Soon she came upon the brine layer and entered. She descended into the long trench until she came upon another layer. The one that covered the lair. Her entry into her home.

Fin swam down the long tunnel until she emerged through the seaweeds and into the dunes. She could see the surrounding area. The bright yellow and orange lava lighting the way. She swam quickly through the heat and gases and emerged from the other side.

I'm here, she thought, as she reached the rock that sat just beneath where her home was. Fin swam up and scaled the rock. She reached the top and walked proudly towards the castle. Arfusei and Ziege were standing with their men. They were both now leaders of Fin's vast army. Panga and Piratchu had sent their men. The men pointed. "It's Fin! She has returned," Ziege said. Arfusei and several of the men ran to her. Fin was happy to see her men. She ran to meet them half way. "Queen," Arfusei greeted. "Arfusei. Ziege. Clem," she said, as she looked at her men. Their love for her was obvious. Fin smiled as she scanned the faces of the men. She was personable. Vulnerable. It was refreshing. It was magnetic. The men didn't understand their attraction to her. It wasn't sexual. Their spirits had been voided of such desires. But there was something about her that drew them to her. Fin was awakening them. She could see it. But they were not ready for the total awakening of their souls. That would come later.

"Where is Lark?" she asked. "He has a group of men in the water. They are practicing in the Trojian," Ziege stated. Fin was pleased. Things were moving along. "Has anyone heard back from Halacai?" she asked. Arfusei shook his head slowly. Fin sighed. Halacai was their eyes and ears. He had acted as prime minister for the cities. And none used his intellect and inside information as much as Eulachon. Halacai had seemed invaluable to them. He was the voice of reason for any city who felt undervalued or treated unfairly. It was the most coveted role of all positions within the kingdoms.

But Andreus had tried to use his services to gain insight for purposes other than political. He was stacking information to use against the city. And Fin was his target. Something she was now aware of. The marriage was a marriage he pushed for with a more sinister agenda involved.

Something his own father was not aware of. And so here they were. Prepared to answer the call of a madman with no one to stop him. No one, except Fin.

The waters were calm. Movement was easier to pick up when the waves were less prominent. Halacai feared being detected by uaru soldiers. He swam close to the surface, attempting to go undetected. He got close to Eulachon and slowed. He dipped down and descended into the depths of the Palimora and looked around. No uaru was near. His travels were successful. He couldn't explain his unannounced entry into Eulachon territory. He would be forced to turn around, escorted by at least a dozen of them.

Halacai swam back up and peeked his head above the water. He saw men gathering at the water's edge. He saw King Andreus walking past them. His face appearing tight. Serious. He looked to be in serious talks. The men stood to attention. Rows of them. A large group, as if preparing for something grand. Halacai stared intensely. Andreus had his *lieutenants in command* walking through the rows. It was a spectacular and scary sight. The men looked menacing. Intimidating. "I must warn them," Halacai said, as he turned and swam back to Mojarro.

Fin sat alone in her room. The time was near. She felt it. Andreus was a restless man. He was coming. She thought of Lance and Isla. She thought of Zander and Aterra. "Oh dad. Mom. This is terrible. I am trying to look unafraid. But I am. I wish you were still here. Dad…You would know what to do. You were so brave. So smart. And mom, we had so much more to discover about one another. So much to talk about. You would have adored Isla. She's so special. She looks just like you. She is so beautiful. I wish you could have met her," she said, as she looked out at the sky.

Fin reflected on her past. On her mother. All the good and bad times. And all the secrets. Suddenly a thought came to her. The room. It was still locked. Its contents still a mystery. She didn't know why she still walked past it. Not willing to get inside. Every time she looked at the door, she could hear his voice reminding her that the room was off limits.

"Guards," she shouted. Clem came running. He opened her door. "Yes, Your Highness," he replied. "Clem. There is something urgent I need. Please get Lark if he has returned. Or Ziege. Please have one of them come to me," she said. Clem left her room immediately and went behind the castle.

"It's getting late. Can you have the team come out the water. Tell them that's enough for the day. They need to rest," Lark said to one of the soldiers from Panga. A man named Darr, who was proving to be a great addition to their army. He was quick, strong and follow every command without any hesitation. "Yes sir," he said, as he turned and headed for the Trojian.

Lark saw Clem approaching. "Sir. The Queen needs your assistance," he said. Lark walked past him and back to the castle. Clem lagged behind, following him back in case he was still needed. "Queen," he said, as he approached Fin. "Don't call me that. Not you," she said, as she turned and walked away. Lark followed her. "What do you need Fin. I have to address the men when they return. Clem said you needed to see me," he said. "Yes. Follow me," she replied.

Lark walked closely behind. "And what am I to call you?" he asked, the conversation now uncomfortable with Clem around. "Fin. You call me Fin. Everyone else can address me by title. Not you," she repeated. Lark continued to follow her. He smiled out of her view. He liked her correction of his formal way of greeting her. They weren't formal. But he wondered. And it was something they'd never spoke on.

"I need this door opened. I have looked everywhere for the key. I cannot find it," she said, looking Lark directly in the eyes. "What?" he said, confused as to what she was asking. "Break it down Lark. That's what I am saying. I need you to kick it in," she replied. Lark narrowed his brow. "You want me to destroy the door?" he asked. "Well...Yes," she replied. Lark looked at Clem then back at Fin. "This is a strange request. And I am uncomfortable doing it Fin. I cannot do that. This is the room the King said was off limits. I can't," he said. "Clem..." she said, looking at him and hoping he would agree to kick the door in. Clem hesitated. "Clem...I order you to kick this door in."

Clem was caught in the middle. But she had ordered him. Lark paced the floor. He didn't like it. He wasn't sure how he felt about it. Clem moved in position and braced himself. He raised his leg. And with a quick thrust forward, kicked the door, causing a piece of metal to fall off.

"Again," Fin ordered. Clem kicked again, and the power of his leg opened the door slightly. Clem looked at Fin and then kicked again. The door fell inward and to the floor. Lark went inside the room and moved the door to the side. Fin walked in behind him. She looked around. It was unbelievable. "Leave me now please," Fin said. Lark paused, then exited with Clem behind him.

The room was enchanting. The walls covered in orange taffeta applied with glue. It gave the room a multidimensional feel. The ceiling was adorned with orange and green leaves. It was exquisite. "Wow," Fin said, as she looked around. A bag on a table caught her eye. It was a familiar item. She had seen one before. Back in the new world at a plaza Lance took her to. Fin walked over to the bag slowly. She was in disbelief. It was not of their world. "What!" she said, as she got closer. The details undeniable. Small bears lined the top half of the pink and brown bag.

Fin unzipped it. She peeked in. She gasped at the items. The bag was filled with items that were not from Madaka. Items she recognized. Lance had purchased all the same things for Isla. The items were from Earth. The world above them. Fin pulled the baby bottle and pacifier out. She sat them on the table.

"Whose stuff is this? Where did it come from?" she said in a low voice. Inside the bag were baby clothes, a pink bib, a white skull cap and crumbled old diapers. A woman's clutch, jewelry and a wallet were also inside.

"No. This can't be," Fin said. Still in disbelief. She opened the wallet. It had been destroyed from the dried salt water. Inside were tattered papers and several pictures. One picture had been remarkably well preserved. The one in the middle was in the best condition. Images on the others were hard to see. Fin stared at the picture of the man, woman and child. A child with red hair and freckles. A baby that looked a lot like her mother. A tear rolled down her cheek.

"Mom," Fin mumbled in a breathless and fading voice. Her pain wiping out any strength she had. She rubbed the outline of Aterra's face. She stared at the grandparents she never met. It all made sense. Fin was flooded with emotion. She understood Aterra's silence. Her inability to swim. Her reason for avoiding the water. Fin wished her mother would have talked to her. It would have been ok. She would have kept her mother's secret. And as Fin realized who her mother was, another realization was made. That she too, was human. Part nermein and part human. She smiled. Her and Lance had a lot more in common than she could have imagined. He wasn't so different from her. Her bloodline traced back to the new world. Fin wondered if everyone in Madaka had a human connection. She wondered what happened that resulted in their differences. She could only guess.

She could not have imagined her history. That they were the offspring of gods and demigods banned to the sea. There was a human connection. Fin felt it. It was becoming more evident in the way her soldiers responded to her. Something that was taken from them was still there. Hidden in the depths of their souls. It was in their eyes. They just needed to be awakened. There was a void. Fin gasped. This had to be the result of the sins of our forefathers. *We were punished. Sent here. And stripped of the ability to feel deeply*, she thought, as she looked off. A revelation spoken to her from her great grandmother. Her guardian angel. Fin wasn't sure why the thoughts came together so vividly. As if told to her directly. But she knew what had happened. She could see it clear as day. And she had a new found duty. A responsibility to her people.

Fin placed the items back in the bag. "Clem!" she shouted. After several minutes she could hear him running down the hall. "Yes, Your Highness," he replied, out of breath from the sprint. "Please have someone put the door back on. Shut it. Then seal it. And have Lark gather the men. I need to meet with them."

The lieutenants of her army wondered what the meeting was about. Fin said nothing as she walked from the castle, looking like a woman with a lot on her mind. She approached the large assembly. It was men from three cities. Among the crowd was the Pangian and the Piratchuian army. Several thousand men. Too many to address individually. Her message would need to be relayed by men designated to get her words to those not within hearing distance.

Lark stood close, confident in what Fin would say. She had become a wise and fierce leader in a short time. It was obvious that she was affected by someone on the outside. He wondered who had her so confident as a woman. Who had her heart. She was there, but she was also absent. Fin looked at him. She glanced at Arfusei, Ziege and Clem. Missing was Sparrow. She wished he was there. He was older and wise. He knew things that she wished she had the privilege of learning. He had been in war. And he was her father's friend and greatest protector. But she had her own confidants. Arfusei was also one of her father's closest guards. So was Lark. Clem was the youngest and newest member of the army. But he was loyal all the same.

These were the men who would lead the others. The key players of her power. The main men in her life who would need to be the first ones freed from what bound them. An invisible shackle. Unlocking it meant an understanding of themselves. And intimate knowledge of love and protection. It would make them more fierce. They would have greater purpose. Instead of doing what was expected of them and fulfilling a duty. She needed them to fight from the heart. To fear death. It would make them more acute. They would be more powerful fighters.

"I called everyone here because I have something important to say before we head to the Palimora Sea. I am looking at the faces of many brave men. Your courage is outstanding. Your fearlessness admirable. And as we set out on a mission to save our cities, we must first reflect on what this battle is really about. It is more than protecting the loss of assets. Or saving our way of life. This is about our love for this great world. Our love of family. It is bigger than the individual. We do this as one. I know you hear me. But you don't really understand me. Your idea of unity is clouded. We are like ants. Have you ever paid attention to them. They exist as one. But there is no witnessed love between them. When one dies, they continue on. Walking over it. Like discarded trash. They move the dead out of their way. And they continue working towards a cause. Survival," she said, as she paced slowly from one side of the neatly divided rows to the other.

"I am here to tell you that there is more. Our culture shuns physical contact. Our eyes have been closed. But if you touch, you can feel. And if you feel, you will have desires. Life will have a different meaning," she assured. Fin walked to Arfusei. He furrowed his brow then looked at Lark.

"Hold out your hand," Fin said, as she extended hers. Arfusei glanced at the faces of his men. He became nervous. "It's okay. Touch my hand," she said. Arfusei slowly raised his hand. Fin stepped close to him. She took his hand and held it firm. He stared into her eyes. Lark's feeling went from intrigue to jealousy. Fin smiled at Arfusei. He closed his eyes. He was overcome with a new sense of awareness. He opened his eyes. Fin got closer. She hugged him then leaned back, keeping her hands on his shoulders. "Do you see?" she asked. Arfusei nodded. A tear came to his eye. Fin could see he was aware. She stepped back. She could see Lark was upset. She would deal with him after the men were enlightened. He was already aware. He just didn't know it. She had inadvertently awakened him long before this day. His jealousy told her that.

The men stood around in shock. Arfusei looked around for his younger brother Rotiro. He spotted him and walked to him. Rotiro became nervous. Arfusei held out his hand. Rotiro reluctantly reached out after a nod from Fin. It would be disrespectful not to follow her lead. But he was uncomfortable with the idea of touching his brother.

"It is okay. You will see," he said to him. Rotiro raised his hand higher. Arfusei took it. Rotiro felt an overwhelming sense of self. He smiled. Fin watched as one by one, the men shook each other's hand. A domino effect that started from one enlightened spirit to another. Fin was the daughter of Zander. Who was the son of Zaire. Who was the son of Veltorro and the grandson of Spurgis. A line of descendants from the founding god and goddess of Madaka, Hershiel and Contessa. And the only one with pure human DNA in her blood. Not altered, as was her people. She was anointed. Her awakening would be the catalyst. Her touch, their liberation.

"Their ready," she said to Ziege, as she touched his shoulder. She looked intensely at him. He looked back into her eyes. A connection was made. Fin walked away as her army became acquainted with one another. They would be ready for war. But not before each man was shown his heart. His soul.

"Is the queen in?" Halacai said, his head shrouded in a loose hood. Clem showed him in. He escorted the odd man to Fin's meeting chambers. "Your Highness," he announced, as he knocked lightly on her door. "Come in."

Clem opened the door and Halacai walked in. Fin sat at her father's throne. Now her throne. Her men standing around her, all in deep discussion. They ceased their talks when Halacai entered. Lark, Ziege and Arfusei had been meeting, off and on, all morning. They were updating Fin on the progress. Her army was ready.

"Yes," she said, as she as she turned and looked at him. Halacai approached but was stopped by Lark. A face he had known all his life. Lark new him well. Halacai didn't understand the change. The need to hold him back first. "He may approach," Fin said. Lark moved from his path.

"It is about Eulachon," he said, looking around at the men. He wasn't sure it was ok to speak in front of the guards. Fin assured him he could. "These are the men who will face the men of Eulachon. You may speak in their presence," she replied. Arfusei looked at Ziege. The men grinned. King Zander met in private. And delivered the news to his men. Only Lark was allowed such privileges. But Fin was a different kind of leader. Her men loved her inclusion of them. They were honored that she had trust and faith in them.

"Your highness. Men are gathering at the shore. They are preparing to enter the water," he said. His voice shaky. His eyes darting beneath the cover of his hood. "How many?" she asked. "All of them," he replied.

Lark looked at his men. Fin stood up. She felt instantly light headed. Her strength had drained from her. But she stood strong. She would not let them see any weakness. "Gather the men. Its time," she said.

Fin wrapped her legs. She put her father's vest on. It was large and hung off of her, but she couldn't go into battle without it. "Umm," she whimpered as she felt a sharp pain. It was a familiar feeling. "She looked off. "No. Nooo," she said. A knock on her door startled her. "Yes," she said. Lark opened the door. "They're ready," he said. Fin looked back. "Ok. I'm ready," she said. Lark looked at her. She didn't look good.

"We don't need you. Please stay here. Address the citizens. Your job is here. Keeping everyone calm. I promise to send word back," he said. Fin walked to him. She smiled. He was the kindest and most caring man in Madaka. She was sure he would have won her heart if it weren't already spoken for.

"I must fight. This started with me. And even though he has married, he still holds a grudge. He still wants the land that would have been his. And he killed my father. I can't stay back. Don't ask me to," she said, turning from him. Fin looked herself over in the mirror. Her reflection not as clear as the refined mirrors of the new world. But Madaka had been efficient in their own right. It was made of aluminum and other naturals metals. Metals found in Panga and in the mountains all over their world. Lark watched her get ready. Fin turned back to him.

"I know how you feel. You have cared about me your whole life. And now you worry about my safety. Part of me doesn't want to go because I know you won't be able to focus with me there. But you must. Because I won't be any good to the people here, knowing that you are out there. I will be alright," she said, as she leaned forward. Lark grabbed her arm. Fin held her stomach.

"You are ill. Fin! No! You cannot go," he said. Fin smiled. "I'm not sick. I'm pregnant. And I am going. Now go. I want the men in rows of five. Long lines so the people can see their loved ones once more. In case they don't return."

Lark bit his lip. This was a terrible way to start. He was worried. And worse, he was more jealous. He wondered who she had gotten close to. Who she allowed to father another child.

Fin waited for him to leave. The pain bearing down. It was happening too soon from what she recalled. She grabbed her stomach. "Ahhh," she moaned. The pain soon eased. Fin stood straight. A new fear surfaced. She had a child to save. Lark was right. She couldn't go. She and Lance had another baby on the way. She rubbed her belly. Memories of the last time they made love melted her heart.

"I have to get you back home. Okay… I guess I won't go into battle. But I will get them there," she said, as she turned and left out. She planned to pull Lark, Arfusei and Ziege to the side and tell them. It would be welcomed news. They didn't want her there. She would be a distraction.

The streets of Mojarro were filled with citizens. Fin walked front and center, her men surrounding her. Families stood along the sides cheering them on. Fin waved. She was the brave face of the war. Her people admired her perseverance. Men smiled as they passed their families. Some reached out and touched their loved ones. Fin watched as some people looked perplexed. Others seemed to come alive. Fin promised herself that she would stay behind and enlighten them as well. It would be great if when the men returned, their families had a new found love and connection to them. The large and intimidating presence of the Mojarroian Army was fascinating. They walked with a purpose. There was something different about them.

Lark, Ziege and Arfusei proudly led them to the Palimora Sea. The men picked up the pace. They walked in, their powerful legs splashing in the water. They walked until the water hit their chest. Fin stayed with them. She walked in side by side with Lark then suddenly stopped. He looked back at her. Arfusei waved. Her men continue past her. They looked straight ahead. They were focused. Fin was proud. She stayed until the last few men walked by. Fin went in further. She pushed off the sand and swam further in, never changing to her tail. She needed one last look before the battle. Some men would not return. The brutal reality of war. She floated, arms extended, watching the men disappear into the darkness.

"Are you alright Your Highness?" the guard asked. "Yes. I need to address the people. Then I need to rest. I'm tired," she said. Fin walked back into town, flanked by a few guards designated to stay back for her protection. She made her way to the stage her father used, to address the citizens.

She hesitated as she looked around at the sullen faces. She began speaking. She told them about their past. As much as she had figured out. What she believed happened. And how they could be better. Men women and children were affected by Fin's words. Her instructions. It was simple. Touch one another to come alive. That something would be revealed in the touch. Husbands touched their wives. Then their children. Eventually, wives kissed the men. Then hugged and kissed their children. The power that had them unaware of themselves, had been broken. But their new found awareness opened their hearts up. They cried for their sons at war. Fin had to speak with families one on one, and in small groups to give hope. She tried to answer their questions. Eventually the citizens comforted one another. They talked among each other. Fin was drained by the time she returned to the castle. It was the longest and toughest day of her life. And all she could think about was Lance, Isla and now the new baby she was carrying.

12

A New Dawn

The waters swelled with the bodies of men swimming towards Eulachon. King Andreus and his men were also in the water, making their way to Mojarro. The combined force of waves from separate directions, caught the attention of the uaru soldiers. They could feel the shift in the currents.

"Hey something big is coming," one uaru said to another. "I know. Alert the others," the captain said. The men swam around looking for the source of the waves. Lark and his men slowed as they neared the mid-point. Ziege swam down to stand with the men closer to the floor of the sea. Arfusei swam next to Lark. He had already decided that Lark's life was important. He was close to Fin. Possibly their next king. Fin had a fondness for him. And so, he would fight to the death to protect him. And to protect his baby brother Rotiro. The men had an advantage. They had weapons and they had heart. It meant more to them. And they had each other's back.

The uaru saw the Mojarroian soldiers in the water. They swam to the men on the end. "Who is in charge here? Why are you in the water?" he asked. "You need to speak with one of our lieutenants," he replied. The uaru soldier swam past, hundreds of soldiers looking for Lark. He was well known. The uaru knew Lark was the leader of the Mojarroian army. He spent many days and nights looking for the princess when she first went missing. He even spent the last days as one of them.

"Lark," the soldier shouted. Lark left the line and swam to him. "What is going on? Why do you have so many soldiers in the water. I heard the princess is back. Is that what this is about?" he asked. "She is our queen. The last battle that killed our king and ultimately our queen, was just the beginning. Now that Prince Andreus is king, he is attempting a takeover. We are here to defend our territory," he revealed.

The uaru soldier was surprised. It was a bold move. They would have to be prepared to fight as well. Their job was to protect the waters. And keep the citizens from unapproved entry into each other's land. This was a breach of gargantuan proportions. "I will alert my men. We stand with you. If King Andreus shows up. And has no good explanation for his presence, we will assume he is now an enemy of Madaka.

Prince Andreus' senses were keen. He could smell the men. The water current seemed interrupted. "They are here," he said, as they neared the midpoint. Lark was keen as well. He was adept to the Palimora sea. He had spent time there. He was accustomed to the environment. The animals. The feel of the water. His attention perked up. Ziege snarled. Arfusei got in position. Lark could see the men. Soon the others could see them.

King Andreus yelled to his men to blast through and kill any man in their path. Lark and his men held their spears by their sides. They were waiting for their enemy to get closer. The wood had no reflective qualities. It would not be seen by the men until it was too late. "Get ready," Lark said. His hand firmly on his spear.

"Attack," Lark shouted, as his men swam forward and lunged with their spears. Men crashed into one another. The force sending ripples through the water. Spears jousted upward. Many men mortally wounded, as the pointed spears entered into their bellies. Men began floating to the bottom by the dozens. King Andreus stayed back. He could see his men succumbing quickly to something. Blood filled the water. His men were dying swiftly. No one was really fighting. Just thrusting movements from the Mojarroian soldiers and blood. Some of Andreus' men turned the tables on the opposing force and removed the spears from their bodies. They used them in the same manner, wielded the weapons against Lark and his men. Men suffered. The sounds of their pain and dying last words were echoed throughout the water. The smell of their blood picked up by predators and scavengers from miles away.

Lark looked through the crowd. A soldier came at him aggressive and swiftly. He pulled his knife and stuck it into the man's abdomen. He pulled it out. His eyes on Andreus. He sneered at his enemy. He tried to swim to him, but was grabbed from behind and trapped in the soldiers firm grip. Lark tried to wiggle away, but the soldier had him. Arfusei was fighting a large soldier. He was hard to kill. He had stabbed the man twice yet he still had energy and strength.

The man swung his tail knocking Arfusei back a few meters. Arfusei swam towards the man, his knife still in the man's back. He pulled it out and stuck it in again. The man was weakened. Arfusei looked back in Lark's direction. He was losing the battle. Arfusei pulled a second knife. He was not supposed to have it. Too much metal would weigh them down. A sharp wide blade molded out of gold and aluminum. A spare, he was glad he had. He swam over. He stuck the blade in the soldier's neck. He turned around. The look of pain on his face affecting Arfusei deeply.

He was the enemy yet Arfusei felt sorry for him. This was a war they had brought about. It was not necessary. An act of vengeance and greed had their king sacrificing many for his own, for his personal satisfaction. Arfusei stared the man down. He watched the life drain from the young man's face. A man young enough to be his son. Lark nodded and went after Andreus. Arfusei turned to check on Rotiro. A blade from a spear he fashioned entered his groin. Lark heard his cry and turned around. "Nooooo," he shouted, as he swam back to his wounded lifelong friend. Lark removed his blade and swiped it across the soldier's throat, opening his neck and killing him. He grabbed Arfusei.

"Hold on. I will get you home," he said. He held onto him and then ordered a soldier to take him back. "We can't lose him. Take him back. And tell the queen we are still battling. We are winning. But it is far from over. I have to find Andreus."

The soldier grabbed Arfusei by the arm and swam back. Lark dropped down to the bottom. He swam slowly. Looking around at all the dead bodies. Some were the bodies of his enemy. Some were the familiar faces of his own. Lark was devastated. It had been a hard-fought battle. There were many dead men from Mojarro. More than he expected to lose. As he continued looking around, he noticed a soldier with his clothing missing. Lark stopped. He looked around. It was a soldier from Panga. But the uniform was Mojarroian. Lark's mind raced.

"Oh no," he said, as he took off for the castle. He believed Andreus removed it and was now wearing it to gain access to the castle.

Andreus swam close to the surface and made it past the slaughter. He dropped down to the bottom and continued swimming towards Fin's home. He had walked his men into a tough battle that numbers alone did not win. Angered and ready for the ultimate revenge, he hoped to get to Fin. She was now his mortal enemy. He swore to kill her slowly. He had lost many men. He wondered about the items they used to take his men out so swiftly. Some of his soldiers retreated. The battle was lost. But it was not over.

Lillia ran into Fin's room. "Your Highness. Its Arfusei," she frantically said. "What!" Fin said, as she awakened from a deep sleep. Fin jumped out of bed and ran behind Lillia to the kitchen. The soldier stood over him. "Get the healer. Quick!" she ordered. The soldier ran out of the castle, headed to the home of a local medicine woman.

"Which herb is for blood?" she asked Lillia. Her lady's maid was too shocked to answer. Fin knew Lillia had a long-standing crush on Arfusei. He never seemed to notice. And Fin felt sorry for her. He would notice now. He was an awakened soul.

"Lillia," she blurted. "Huh," she answered. "Get me herbs. He will be fine. He needs our help. Focus! Go get the things you used when the guard got attacked and injured by the Tetra," Fin said. Lillia ran to the garden.

"Arfusei? Can you hear me? Say something. Please," she pleaded. "You can't leave us. We need you. Lark needs your guidance. And Lillia has always loved you. Come on. Don't die," Fin cried.

"Okay. I found everything but willow and blackroot," Lillia noted. "What does that mean. Will it work without those?" Fin asked. "I don't know Your Highness. I will try," she replied.

Lillia grabbed bedding and covered Arfusei. They decided to leave him on the kitchen floor. The healer arrived and made a potion of her own. She rubbed herbs on his wounds then poured some in his mouth. The only thing to do was wait. Fin stood back. She felt weak. "I must lay down. Please take care of him. Wake me if anything happens," she said. "Yes. I will," Lillia replied. Fin returned to her room and crawled back in her bed. She fell asleep as soon as her head hit the fabric filled pillow. Lillia lay on the floor next to Arfusei. Her hand on his hand. Praying for his recovery. She too had been awakened by the touch of Fin.

"Your Highness," Ziege said, as he stood over Fin. He had a deep gash on his arm and bite wounds to his legs, but otherwise was fine. Fin opened her eyes then sprung up. "What happened?" she asked. Ziege smiled.

"Is it over? Is it really? We won?" she asked. "Yes, Your Majesty. The war is over. We lost many men. They lost more. Many of them retreated," he said. Fin smiled. "Oh Ziege. That is wonderful."

Fin's smile turned to a look of concern. Ziege looked upset. Something was wrong. Fin shook her head slowly. "No. Don't say it. No! Where is he?" she asked. Ziege continued to shake his head. "I don't know. There are many bodies on the sea floor. We tried to locate him. Clem is among them. But there was too many to find Lark. Plus Tetra came. Many of them. They began to eat the dead. We tried to stop them. Then we tried pushing some of the soldiers into the ground. We were able to bury some. But we never located him. I am sorry Your Highness. We will wait and go back once it is safe."

Fin grabbed her vest and a knife. "No. He is alive. He is strong. Smart. He is out there alone. Maybe wounded. We can't look later. I must find him now," she said. "Your Highness no! I will take men back in the morning. It is dark. You won't be able to see clearly unless there are sea animals around to light the way. Please," he begged. Fin walked past him, stubborn and determined. "No one knows the bottom of the Palimora like I do. I will go," she said, as she ran to the door.

Ziege ran to the soldiers quarters. He ordered two of his best soldiers to help him catch up with Fin and aide her in the recovery of Lark. Most of his soldiers were either injured or fatigued from battle. It was a difficult request. The men needed rest. Food. But the queen was already on her way.

The water was black. Fin wondered how she would see the surface, let alone the bottom. "Come on. Let there be life," she said, as she dove in and changed to her powerful blue tail. Fin swam, staying close to the bottom. Illuminated sea animals were scattered about. Not enough to light the area. It would be a difficult task. She hoped he could hear her. She planned on getting close to the area and then calling Lark's name until she found him.

Andreus hung around until he was sure the soldiers were gone. He had a plan. One that he hoped would work. He had everything he need. "I have no army. So, they will have no queen," he angrily promised himself. He cared about nothing but revenge. His new wife was a few months pregnant. He had other soldiers that relied on his leadership. But his evil heart had consumed him. His desire to force his ways on the world had him throwing it all away. He was willing to die, trying to kill Fin. She would be surrounded by guards. They would tear him apart if they caught him. But he blamed her. And so, she had to die.

"Please be safe," Fin said to herself as she searched the sea floor for Lark. He could be anywhere. She knew it was a long shot. But she could not sit by, knowing he was in trouble. "Lark!" she yelled out. "Lark!" she shouted again. The water seemed peaceful. It was hard to imagine a war had just been fought there. Soon the faint smell of blood filled the surrounding area. It was heavy. Fin was crushed. She could tell a lot of men had died. It was unnecessary. She felt bad for the families. And she could only hope Andreus was among the dead. She didn't think to ask Ziege in her frantic haste. Lark was a priority.

"Lark!" Fin continued to shout. She yelled his name every few meters and listened intently for some sort of response. Soon she could feel a change in the current. Something was coming. It was approaching fast. Fin smiled. It was Lark. He heard her.

"Lark! It's me, Fin. I thought you were dead," she said, as she rushed to him. Sediment had been stirred by the movement. The illumination of sea creatures weren't enough. Fin squinted as the sediment got into her eyes. She called his name again. She wondered why he didn't answer. She hoped he wasn't injured. Suddenly an arm grabbed her around the neck. It was Andreus. He tightened his grip as Fin chocked and squirmed to get away.

"Princess. How nice. You read my mind," he said, as he took pleasure in squeezing the life out of her. Fin struggled to pull away as he laughed at her efforts. "So, you stay behind while a slaughter commenced. One that you commanded. At least your father was brave enough to enter the water and face his enemies. You women... Natural born cowards," he snarled.

Fin could feel herself losing focus. She feared for her life and the life of her unborn child. Andreus had her in a tight grip. She was unable to speak. Unable to yell out. Fin thought of using telepathy to communicate. She hadn't used it since she was a child. She never had the need. Nermeins had the ability to speak under water. And so, it was an unused talent. And not all nermeins had the capability.

She tried talking to Andreus. She tried pleading for her life. But it didn't work. He continued to taunt her using his voice. *Oh Lark. Please be ok. Please*, she thought. Fin had never tried telepathy with Lark. She was unaware if he had the gift.

Fin felt herself slipping away. She suddenly dug her sharp nails into his hand, severing a finger. "Ahh," he blurted, as he released his grip. She tried to swim away but he chased her down and swung his tail around knocking her back. Fin was disoriented from the blow. Andreus smirked then attacked her tail and fin. He ripped her fin into shreds and dug his razor-sharp nails into her tail, badly damaging it. Fin yelled out in pain. Already in a weakened state, she didn't have the energy to flee or protect herself from harm. It didn't take much effort for Andreus to severely wound her.

"This blue tail you love so much. That you think distinguishes you from the others. Look at it now. You will never be able to use it again," he teased. Fin could not see the damage. But she could feel the immense pain coming from her lower half. "Please! I have done nothing to you," she said. "You have. It all started the day you shunned me. And now you will pay. Too bad so many had to suffer," he replied.

Andreus prepared to finish her. Fin could barely see him. She felt herself getting weaker. She was losing blood. She prayed to the gods to spare her child's life. That she would sacrifice herself for the life of her child. She closed her eyes. Ready to die. She hoped Lark would happen upon her and take the baby from her body. "You'll die slowly like my men.," he said, as he approached her. "Please. I am with child. You started this war. Why are you so determined to make me suffer?" she asked. Andreus slowed. "With child. Then the child will die with you," he angrily said, as he charged her.

Suddenly Lark emerged from the sediment. He swung his powerful tail around, smacking Andreus in the head. The blow stunned Andreus. He shook it off and charged at Lark. The men tussled against the ground. Lark grabbed for his knife. It was missing from the holder. Andreus grabbed him and twisted around him, wrapping his arms around his neck. Lark struggled to break free. "Is she worth dying over. Are you to blame? Are you the father of her child? You wanted her? I saw it in your face, the first day I met you. It's you. And you will die with her," he said, as he tightened his grip.

Lark glanced at Fin. She was floating on the bottom. Her body bobbing with the currents. He felt himself succumbing to Andreus' strong hold. He looked back at Fin.

They couldn't die together. It seemed unfair when they never even lived together. As one. He loved her. And Andreus was partially right. He did want her. He needed to see her once again. He was responsible for her. He promised Zander that he would take care of her. "Fin," he mumbled. The sight of her lifeless body enraging him.

Lark twisted around and grabbed Andreus by throat. The men had each other. It was now a match of wills. Who would stop breathing first. Who would black out first. The men stared into each other's eyes, enraged, as they tightened their grips on each other's neck. Andreus began closing his eyes but his grip stayed firm. Lark growled. Andreus' grip began to loosen. Ziege swam up from behind and punch Andreus in the spine. The force, injuring him severely. His body floating as he started to move again. He was coming back around. He tried to swim away. But was grabbed by the neck once more. Lark swam quickly towards an area he knew well. The Palimora Sea blades. He remembered seeing two Tetra there. They were feeding on a carcass.

Andreus was too weak to fight back. His weakened body being pulled by Lark to the sea blades. An area that was a known habitat for Tetra. When he neared, he bit a chuck from Andreus' neck and tossed him in. He floated backwards.

He waited. The fresh blood caused a frenzied attack. "Ahhhhh," Andreus yelled out, as the Tetra bit chunks of him until he was consumed. Lark swam away. He had to get to Fin.

"Fin!" he said, as he took her from Ziege's arms. "You are weak. Injured. Let us carry her," Ziege said. "No! I can," he assured. "Are you ok?" Ziege asked. "Yeah. Thanks," he replied, as he placed his hand on his friend's shoulder. "What about Arfusei?" he asked. "He's still out. It's hard to say. Lillia has bandaged his wounds. And the healer is there," he said. Lark felt confident Arfusei would be okay. "Tetra's are still in the area. We need to get her out of the water," Lark noted.

He took Fin gently in his arms and swam back to the Mojarro shore. The men walked through the town. The soldiers worried. Their queen wasn't moving. They bowed their heads as Lark passed, carrying her body. Fin was injured severely. It would take a miracle to save her. All they could do was hope.

*F*in awakened to a bright day. The flowers were in full bloom. The new hues of purple and red were delightful. There was so much yellow green and blue that the new colors brought life into the area surrounding the castle. The red flowers were gifts from Panga. And Queen Rasbora sent purple gleamers to compliment the red. Lark had to step in as acting leader since Fin was still too weak to run the city. And she asked Lark to take on her duties while she tried to get well. The truth was it was a permanent position. She didn't want Mojarro under her power. He had earned the position. He was her father's closest confidant. The son he never had. It was as it should be. He would be king.

Eulachon had settled. Fin asked Guida to take her seat at her husband's throne. She was reluctant to take the position. She wasn't the type to lead. But she agreed to take on the duty for the sake of her unborn child. Fin and Guida forged a bond and she eventually introduced her to Lark. Fin could see a sparkle in Guida's eye for the handsome, well-mannered and powerful new leader of Mojarro. She smiled, as the two shook hands and made small talk. Lark apologized to Guida for the war. She spoke of being aware that Andreus was planning something terrible and apologized for the loss of men. Lark seemed intrigued by the interesting and beautiful new queen. But then suddenly cleared his throat and turned his attention back to Fin. She didn't mind. He was awakened. He was now mentally free to be attracted to women.

Guida held no one responsible for her husband's death. His obsession with Fin and a city he coveted, was his undoing. Guida was the daughter of Halacai. A secret only Zander and Lark knew. His secret visits to see Mayat was easy since she stayed so close to the sea. Halacai moved to Eulachon to act as his daughter's advisor. Fin was glad. He was a good man. He only ever wanted everyone to get along. She would continue to let him work as prime minister between the cities. He was good at it. Eulachon would be better with him there.

It was a long rough road. Fin was still healing every day. Arfusei had healed and returned to his post. A scar on his head the only reminder of his near-death injuries. But Fin had not healed completely. And Lillia was tending to her daily.

"How is she today?" Lark asked. "Better. The healer has stopped giving her pain herbs. And she is much more alert. She is depressed. She just found out the baby didn't make it," she said. Lark sighed. That was a blow. Fin would never be okay. "Can I talk to her?" he asked. "Sure. But keep it brief. She still has some pain. She needs her rest," she urged.

"Fin," Lark called out, as he knocked and then entered. Fin was not responding. And it instantly caused him alarm. "Fin," he repeated, as he slowly walked to her bed. Fin moaned and turned on her side. Lark watched her. She was as beautiful as ever. He wondered if she had plans to reunite with the man who obviously had her heart. He hoped she would wait. Think it through. He could make her happy. She never gave him the chance. Lark was certain Zander would approve. He had asked him if he loved Fin. Because he already knew the answer.

"Fin," he said again, in a low tone. Finora opened her eyes. She blinked quickly as she tried to focus on his face. The strong herbs that the healer had her taking, had her groggy. Fin cleared her eyes. She focused on his face. She turned from him. The sight of him caused intense emotions. Lark sighed. Lark reminded her of Lance. They were both handsome, strong, wonderfully built men with powerful sex appeal and magnetic eyes. But Lark wasn't Lance. There was no comparison. Lance was her heart. No one could take his place. Not even the one man who loved her all her life.

"Can we talk. I have something to say," he asked. Fin nodded. Lark sat down.

"I've been waiting for months for you to get better. So I could tell you that I care for you. I know you have feelings for someone else. But I'm here. I've always been here Fin," he said. Fin opened her eyes and turned back to him. She sat up. She paused as she thought of what to say.

"I could never love anyone the way I love him. I have to return. I have a child. I miss my family. When I am well, I plan on returning. Please understand," she said. Lark didn't understand. "Is it Arfusei?" he asked. Fin chuckled.

"No. And besides Arfusei loves Lillia. No…The man I love, doesn't live here. One day when I am well, I will show you something. I am only showing you because you will be king. And as king, you need to know every corner of the land. But it is not safe for our kind. It is a world that is harsh and unfriendly to outsiders. They will capture and hold anything that doesn't belong. Not out of spite. But out of safety for their own kind. I have to stay hidden when I go back. Away from their prying eyes. So, you must promise me you will not share the location with anyone," she said. Lark was confused. But he agreed anyway. He wasn't sure what she meant.

"Of course Fin. But I don't understand. What do you mean somewhere else?" he said. "He lives through the dunes. Through the lair. Another place. A place you have never seen nor could ever imagine. It is forbidden. And you must promise not to show anyone. Promise me?" she demanded. "I promise."

Fin told Lark about the lair. And the world on the other side. Lark didn't like the world she was describing. It sounded harsh. Critical. Unconnected. And violent. He was sure he would never tell anyone. It was a world where the people took what they wanted. They would consider Madaka part of their property. The ocean was theirs and so anything in it was fair game. Fin assured him that they would come for the treasures. That the items were rare and valuable. And if they knew Madaka had them in abundance, it would cause many treasure seekers to find a way into their world. And they had the weapons and possibly the means to do so.

"That is unbelievable. I just can't see why you would want to live there," he said. Fin smiled. "For them. For my family. Not for me. I love Madaka."

13

The Power of Love

"You're almost there.," Lark encouraged, as he helped Fin through the garden. Her feet hadn't healed properly. And as a result, she had trouble getting around. She was afraid to get in the water and see what her tail and fin looked like. She was sure it was worse. It was probably ravaged. And swimming would probably be a chore.

She tried every remedy and homemade solution on her legs and feet. Items given to her by other nermeins who had also damaged their tails. But Fin was different. Her bloodline included too much human DNA for the remedies to work. Her Fin was permanently damaged. And she had settled on a life at the castle. She could not get back to Lance. The human part of her that made tolerating the gases possible, was the same part that made healing from such damage to her body, nearly impossible.

Lark helped her to a chair. A handmade wood bench she designed, and he made for her. Lark was secretly overjoyed. He kept his delight from her. He was sure Fin would be angered at his happiness over her immobility. That he was glad she could not get to her lover. Lark wanted to make love to her. It was a new discovery. Many children were being born. Madaka was growing at a rapid rate. As the nermeins were released from the powers that kept them in the dark, they discovered they were sexual beings. They became more body conscience. They were attracted to one another. Fin hoped there would be no rise in infidelity with the new sexual appetites that their people found themselves preoccupied with. Lark had heard about it. And he was anxious to get closer to Fin.

Fin was starting to look at him as a possible mate. She had begun to imagine a life without Lance. Without her daughter. She found comfort in knowing that her baby was with the best father on the planet. She missed Isla. And she was brokenhearted at the love she lost with Lance. But the pain of her loss caused her to send mixed signals. And Lark had become frustrated.

"You are quiet today," Lark said. Fin looked out at the ocean. She stared out at the water. She seemed agitated at the light breeze. Lark tried to keep neutral. He walked on eggshells with her. Fin was starting to pull away from conversations about a future with him again. And she desperately wanted him to move on. "Yeah. I'm ok," she softly replied. Fin wanted to be alone. And she would get her wish. Lark had something to do. He would be gone most of the day.

Flashed of darkness and faces of men entered Fin's dream. She tossed and turned, moaning as she fought back the tension of a nightmare. Fin kicked her cover off then suddenly awoke. She was in a cold sweat. She bolted up. She grabbed her chest. Her heart was beating at a quick pace. Fin caught her breath. "I need water," she said. She opened her door. Her personal guard immediately stood up. He wiped his tired eyes. "You need something Your Highness," he said. "No. Stay here. Everything is fine. I just want a glass of water," Fin said.

The soldier sat back down. He was tired. He slowly drifted back to sleep. Fin looked back at him. She turned and walked down the stairs and into the kitchen. She tried to be quiet. Lillia's room was near the kitchen. She drank the water then looked around. Her foot was sore. She still had a slight limp. She was glad that the pain was slight. Her foot was healing and her walking had improved.

Fin stood at her pantry. She wiped a tear then shook her head in disbelief. Isla would be turning two soon. She was having a nervous breakdown. "I can't...I can't do this," she cried, as she tried talking herself out of the idea, of trying to get to Malibu. Fin covered her mouth and cried into her hand. She was out of control.

I'm coming baby. I'm not missing anymore birthdays, she thought, as she slowly walked to the door and opened it. She could see two guards laughing. Fin closed the door back and decided to leave out the back door. She walked through the pantry and out the back door. A guard stood leaning against the wall. His eyes closed. Fin closed the door halfway and walked quietly through the grass. She looked back at him as she got further away.

She took off running for the cliff. The same sprint she ran as a six-year-old, frustrated and anxious child. Fin stopped at the cliffs edge. The sea was turbulent. The waves crashed along the bottom rock. Fin looked back. She took a deep breath. She hadn't seen her tail in over a year. The last time she tried to change she was devastated with the condition of the fin and vowed to never try again.

"Okay. This is it," she said, as she leaped. Fin hit the dark waters. She used her arms to float vertically while she overcame her anxiety and changed her legs to her tail. Fin swam using her legs then changed into her tail. "Noooo," she said, at the sight of her tail. It was worse than she imagined. Her fin was torn in many places and the tail had gashes and chunks of flesh missing. Fin was saddened at the sight. It was a devastating blow. Her beautiful and unique tail unrecognizable. The damage rendering it useless. Fin struggled to move through the water although it was not impossible.

"I can do this," she said, as she empowered herself. Fin took longer than anticipated to reach the dunes. She worried about spending such a long time over the gases. It was a swim that she always did quickly, to keep from having too much exposure to the gases. "I can do this," she repeated, as she prepared herself.

Fin took a few breaths, then held it and started across the hot and gaseous area. She could tell she was taking too long and her body was not in the same shape. She struggled to continue holding her breath and released the water, then took in a breath of the gas and oxygen mixed water. Fin continued on. She didn't feel herself becoming ill. "Just a little more and

I'm there," she said, as she took small shallow breaths hoping it made a difference.

The lair was close. She could see the opening. But her tail was ineffective. Fin decided to change back to her legs. She hoped it her legs would propel her better and faster. She hadn't used them very often. But she was willing to try anything.

She made it to the lair and swam up. It was heavily concentrated with trapped gas. Fin felt herself getting nauseated. She panicked. She tried to speed up. Soon she felt herself losing her momentum. "Oh no! Please! Help me," she said, as she faded in and out of consciousness. Fin stopped and held onto the rock. She tried pulling herself up and out. But it was too late. The extreme environment had no oxygen. And her slow movements had her in its toxic water too long. Fin was losing her reserve. She held onto the rock, unable to move, as her oxygen levels continued to deplete. Fin managed to climb three more meters before coming to another rest. Her breathing shallow and labored. *I can't die here. Alone. No one will know I'm here,* she thought, as she pulled herself up a meter more. Fin was determined to get through. She had to.

*T*raffic was congested. Lance was on his way to *Tot Time Daycare*. He had just finished for the day and left his office early after hearing a voice message left by Isla's aide, Brigitte. The voice message stated that Isla had a rough day. That she had stated she wanted her mother. Lance was surprised. She had not called out for Fin in months. They both had a rough couple of years since Fin had left. Lance was convinced she was dead. He was certain that there was no way she would voluntarily stay away from her husband and her child. She was going to train her men on how to fight, select someone to run the city and return. But his worst nightmare had come true. He hated to interfere with Fin's plans but this was exactly what he thought would happen. A war with true, hand to hand combat, was a man's fight. And now he and his baby girl, were living life without the woman they loved. It was a major adjustment. And Isla had come a long way.

She seemed to be doing fine. But today was a setback. He wondered what triggered it. Possibly the picture of a mermaid. Or perhaps a television program. Maybe a cartoon. One about an undersea world. One that included mermaids.

"Today was not a good day. She cried a lot. She repeatedly asked for her mom. We tried calling you," Brigitte said, as Lance walked through the door. Brigitte took a special interest in the single dad and his beautiful daughter. Lance was handsome. He was charming. His child was gorgeous. She was the little girl whose looks were television worthy. A reputation noted when a photo of her went viral. A photo one of the teachers took when the class made pottery, and posted it. A director interested in putting the child in a movie contacted Brigitte. And when she mentioned it to Lance, his response was anything but pleasant.

The incident was behind them now. And Brigitte removed all photos of her class from her account. She was horrified at his reaction. The look on his face. She thought he would jump at the chance to put his child in pictures. Over time she could see she was wrong. Lance was a man who liked life simple. And he was wealthy enough not to chase the trappings of Hollywood. He looked like a star himself. And Brigitte was interested in him. And it helped that she adored Isla.

"How is she now?" he asked, as he looked over her shoulder. Isla's classroom was right behind her. "She's fine. She took a nap. And we just had snack time. She just needed a little extra attention," she replied. Lance smiled. He was relieved. He was on the fence about whether he should pull her from the childcare center. It was convenient and it was a well ran children's center. A sophisticated facility down the street from his office. Equipped with an indoor playground, state of the art amenities and some of the best teachers one could ask for. The owners were child psychologist with PhD's in child development and behavioral studies. But Isla was sensitive. She was an emotional child. And she was still very young. Lance thought of hiring a nanny. It was all overwhelming.

"Listen…I know you worry about her. She is fine. Sometimes children who lose a parent will have moments of emotional breakdown. They mourn differently. And different things can trigger a thought. A feeling. She will be fine," Brigitte said, as she touched his shoulder. "Thanks," he said. Lance could see Brigitte was interested. She had shown him on several occasions and was not shy about it. She was beautiful. She looked more like a fashion model than the licensed child psychiatrist that she was. She was brilliant, smart, outspoken and aggressive. Everything he liked in a woman. She just wasn't Fin.

"Were you still thinking of pulling her out of Tiny Tots?" she asked. She hoped not. Isla needed other children. It would help in her development. "I don't know. I will think about what to do," he replied. Bridgette smiled. "Well. You have options. Let me know if I can be of help," she said.

"Daddy," Isla shouted, as she ran to her father. She displayed no sign of having had a rough day. If she did, he would never see it. She always perked up whenever her father entered the room. "Baby girl," he said, as he reached down and picked her up. "Did you tell your teacher your birthday is in a few days?" he asked. Isla blushed, then buried her head in her father's neck. "Oh wow Issie! We'll have cupcakes and ice cream," Brigitte exclaimed.

"Go get your things," Lance said, as he put her down. Isla raced off, another child running right behind her. Lance sighed. He couldn't really imagine pulling her from the daycare center. It was really the best thing for her. "She'll be alright. I know you worry. It has to be hard being a single dad," Brigitte said. Isla ran to her cubby and grabbed her mini bookbag and her sweater. Lance was proud of her. She was smart. Brave like her mother. And mature. She seemed to have an innate sense of what their life entailed. She stopped showing him how much her heart ached for Fin. As if she wanted to cheer him up instead of the other way around. But Lance knew better. She too, missed Fin immensely.

Lance walked through the door as Isla ran through the hall into the great room. He followed her in and turned on the television. Isla danced in anticipation of *The Little Mermaids*. "Okay. Okay," he said, as he tried to find the channel. She was excited. Soon the familiar songs and characters were on the screen. Isla looked back at her father. He was her hero. He knew exactly how to soothe her broken heart. And her huge smile was enough for him.

The sun was setting. Lance chuckled as Isla wiggled her small frame from side to side. The music from the mermaid cartoon had her in her element. She loved to dance and join in, as the characters asked questions of the audience. Lance walked to the open kitchen and picked up his cell phone. He was in no mood to cook. He planned on ordering take out for Isla and himself.

"Issie. How about burgers?" he asked. Isla didn't respond, as she danced and turned in circles. "Iss. You hear me? What about burgers sweetheart?" he repeated. "Uhuh," she said, as she followed along with the moves of the mermaids. Lance placed his order online and typed in his credit card. He tossed the phone on the table and laid down across the couch. He was tired. It had been a long day. This was the first chance he had to relax. And Isla was fine.

The sound of an infomercial awakened Lance from a long nap. Isla lay on the couch next to him. He looked at his watch. He missed the delivery of food. Lance sighed. He couldn't believe he was so tired that he slept through the man knocking at his door. Isla had already eaten earlier at the daycare. Lance figured she wasn't that hungry. She had a small appetite and he didn't think she would have eaten much of her burger. But he was hungry. He hadn't eaten since lunch. Lance sighed. He eased off the couch and stretched. He reached down and slowly picked Isla up.

"Umm," Isla uttered, as her father carried her up the stairs. He walked to her room and over to her bed. She had a bed fit for a princess. A custom-made chariot complete with two wood carved horses and all the accessories to make her fantasy a reality. The massive sized bedroom set had to be shipped in from Italy. Lance went above and beyond to have it made. She was a princess. The real-life daughter of a queen of the ocean.

He would have to explain it all to her someday. But she would have a head start. The book created for him by his psychologist Helen Karpowski, was written to keep her story alive. To keep Fin in Isla's thoughts. Lance was forever grateful to Helen. She took his story and with his permission, wrote a children's book. Lance didn't mind. It was perfect for Isla. And with Allan drawing the likeness of Fin on the inside page, the book had much more meaning for him.

"Goodnight precious," he whispered, as he turned to leave out. He made a point of cutting on night lights in case she awakened in the middle of the night. Lance went back to his kitchen and pulled roasted turkey from the fridge. He made a sandwich and ate it as he scaled the stairs back to the second level of his home. He walked the long dimly lit hall to his room and climbed into bed. It was one in the morning. And he was ready for a full night's sleep. It was the weekend. He could relax all day. Maybe take Isla to a park. They both could use an outing.

"Daddy," Isla whispered, as she shook his arm. Lance awakened and rolled over. "Hey. What are you doing out of bed?" he asked. Isla stared. Her usually animated face showing no emotion. Lance sat up. The nightlight in his room not bright enough and he was unable to read the strange cues coming from his daughter. "What wrong?" he said, as he searched her eyes for an answer. Isla stared as if in shock. Not speaking and not giving any visual cues to her stress. Lance jumped up. He feared someone in his house. Her behavior had him now freaking out.

"Issie talk to me. What wrong sweetheart," he said, as he moved room to room, with little Issie walking right behind him. He walked around the house, checking every window and door. He looked back. Isla was no longer behind him. He heard the refrigerator open and walked hurriedly into the kitchen. He watched as she pulled open the crisper drawer and pull the package of strawberries from inside. "Oh! You hungry. I'm sorry baby., I thought you were ok. I'm sorry about the burgers I ordered earlier. Daddy slept through the delivery," he said.

"Mommy," Isla said, as she pulled several strawberries from the container and ran to the glass sliding door. Lance stared at her. His heart dropped. He thought she was okay after her melt down earlier that day. But he could see she was not. "Iss... Where are you going? We can't put strawberries in the water tonight. Mommy's not there," he said, the words difficult for him to say. He felt like a failure where her mother was concerned. If only he had fought to keep her home. Maybe she would have stayed, if he had made a bigger fuss about leaving. But he didn't. And now he was in mourning and so was his daughter. Their lives, shattered.

"How about we sit on the dock tomorrow when the sun is out. We'll put berries in the water then. Okay. Now let's go to bed," he said. Isla turned from him. As if disappointed. She teared up. Her silent contempt hurt Lance. "Come on Iss. I promise we will go to the end of the dock tomorrow," he said. Isla stood still, staring out into the darkness. The lights from their patio and surrounding landscape shielding her view of the dock. "Mommy," she said again, as she reached up to open the door. Lance wasn't worried. It had a special lock. Toddler-proof and not easy to open. It was necessary since they lived around water. A fact that would be changing soon. Lance didn't have the heart to break it to her. He feared a major meltdown. She looked to the water every day. She was still expecting Fin to rise from it. They were still walking to the end of the dock daily, to sit on its edge and hope. Isla throwing strawberries in. Even getting mad if a fish ate it. "Issie. Come on. Back to bed."

Isla looked at him. Her eyes watery and saddened. Lance sighed. "Ok. We'll go to the dock. Just for a moment. You can put the berries in. But then we go to bed Issie," he said as he walked up. Isla looked at her father towering above her. He was her hero once more. She smiled and wiped her eyes. She didn't want him to see her sad. Her tears sometimes led to his tears and she didn't want to see her daddy cry. She just wanted to go to the dock.

Lance pulled the door. A gush of wind came in. "Oh wait Iss. It's cold tonight. I have to get your sweater. Wait here," he said. Isla held the berries as she patiently waited for her father to grab her sweater. Soon her patience disappeared. Isla pushed the door back open and darted out. Lance opened her drawer. He closed it and opened another. "There it is," he said, as he grabbed her sweater. He walked down the steps.

Soon he could see the door. It was open. He stopped and looked around.

"Oh shit. Noo," he said, as he bolted from the steps, almost falling, as he frantically tried to reach the outside. He knew where she was. She had gone to the docks. And it was pitch black since he forgot to turn the lights on. He didn't have time. The light switch seemed miles away. It only would take a second for her to fall into the water. Lance bolted through the door. He needed to get to Isla.

"Issie!" he said, as he ran onto the patio. He reached the dock and stopped. Isla was on her knees. She was bent down, practically lying on the planks. Lance slowed. "Issie," he shouted as he ran again. Something was on the dock. Lance ran up and stopped dead in his tracks. His heart pounding. It wasn't real. It couldn't be. Lance dropped to his knees and began kissing Fin.

"Fin!" he said, as he rubbed her face. "Fin...Fin...Baby wake up," he pleaded. Isla smiled, as she tried pushing a berry into her mother's mouth. Lance kissed Fin over and over. She was cold as ice. He wasn't sure she was alive. She didn't appear to be breathing. Her skin was cold. She looked lifeless. Lance cried and closed his eyes and he continued kissing her. "We have to get mommy inside," he said. Lance stood and picked Fin up.

"Hold onto my pants leg," he instructed his baby. He couldn't grab her hand and he didn't want to leave her while he took Fin inside. Isla gabbed his pant leg. Lance walked slowly, making sure to keep to the middle, away from the edge. Suddenly something caught his eye. Something in the water. Lance squinted. He wondered what it was. He soon realized it was the head of a man. The man was staring at him. Lance stopped. The man stared for a second longer then dipped into the water. Lance looked down at Isla. She was beaming. He forced a smile. He wasn't sure her mother was alive and he couldn't be happy yet.

"Go in," he said to Isla, as he walked in behind her and laid Fin down on the couch. Isla got in Fin's face. She tried to open one of her mother's eyes. She lifted her eye lid and then smiled. "Mommy,"[i] she said. Lance stood over Fin. She was not responsive. He walked away and started pacing back and forth. "I can't take her to the hospital. What if they take her blood. They always take blood. They will realize she isn't human. At least not completely," he said, as he talked to himself. He was unsure of what to do. Lance stopped and stared, hoping for some sign of life. Fin lay there motionless.

Not breathing. Not moving. Panic set in. And Lance's mood changed abruptly. He was overcome with emotion.

He sat down on a second couch and dropped his head. Isla looked back at him. She looked at Fin then back at him again. She ran to him.

"Mommy needs a warm bath," she said. Lance's tears hit the floor. He didn't hear his daughter completely. He was in shock. "Huh," he said, removing his hands from his face. He looked at her. Isla wiped his face.

"Mommy want a warm bath daddy," she repeated. Lance furrowed. "What? A bath?" he said, glancing over at his wife. "Iss. She's gone," he said. Isla smiled.

"No daddy. Bath," she said. "You want me to put her in the bath?" he said, not sure why his child thought that was a good idea. A thought came across his mind. Isla was alone with Fin for a few minutes. He realized there was some time between him getting the sweater and Isla finding her. His mind raced. Perhaps Fin was awake when Isla first happened upon her. Maybe she told her to have him put her in warm water. Lance jumped up. He ran to the bathroom. Isla shuffled her feet in anticipation.

The water streamed out. Lance had it turned all the way up. The tub was filling quickly. Lance raced back and picked Fin up. Her limp body falling easily into his arms. He hoped Isla was right. He hoped the baby was on to something. Lance removed Fin's thin sheer dress and placed her in the water. He moved her hair from her face and kissed her. He laid her head back. Isla moved in front of him. She continued pulling up Fin's eyelid. Lance waited patiently. "Mommy," Isla called to her.

Lance's eye widened. Fin moved. "Fin!" he said, as he touched her face. "Can you hear me?" he said in her ear. He waited for another sign. Another sound. He kissed her, then moved so Isla could kiss her. Fin moaned. Isla turned quickly to her father and giggled. Lance touched Isla's little cheeks. Fin was alive. They were both elated. She was back. Lance looked her over. He could see her feet were scarred. He reached over and touched them softly. His mind picturing images of the pain and suffering she went through. He looked at her. Her bravery was admirable.

"Come on," Lance said, as he waited for her to open her eyes. Fin mover her head side to side. She slowly opened her eyes, rapidly blinking as she tried to adjust her vision. Fin got her bearings. She looked at Lance and Isla. They were both mere inches from her face. Their smiles, melting her heart.

Fin burst into tears and kissed Isla then her husband. She kissed him again. She looked at him in disbelief. She looked around astonished. "How did I get here?" she asked, as she thought hard. Suddenly she remembered. She put her hands over her face. "It's ok mommy. Daddy saved you," Isla said. Fin removed her hands and grabbed her baby. "Yes he did," she replied, looking at him. "Someone was in the water," Lance said. Fin looked at him intensely then nodded. She knew who he was talking about. She remembered.

"I didn't think he would. He pulled me out of the lair. He saved my life. All I remember is pointing the way. I must have passed out after that. He must have pulled me the entire way," she said, amazed and wishing she could thank Lark. She wondered how he pulled it off. How he survived the dunes and the lair and was able to get her home. He was the most remarkable of all. His ability to forsake his own heart, and help her get to hers. Her family was her heart. Her life. And Lark deserved the kingdom she left him. He was a great man. And she wished him happiness. She hoped the spark that she knew would occur between him and Guida, would turn into something wonderful. He deserved it all. And she was grateful that he got her home.

It was worth the risk for her to try. Fin knew she would have died of a broken heart. Lance was her greatest love. And the way he was gazing into her eyes at that moment, showed her how deeply she was loved. Her life could begin again. She was home. Her baby was healthy and happy. Her husband stable and strong. They had been through a lot. Each one of them. But it would all be better now.

The waves were crashing gently against the rocks. Fin stood in the dark, rubbing her belly, looking out at the Pacific Ocean. Lance exited the shower and opened their door. Fin glanced back then looked back to the water. He dried himself then wrapped the towel around his waist. "You alright?" he asked, as he walked to her then stood behind her. "Yeah," she said assuredly. Lance put his arms around her and smelled her hair. Fin leaned back into him.

"Are you worried about them?" he asked. "No. Lark and the others are leaders. They will guide everyone. They lead with their hearts now. Madaka is different. Their lives and their families will mean so much more to them now," she said. Lance looked at the moon, the water casting it's broken image on the rough waves. "You would have resented me if I kept you from going. But I was angry that I let you go," Lance confessed. Fin turned to him.

"Thank you for believing in me. I know it was difficult. And I'm sorry I didn't take better care. I almost didn't get back," she said, laying her head on his chest. Lance rested his head on hers. They stood holding each other. Still in shock at the events that got them to this point. "I love you," she said. Lance kissed her head. He was grateful to Lark. A man he never met. A man he was sure loved Fin. Why else would he risk his life. Risk coming to a strange world. He understood. Fin was phenomenal. "I love you too."

$\mathcal{F}$in stood at the window, a cup of warm tea in her hand. Isla sat at the kitchen table doing her lessons. "A…B…C…D…," she said, as she went through the whole alphabet. Fin listened with pride. Her baby was smart. Gifted, according to her husband. Maybe due to being part nermein. Whatever the reason, she was bright beyond her years.

"Good job Issie. Now count to fifty," she said. Isla chuckled. She liked doing her lessons with her mother. In a way, Fin was learning them herself. She had the language but not the letters. Isla said them loudly. Fin smiled. She could hear the front door open. Lance was carrying another box out to the moving van. This was the last day in the house off the water. It was bittersweet. She and Lance agreed that they were ready to be in a safer environment for Isla. And the timing was perfect. Fin was pregnant again. And their growing family would need land, trees, backyards and parks. A family setting for their children. She didn't have the heart to tell him about the baby she'd lost Not yet. Lance wanted a big family. And Fin had plans of filing their house with children.

Isla jumped down from the chair and ran to the television. Fin picked up the remote and turned to Little Mermaids. Isla danced to the theme song as her mother put a few more of her personal items in a box. She picked up the tape and began sealing the edges. She stopped and looked inside. Something caught her attention. Among her items, was a book. Fin pulled it out and looked it over. She had just started learning how to read the English language. Lance was teaching her every day how to read and write. And she had excelled at it.

She looked at the title. It read; *Pretty Fin*. She fought back tears as she opened the page. The beautifully etched drawing of her was overwhelming. Fin smiled. It was like looking in a mirror. She turned to the next page. She read a much as she could. It was the story of her life. A book created out of need. And one that had not been read since her return. Fin looked at her baby. She placed the book in with Isla's belongings and sealed both boxes.

"We ready," Lance said, as he touched her belly and kissed her forehead. "Yes. I guess so. You coming back to get the rest?" she asked. "Yeah. The movers will. They have to box and tape everything else."

Lance strapped Isla in her car seat. She drank from her juice bottle as she watched Fin exit out the door. "You ready to go to your new house?" he asked Isla. "Uhuh," she replied. Fin got in and shut the door. She fastened her seat belt then glanced back at Isla and smiled. She reached back and handed her a bag of strawberries. Isla took them and bit into one. Fin turned back around. Her mind wandering. She had read the part in the book about the strawberries. It was the first time she realized that the berry had a significance in their union. That it was a constant in their life from day one.

It was the berries that drew her in and made her comfortable. Something the man from the dock, who had her intrigued, shared with her without even knowing it. It was something to look forward to. He would be there. And he would have them. Discarding them innocently, as she held out her hand. If only he knew the importance of the berry.

But he did. Lance was suddenly there, in the water, staring at her. The berries in his hand. His spirit meshing with hers almost automatically. As if they were meant to be. Fin smiled. There's was a great love story. She remembered the day vividly. Everything about him. What he had on. What he smelled like. His voice. His eyes. His strong masculine energy. And she could tell the book was as much for him as it was for her daughter. She could see it in the writing. The way he told the story. As if he possibly dreamed it and having Isla validated it as his reality. It was a fairytale that came true. He had fallen in love with a mermaid. And she was real.

"Ok. Let's go," Lance said, as he got in. He started the car and looked around. He backed out and drove away, waving at his neighbors as he drove towards the highway. He reached over and grabbed Fin's hand. He held it tight. He checked Isla in his rear-view mirror. He was happy to go. He had children to care for. A wife to love and cherish. Home could be anywhere. It could be inside a cardboard box for all Lance cared. As long as they were together, their lives would be a real-life fairytale.

Please leave a **Review** of the book!

By logging into your Amazon account and giving honest feedback. Thank you!

Smokey Moment

BookBabe

For information on use of this material or for help with indie publishing needs contact Smokey Moment.

Email us at: bookbabepublishing@gmail.com

Thank you!

Smokey Moment

CPSIA information can be obtained
at www.ICGtesting.com
Printed in the USA
LVHW041546140120
643593LV00001B/37

9 781652 594116